Enoree

Jerry Mullinax

Dedication

To Buddy and Anne Mullinax,
parents who trained up a child in the way he should go
leaving to him his own departures.

Acknowledgments

To Gerry Corn who suggested *Pelham Hill,* a series of Jerry's often-shared stories, as the title of a book.

Table of Contents

1

I wasn't born in Pelham. I only came there because my daddy preached and that's where we all landed when his time came to pastor the Baptist church there. My daddy was a hard country-fireball preacher who was known to take his jacket off and loosen his tie when he preached. He loved it. "The foolishness of preachin' is what saves them that are lost!" I heard him shout that a few times from the pulpit.

There were six of us in our family, a daddy, a mother, and four kids: three older boys and a baby girl. Years later, when time would come for us to move away from Pelham, there would be two more girls added to the litter. I was the middle boy, Jake.

Traversing from the mountains to this little spot on earth, my family relocated to Pelham in 1957 when I was entering the third grade. From God's perspective looking down, Pelham's northern most point, like the sharp end of an anvil, gradually widened downhill along Highway 14 into the heart of the final stages of a former mill village, across the Enoree River over the Highway 14 Bridge, past the Enoree Dam, squaring out into Blountville at the southern blunt end. Along the way, Highway 14 passed the Leopard's cotton field, the schoolhouse, the parsonage, the Lee's house, the Stuart's general store, the other church, our church, the Moxley's store and post office, and the other side of the bridge.

Many a car had negotiated the highway and jarred along the cracked surface of aged and poorly-striped concrete through and out of Pelham without even noticing the symptoms of life on either sides of the road and river.

Gabriel, my fourth-grade brother, groaning from the back seat of our 1950 Buick, said, "You gotta be kiddin' me!"

"What, Gabriel? What is it?" I asked. I turned on my knees to see out the rear window where he was staring. "What?" Our Buick was just coming to a complete stop.

My younger brother Daniel, blessed with quickness of feet and nimbleness of body, had already spun around and was standing up in the seat.

"There's the school, next to our house," Gabriel explained. "We're going to live right next to the Pelham School." Our three heads collectively adjusted to see past the eight-inch adhesive letters, spelling out *Jesus Saves*, adhered to the rear window of the car. "Next to the school," Gabriel said.

"Nest to da skool?" Daniel exclaimed in his baby voice. Daniel would be starting his first year in school. He wasn't aware of the dilemmas that living right next to the school could bring. Me and Gabriel would almost barf whenever Daniel would switch from his regular-talking voice into his *baby* voice. Daniel knew exactly how to play the adults to his advantage with his pretended tenor.

"Boys!" my daddy said, "help your mother get the stuff into the house!" His boisterous voice twisted us around and down into our seats, excepting Daniel, who still stared at the school through the car's rear window.

Pointing toward the school with his other arm, Daniel turned back to the front seat. "Nest to da skool, Daddy!" It was obvious he wasn't receiving the attention he had wanted.

"Okay, son," Daddy spoke, eyeing Daniel in the rearview mirror. "Help your brothers, but stay out of the way."

Gabriel and me reached for the car door, pulling it open. Both of us unfolded out of the car at the same time, plopping onto the partially white-rocked driveway. We hopped up, brushing our hands off on our jeans.

The parsonage had a fresh trimming of white paint around some grainy red bricks, giving a new-fangled smell to the house. Daddy stood near a small screened-in back porch and looked the house over. Three days earlier, he and the deacons of Pelham Baptist Church had convened at the

South House Restaurant in Greer, South Carolina to finalize the asking of him to become pastor the Pelham church.

At the meeting, Mr. Elijah Green, chairman of the deacons, almost ninety-years-old and barely mobile, said, “Pelham loves God, Preacher…and God loves us all, and we wish to keep it that way.” Mr. Green had been a deacon at the Baptist church since he was twenty-eight-years old and chairman since he was fifty-five.

The deacons and Daddy sat around the table, conversing softly, relating to each other with laughs and considerate joking. The deacons kept their eyes glued to my daddy, noticing how he picked up his fork or how he drank his iced tea, looking to see if he wiped his mouth with the napkin, or if he folded it or just let it drop on top of the table like a collapsed gospel tent. While Daddy was gone to the deacons' meal, I asked Momma if they were having the last supper. She didn't find my question at all amusing. The deacons picked up my daddy's check, even the dessert, without asking him to tip the waitress. It was a done deal; we were going to Pelham to be the first family of the Baptist church. He didn't have to sign a contract or initial an agreement. The deacons and him smiled and shook hands. "Welcome, Pastor!"

"Lillian, honey, catch that stuff in the trunk!" Daddy hollered at my momma from across the yard. "I'm going to the front door and let y'all in through the basement." Daddy briskly disappeared around a large green row of hedges that covered up the bottom half on the front of the parsonage.

Trying his best to get anyone to listen to him, Daniel still yelled from the back seat, "Nest to da school!"

Momma opened the trunk with the car key, as me and Gabriel waited for our first load of things to carry.

"Where's our furniture and stuff, Momma?" I asked her.

"The big truck's bringing it," she said. She stood thinking about what to lift up out of the trunk first.

The big moving truck had been at our small apartment in the mountains the day before. The big-armed black men had gently packed and hoisted our furniture, large and small, into the long truck while the white man casually filled out papers. Gabriel and me liked to watch the black men work. We had never seen black people so close up before. They had mammoth muscles sticking out of their tight and dirty shirtsleeves. Their skin was oily dark like a bucket of wet coal. They had teeth like pearls.

We dared not talk out loud to 'em. Our great grandmother had told us not to talk to black people. She never told us why, but I think it had something to do with a story she always told us about *Little Black Sambo* that lived in the closet in her back bedroom at my grandmother's house.

The only black people we had ever been up close to was Mitch and Nora. They visited my grandmother's house on occasion to get my grandmother's old newspapers and stuff. They used the papers to start their winter fires. Grandmother always gave Nora some extra stuff too, like fruit preserves and miscellaneous food items. Mitch would never get out of the car. He wouldn't even drive his car into my grandmother's yard, but parked it under some trees at a considerable walking distance. Nora took her time meandering up to the front porch, and later, back to the car.

When Nora saw us at Grandmother's house, she would say, "You chilluns sho' has gro'an up consid'rable...yes you has." To me, she would whisper, "My Lawd, Jake, you setch a *pur-tee* lit'l man, my, my my." I would blush when she talked to me like that. It made me want to run four times as fast as I could around the outside of Grandmother's house, and I did. Something about her shy, sincere smile that pulled me into her soul. Something about her dry lips and how they moved as she talked. Even though I had no idea of slavery or the emancipation, Nora's face reflected a deep-furrowed injustice in my heart. I rarely blinked my eyes when she was in Grandmother's house.

My grandparents on my momma's side were the ones who were bringing my baby sister down to Pelham in two days once the rest of us got settled in.

Daniel jumped from the rear seat, out of the back door of the 1950 Buick, and onto his feet without even stumbling. He leaned backwards into the door, forcing it shut with his behind. My momma peeped quickly around the trunk in case the shutting noise had been on his fingers. “That boy,” she said. “Be careful, Daniel!”

“Here, Jake,” she said. “Take this to the basement door. Hold the bottom, ‘cause it’s drinking glasses.”

I reached to the box and squeezed it to my stomach, holding it tight.

“No,” Momma warned me, “not like that…hold the *bottom* of the box!” she added.

I moved my hands down and cupped the bottom. The glasses rattled their relief.

Gabriel ended up with a box of table dishes. “Dishes are heavier than glasses,” he told me. I didn’t believe him. While we waited for Daddy to unlock the basement door, Gabriel grunted and swayed side to side more than I did. He utilized his lifted leg to reposition the box in his arms for a better grip. Daniel toted a tiny bathroom rug, rolled up and secured with a black belt. I supposed it was my belt, since I had my brown one on at the time.

Suddenly, the basement door clanked and twisted. Upward, it began its creaking and folding sound. Daddy's hands held on to give the door a last shove. He pushed it. "There she goes, boys. Now, ask your mom where she wants this stuff. I'm not the one who knows that," Daddy said. He smiled at Momma who was loading up her own arms with kitchen supplies.

My momma and daddy both seemed in high spirits--moving into a brick house--as if they were exchanging anniversary presents with each other. They smiled and touched each time they passed. On one of my trips up and down the stairs, I caught them playfully kissing in the garage. Our family had never lived in a brick house before. From the mountains, we had moved from a white garage apartment, whose thin walls were scaly and chipped, and now, we were going to be living in the Pelham Parsonage, of the First Baptist Church. Who'd a ever thought it!

"Momma, where? These glasses?" I moaned, pulling my head back to exaggerate my discomfort for sympathy. "Where do you want these glasses?"

"Take them up the steps to the kitchen. Watch those steps though," she instructed.

Gabriel and me stutter-stepped across the cool concrete basement floor, then carried the boxes up the steps, one at a time. At the top of the fourteen steps, we entered the hallway's long wood floors where later we would run and slide down with our friends. Down the hall and to the right was the kitchen, where me and Gabriel gladly emptied our loads onto the counter top and partnered each other throughout the empty house for our exclusive short tour. Each step was yielded soft echoes.

At the south exit of the kitchen was a smaller-than-usual door, closet-like.

"What's this, I wonder?" Gabriel asked aloud.

"Don't know. Try it. A closet?" I asked, not so sure.

He reached for the doorknob and turned. The door seemed stuck, suctioned. Pulling against it, Gabriel forced it open. The mustiness behind the door emptied right past us into the rest of the house like white rice when an Uncle Ben box topples.

"Eww. What is that?" I asked Gabriel.

"A attic. Our house has a attic."

"Attic?"

We both froze for a second. Into the threshold we leaned as one. The sun, slicing through the eave vent, highlighted the roused dust that swirled in confused circles and showered the climbing steps with an eerie atmosphere. Above the first couple of steps, unaffected by the hallway lighting, the obscure shadows lounged secluded, untouched. Smells of overused insulation permeated the space above the stairs. Gabriel immediately shut the door. We walked quickly into the living room without speaking to each other.

Unexpectedly, Daniel bounced into our path, startling us. “Momma said come get your next box. She said she means it,” he said. Having done his assigned duty, Daniel turned on a dime, vanishing out of sight.

Gabriel and me moved down the steps, through the garage-door opening, listening for Momma's next instructions.

Daddy was working inside a small room off to the side of the basement. He had already chosen this room to be his at-home office. This is where in years to come, he would relentlessly practice his trumpet and read his Bible to make preaching messages for Sundays and Wednesdays at church. Quite often and loud, he would pray there, too.

Momma had already mostly transported most of the car-trunk stuff inside the house. She walked methodically back and forth along the same path from trunk to kitchen, kitchen to trunk like an ant relocating bread crumbs to the nest. Momma had told Daddy before we left the mountains, “If we can take our kitchen things with us, Adam, we can at least do some cooking at the house." My daddy wasn't born Adam. He was called Adam as a nickname. It had stuck to him.

With only a few items having been placed into our house, and the big moving truck not yet having arrived, my daddy was already practicing with his trumpet in his new, not-quite-ready-to-use home office. He used two unpacked boxes as a concert chair. The shrilling sound bounced from cement block to concrete floor and out of the wide garage-door opening and into the lower ground behind our house. I had never heard *In the Garden* played so beautifully. Daddy's lips were hard pressed to perform such an impromptu rendition.

In my own mind, I hummed the words. "I come to the garden alone, while the dew is still on the roses..." and then the words faded off with Daniel's piercing voice.

Jumping in place on his toes, he asked, "Jake, did you see the woods?" His buggy eyes, bright and clear, peeped right below his yellow-blonde hairline in jagged bangs and strands. “Did you see ‘em? Woods!”

I peered around Daniel toward the green, kinda-long grass in our back yard. An open field, hay- and briar-filled, and a thick tree row, outlined the distant horizon near the river. To my immediate right, only a few running steps past the parsonage property, sat the elementary school building, long and rectangular. The school's driveway extended from Highway 14 down a hill next to the parsonage, circled in front of the school for depositing school children and back up the incline on the opposite side. This leaning horseshoe hill would provide many great adventures for me and my brothers while living in Pelham.

“Wow, them’s some woods, Daniel. We’ll have to go down there sometime,” I answered him.

“Now? Can we go now?” he asked.

“No, we can’t go now, ‘cause Daddy’s practicing and Momma’s cleaning, and Gabriel’s...” I didn’t know what Gabriel was doing. Rethinking the situation, I added, “Let’s find out what Gabriel's doing. Maybe he'll take us down there." Me and Daniel jogged south around the back of the house away from the school on the white rock driveway that outlined the back blunt perimeter of the side yard, like a rounded chin for the front yard's face. The circling corner was outlined with a wall of river stones, about four or five feet high, held together by gray cement, which shored up the dirt up on the front lawn. Me and Daniel started in a sprint looking for Gabriel, ending up in a hard race to the end of the driveway near the paved border of Highway 14. Only barely in formal school, Daniel still liked to have beat me to the highway. He would always be faster than most kids his or my age. God blessed him with physical agility. He blessed me with physical limitations.

Engaged too intently in our race, me and Daniel suddenly stopped, directly confronted by the highway. We had never seen a paved state road this close before. Faded white painted lines, languishing, decorated the pale gray surface of Highway 14 like leftover streamers at last year's homecoming game. At our white garage apartment in the mountains, we had been a good distance away from a real highway, barely able to detect the humming sounds of automobile tires moving up and down the road. On some occasions, standing on our grandpa's fence next door to our apartment, we could distinguish the tops of the cars passing by.

And now, a few blades of our own front-yard grass of the parsonage actually curled out into and over the nearside white line of Highway 14. We were *too* close for comfort. Our lives would touch this paved pathway.

All of a sudden, Momma screamed from the front porch of the parsonage. "Get away from that road! Get over here now...both of you!" Momma, already apron-adorned, stood on the brick-fashioned, square, roofless porch. Her light-colored cotton dress flapped slightly with the warm breeze like a bed sheet on a March clothes line, out of rhythm with her tapping right foot. Her hands rested on her hips.

Daniel and me ran as quick as we could. I beat him again.

"What, Momma?" I asked, as if I couldn't remember where I was just standing a few seconds earlier.

Seizing our full attention, she said, "You two look at me and listen to what I'm gonna tell you," Meanwhile, Gabriel rounded the house in a slow walk, kicking a pinecone in front of him. Momma added, "You come here too, Gabriel. You need to hear this."

Daniel and me looked at Gabriel with one of those we're-being-talked-to looks. Gabriel moved in beside Daniel, sandwiching Daniel between him and me like an un-matched fence post.

Kinda lawyer-sounding, Gabriel asked, "What, Momma? What did I do? I was just kicking the---"

"None of you have done anything wrong. I need to talk to you about this new place we live in." She moved down the three steps and onto the grass. "Sit down," she requested. "...on the steps." We were dumbfounded by her order. Side by side, we sat like three see-hear-and-say-no-evil monkeys.

Momma pivoted like General Patton and began. "That," pointing toward the road, "is Highway 14. It's the only way that people can get from Columbia to Greer. A lot of cars travel that highway. It's dangerous. As long as we stay here in this house..." My momma's voice maintained the same pitch but began to fade beneath the clickety-clack of automobile tires that rumbled across the sectioned patterns of the aging asphalt.

"That car's headed toward Columbia," Gabriel said. Momma turned and watched the car pass the house and out of sight. Daniel stood up on the bottom step and leaned around Momma's skirt, hanging on to see the car vanish out of sight. Momma reached out to balance Daniel, not even looking at him but noticing the car too.

"Columbia?" Daniel whispered, as if Columbia was a sacred, mystical destination. Actually, it was the capital of our new state and was home to a lot of the important events for everyone in the state. But after all, it was *just* Columbia, not Hollywood or heaven or anything.

"Okay," Momma inserted. "Look at me...and...Daniel, sit down." She paused enough to push a cloud of hair back into a loose bobby pin. "Did you see that car?" she asked. "Many cars will pass on that highway while we live here in this house. That's what makes the highway dangerous...*very* dangerous."

This is where my momma changed her tone of voice to sound like God of a feminine persuasion, calling us by our complete given names. "Robert Gabriel, Jacob Levite, and Daniel Bentley, look and listen to what I'm saying to you." With those words, our spines straightened and our eyes blinked not. "You are to *never* go near that highway. Do you hear me?"

Gabriel and me answered, "Yes, ma'am." Daniel just shook his head, turning to see why our heads were not shaking too.

Momma continued. "I'm glad we all understand each other, boys. Your little sister will be watching you, and if you get near the highway, she might try it too, thinking it's alright. Now, you wouldn't want her to go onto that highway, would you?" Momma asked, not really expecting an answer.

We all shook our heads no.

"Then, stay away from it. Keep your distance. You need to respect something that you do not quite comprehend. Okay?" she ordered.

"Yes, ma'am."

She pushed back a couple of other wayward curls from her light brown hair and lifted her apron to catch sweat on her forehead. Taking a refreshing breath, she stepped between us, tapping Daniel lightly on the head, and into the front door of the parsonage.

We all sat still and stared at Highway 14. Daniel leaned against my leg. Mother's speech about the highway gave us a new appreciation and contemplation about the man-made road. The top of the highway was beginning to cook in the searing sunlight. Sizzling steam caused the road top to take on an unnatural appearance, like a wavy, watery sea.

Abruptly, Gabriel said, "You two stay away from that road!" He arose and walked toward the pinecone he'd been kicking. He stopped, picked it up, and moved around the north end of the house, past the hedges and out of sight.

"Where's Columbia, Jake?" Daniel asked. "Where does it go?" His eyes were looking at the south trail of the road that dropped slightly as it passed the edge of our lawn and in front of the neighbors' houses.

"It's another town, a big town, down that way," I explained. "We ain't never going there, so don't worry 'bout it."

"Who's that, Jake?" Daniel abruptly asked.

Down the upper distance of Highway 14 on the other side, trudging, heads down, were three black boys. They never looked up, moving in unison with a solemn stride, keeping their eyes fastened to the shoulder.

"Don't know... don't say nothing though," I said.

"Black people. They have black people here, Jake."

"Shh..."

We watched the three black boys saunter down the highway like the dark wakes at the edge of a paved river, until they were on the Columbia end, their three heads leisurely vanishing out of sight like drowning ellipses.

The breeze picked up another trumpet sound and was carrying it around the parsonage driveway into our ears. The song was "Rescue the Perishing" from the end of my daddy's horn. What a fitting selection for our most recent lecture from Momma. Daniel and me relaxed a little more with the music. I quietly sang a few words. Me and Daniel walked around the south end of the house beside the river rock wall, the way we had raced earlier.

"Rescue the perishing, care for the dying, snatch them in pity from sin and the grave..." I couldn't remember the rest of the words but hummed the tune, even as I beat Daniel again in a sudden sprint toward the front of the black, 1950 Roadmaster Buick that sat parked in the shadow of the parsonage.

2

It took overnight for the driver of the big moving truck to get down to us in Pelham. Daddy had mentioned something to Momma about the driver getting sick. For breakfast, Momma baked fresh biscuits and served them with syrup and butter. “No grits ‘til the table gets here,” she announced.

At the countertop, all of us ate breakfast standing up in the kitchen on the first day. After all, we didn’t have any kitchen table or chairs. That didn’t keep us from doing our regular prayer over the meal, though. Nothing in our lives would ever cancel the before-meal or before-bedtime prayers.

Many things would try to prevent that tradition in our family, but could not.

We mixed the butter and Karo syrup together in our plates until the syrup took on a overcast texture, a more creamy appearance, and then, with a steamy hot biscuit, butter-laden and fresh from the oven, we dipped right into the sugary mixture and pulled the sweetness into our mouths. It was heaven in our hands.

Momma had taught me how to make hot water tea. I drank it just like some of the grownups would drink coffee. My momma drank coffee, but for me, hot water tea was my pretend coffee. I made it with hot water, sugar, and milk. It became a habit-forming breakfast beverage for me. It would be later in my teen years before I could wean myself from hot water tea. I also liked to put my biscuit into the tea and let it get soggy. Then, I'd eat the mushy biscuit with a spoon. Dee-lish!

Without any beds or bedroom furniture, our family had slept on the floor the night before. Momma had made sure to pack some blankets just in case we needed them. Gabriel, Daniel, and me slept for the first time in our bedroom. It was like going camping, except with a roof over our heads. We left the windows cracked and the tree chirpers and clackers outside sang all night long. In an empty house with wooden floors, every movement ricocheted with crisp acoustics. The night sounded like an orchestra with our periodic rotating in bed and groanings, with Daddy's snoring the vibrating bass notes, and with nature's contributing the grandest percussion from the darkness just beyond the stretch of our windowsill.

Typically, me and my brothers would sleep in the same double bed. In all our years of sharing the same room, and that would be until Gabriel would go into the United States Air Force to Vietnam, we would sleep in the same bed. Yes, even through high school. My parents couldn't afford to buy separate beds, and we didn't complain that much about it, since we had never experienced the alternative. We thought all families shared this unique privilege.

Well, I suppose that I should mention my problem that would benefit me sometimes in the bed-sharing process. I wet the bed up until I was in fifth grade, the *later* part of the fifth grade. I had a real bed-wetting problem. So, until I conquered that bad habit, I had a distinct advantage in the double bed. No one wanted to sleep next to me, which would usually pile Gabriel and Daniel atop the other, or at least as uncomfortably close to each other as they could be, so I could have ample space for my exasperating and advantageous disability.

For some reason, unexplained to me at any time, the morning of a bed-wetting incident always found me under the cover, for seclusion, in a perfect circle of yellow. I have never been that good at math, and especially geometry, but how it was always a circle, I can't explain, but I *do* know that the area of that circle was the extension of my power in the double bed. Neither of my brothers wanted to be within the diameter of my perimeter--and I hope I got those arithmetic terms right.

My brothers would fight over the bed space near the wall, because I always asked for the space nearest the floor, "...in case I have to go," I would argue to them. That reason made enough sense to my momma for her to confine them against the wall for their sleeping locale. Once I was securely positioned in the center of my own little surveyed perimeter, I would never get out of the bed to go to the bathroom. To be so snug in the covers was just too territorially pleasing and comfortable to stir myself.

"Momma, make Daniel move over some!" Gabriel would yell as we would all be trying to settle in for the night. "Momma!"

Daniel would use his legs to push against Gabriel and get as close as possible. Gabriel despised Daniel touching him.

By his fifth grade year, Gabriel would produce a tool for survival in bed with Daniel. Gabriel decided to never cut his toenails. They became so lethal that Daniel would sometimes sleep on a narrow space in the bed as if he were perched on his spine onto a single tree limb, balanced to neither fall off toward the claws of death or into a bottomless golden pond. As uncomfortable as that must have seemed to a first grader, Daniel could sleep as sound as a cat—with his eyes wide open. Later in life, I would suggest that Daniel's balancing in bed would contribute to his great poise in the batter's box.

"Daniel," Momma would yell down the wooden floored halls, "move over some and give Gabriel room, or else I'm going to send your daddy down there. You don't want to wake him up, now do you?"

How Momma would always change a statement into a question in mid-sentence never made sense to me. By changing a statement that all of us could generally agree with like "You don't want to wake him up," into a question by adding, "now do you?" simply ruined a perfectly well-developed declarative sentence and placed the power of responsibility in *our* court, or bedroom. Of *course*, we didn't want to *wake him up*. We had accomplished that feat on several other occasions. Once my daddy was well tucked in bed, he usually highly disregarded outside interference in his sleeping mode.

However, once awakened from his well-deserved slumber, his subconscious Pavlov-cal predisposition was to pass the right corner of his bed, lean slightly to the right, bending only minimally at the waist to secure his long black belt from his nightstand, flop his bare number ten-and-a-halves down the cold echoing hallway to enter our haven. Once in the general area of the double bed, on which side I was comfortably secured, he would begin to whip the entire bed, marking specific areas like a hungry black bear, areas that were body-lumped and frantic, and would give his best impersonation of an Egyptian master with three slaves from the tribe of Benjamin.

There was no prescribed length of time for my daddy's *offspring bashing* that occurred on a few instances in the middle of the night. --and I purposely for my daddy's benefit here, chose the root word "scribe" in pre*scribe*d-- The length of time, I did reason over a span of years, was determined by a priestly matriarchal mathematical formula, geometry-related, I might add, and the formula was this: D (L+A) x C = P. Since math was not my strong subject, I had to analyze this formula quite a few years before securing it in its final form.

It means, in layman's terms, eliminating the parentheses first, of course, (Lillian and Adam) times the current problems that Daddy might be experiencing with any (D) *deacons* of the church, multiplied by any (C) *church problems* that my daddy might be having to solve or dream about at night, was equal to the amount of (P) *pain* that me and my brothers were going to have to suffer if my daddy had to get out of bed to get Gabriel and Daniel off each other and away from the wall, and not too close to the edge of my yellow circle. I often thought that it simply did not add up.

One of my most embarrassing moments in the fourth grade was when my momma let my best friend and next-door-neighbor Rocky into my bedroom in order to wake me up to go to school. My brothers had already gotten up and were gone. I lingered behind.

Whenever my bed was sodden on a winter's night, I would typically stay in bed much longer the next morning. There's something about a temporary period of warmth, that when gradually altered to equal the extreme cold in the bedroom, will keep one under the thick covers much longer.

I woke up and looked directly into Rocky's face. He was the last person I expected to see.

"Hey...what *you* doin' in here?" I asked Rocky; my face flushed yellow with confusion, so I moved my covers up around my neck like a body-length shirt. "How'd you get in here?"

"Your mom told me to wake you up," Rocky said. "Come on, Jake, the buses are already at school. You're gonna be late." Rocky's face was all-smiling, but sincere, and he was obviously not budging from his bedside spot. I was hoping he might relocate to the window to look out at the school.

"Okay…I will. Give me a second," I said, not knowing what I would do with that second—that one-sixtieth of a minute--except lay there, under the covers, and hope to God that Rocky would somehow suddenly disappear.

Often in church, when my daddy would be preaching, I would not always directly listen to him. Of course, I would look at him because it was hard *not* to notice him, swinging his arms, shouting praises of the Lord, and slapping his hands together--not to mention that he had called me down before from the pulpit because I was inattentive. Typically, he would pound the pulpit with his hand and raise a leg sometimes to regain the attention of his members who had slipped into post-introduction hypnosis. Even though I would look in his direction, I would not be necessarily listening to him. Oh, I would hear him, yes, but I would not be *hearing* him.

However, it's funny how when I needed to get out of a sticky situation--and me in my circle with Rocky staring at me was definitely sticky, I could remember some of my daddy's words from his Sunday sermons.

I looked up at Rocky and began to pray to myself. "Lord, you say in your Word, and I do believe your Word, especially now, Lord, that if we say to that mountain to be removed, that if we have faith as a grain of mustard seed, that we can say to the mountain *be thou removed*, and the mountain will go somewhere else--I suppose if I had listened more closely, I would have known the last part of that verse, but I adlibbed it to suit my slippery situation. So, Lord, *here goes*. (When it came time for God to do His part, I would always say *here goes*, I guess so He'd know when I'd finished talking so He could get to work on *His* part.)

I guess the Lord would have preferred that I had announced my bed-wetting to my brothers with *here goes*, so I could have warned them of the impending danger and also to let myself know it was time to get out of the bed to go to the bathroom.

Rocky asked me, "So, are you getting up, huh?"

I laid and stared at him, and unbeknownst to him, was silently repeating the aforementioned, specific prayer-related request to God. Then I said, without meaning to say it aloud, "Here goes."

Rocky, noticing the intense, prayerful expression on my face, which appeared like a prostrate nun's with everything covered but her head, answered, "Jake, are you okay?" He continued staring at me, and made one quick glance over his right shoulder as if he were thinking about calling for someone. "Do you want me to get your mom or something?"

Answer to prayer! "Yes! Go get her and tell her." Rocky froze.

"Tell her to count to twenty-five," I said. I almost wanted to praise the Lord for His timely answer to my prayer of desperation. With Rocky still studying my face and with his body language confused as to whether to sprint out the door or to wait to see if I should suddenly rise horizontally upward from the bed like a spiritual séance, muttered, "Twenty-five?"

"Yes." I wanted to say the words *my son* but felt that a little hypocritical. "Tell her to count to twenty-five," I repeated. I began to praise audibly, my eyes semi-rolled back into my head, and to this day, believe I even said, "Thank you, Lord."

Rocky, having been exposed to this devout, sacred moment, even before an earthly school day, whizzed directly through my bedroom door and into the kitchen. I could hear a faint babbled exchange between him and my momma.

I wasted no time. I knew that Momma would occupy Rocky at least for twenty-five seconds, 'cause that had always been my private hint to her to buy me some time. On one occasion, she like to have entered the bathroom 'cause I was taking too much time in the tub. She had given me numerous warnings to *hurry up.* Being that we boys shared the same bath water, it was important that each person would hurry his bath, or else not have to be the final person in the tub. As a last resort and seeing that the doorknob was rotating, I begged, "Give me twenty-five seconds." Since that experience, I had used that same phrase to save a few anxious situations in my young life, a secret of Momma and me.

I must admit that that school day, after the morning religious encounter with Rocky beside my bed, was one of the most miserable days of my school life. You see, I didn't have time to change my fruit of the loom, and at school, they became the *pollute of the room.* However, on the other hand, I *did* gain my own private space in Miss Jenny's class room.

3

So, during breakfast of our first full day in Pelham, a low roar decelerated in front of the parsonage, made a wide turn to the side of the house, and grounded to a screeching halt with a hissing afterthought. The Benson Moving and Storage Company truck parked at the side of the house on the declined school driveway. One of the black men jumped out of the truck and placed a chock under two of the truck's large back tires.

My dad wiped his mouth with his cloth napkin and said, "I'm through, sweetheart. Let me go talk to the mover."

"That's fine."

Dad left.

Gabriel started eating more quickly. He picked up his plate and licked the Karo/butter mixture off the surface of the plate.

"No, Gabriel," Momma said. "You know better than that. Don't lick your plate. That's rude and not very good etiquette."

Gabriel took one last lick when Momma turned around to her own plate. Then, his hand pushed across his chin to catch the last smear of leftover syrup. That made his hand sticky, so he licked it too.

"Can I go with Daddy, Momma?" Gabriel asked; he had partially stepped toward the door already, his napkin still lying upon his sticky plate.

Momma swallowed her bite. "Did you clean your plate?"

Squeezing in a lighter moment to ease the tension, I said, "He tried to with his tongue, Momma."

Momma ignored me and continued. "Okay. Go outside but do not get near the big truck without your father close by."

Gabriel stepped through the open back door and shoved the screen door on the porch's bottom edge, letting it squeal shut with a thud and bang.

"Jake," Momma said, "thank you, but not everything's funny in life." She looked left, then right, out of the front window above the kitchen sink.

"Yes, ma'am," I said.

"Momma," Daniel said, pitifully.

"Yes?"

"What's e-quh-tut?" Daniel asked. "Huh?"

"Et-i-quette, son." She corrected Daniel in a soft voice. "Etiquette is the right way to act at the table. There are certain ways we are to behave when it comes time to eat at the table. Understand?"

Daniel's eyes were confused.

Momma commenced to roll off a whole list of e-quh-tuts in a ten-commandment format: "Always put a napkin in your lap. Keep one hand in your lap when you eat. Never talk with your mouth full. Always say please when you ask someone to pass something to you at the table. Never burp. Say *excuse me* if you do. Do not put more on your plate that you can eat..." she would have gone on forever, had Daniel not interrupted.

"Momma," he said.

Coming to a plausible pause in her proper propaganda, she answered, "Yes?"

Daniel stood on a wooden box near the counter, where he had been standing in order to eat. He spoke. "But, Momma...we don't have a table."

Momma hesitated quietly before answering. "That's right, Daniel, we don't. It's out in the truck, isn't it?" she answered. Momma smiled.

"Momma, can me and Daniel go outside with Gabriel?" I asked.

"Daniel and I," she was quick to correct.

"Oh, so do you and Daniel want to go outside and leave me in here by myself?" I asked. A tentative grin coursed my mouth.

“Why don’t you and Daniel go outside, Jake,” she said. Momma smothered her laugh beneath her fair skin. “I’ll stay here with the kitchen.”

“May I be excused?” I quipped.

“Jake, get outside now, before I---” she said.

Me and Daniel darted off the side porch wide open. Even outside, I could hear my Momma’s wholesome laugh. Her healthy reactions to family situations kept us all relaxed. The love she reserved for all of us was validated by her sense of good humor.

Outside, Daddy was talking to the white man with the hat on. They were discussing where to begin unloading and what to put where. The man pointed, and then Daddy pointed. They seemed to be making good verbal progress as both of them disappeared around the far corner of the house, chattering.

Gabriel was scurrying in the bottom edge of the property near the open field. He was picking up rocks and stacking them in a pile. He had Daddy’s sling blade. Some leafy, green and brown victims of his work were lying unattached and lifeless nearby.

Daniel exploded in a run toward Gabriel. “Gabriel!”

I stood and watched the blonde antelope as he gracefully sprinted toward his elder brother.

“’Scuse me, Sir...” a sudden, unexpected, coarse voice to my backside halted me near the driveway.

I froze in place. Cold chills scattered across my arms and back. I turned slowly, and looking up, saw one of the large black men that worked for the moving company. Words were futile.

He spoke. “Could I pleas’ ax you fo’ a drink o’ watta, Sir?” He had his cap off in his hands, both reverently affixed to the cap’s rim. He was leaning forward and backing up at the same time, in a rocking motion. I couldn’t believe I retained so much detail of a single man in one awkward glance. It was like a negative view of a picture.

I moved my lips but nothing came out. “Yes...okay,” I think I said. My mouth stayed open.

It seemed like an eternal split second that I looked up to study his face. His eyes were roun,d and at their core, surrounded by a white picket fence, were onyx stones, three-quarters buried.

"Thanks ye, Sir, thanks ye," he very politely said, with an inhibited smile. He turned toward the large truck and signaled with his hand to the other black man. The other black mover eased shyly around the back of the truck.

I didn't know what to do. I walked toward the house. Suddenly, I realized Momma would be a little thrown back if I walked into our empty, just-eaten-in kitchen with two large black men trailing behind me. I paused near the back porch door and breathed an alternate plan. Turning back toward the thirsty men, head down, I split them by walking toward the well house.

The well house was bricked up about four feet high, capped off with a flat-shingled roof. Sticking out from its side, I was glad to see, was a water spigot. I was hoping I could turn the knob to make the water come out. Once I headed in that direction, I didn't break stride, putting my hand on the spigot. I attempted to turn it. It didn't budge.

I was wondering where my daddy and the white man had gone. They had disappeared somewhere inside the basement. I kept looking underneath my arm toward that direction, hoping to see them. *Come on, Daddy. I need your help.* I don't know why I was so nervous. I could see Gabriel swing blading; Daniel had found a few scattered stones and was tossing them into the open field. I tried again to turn the water on. No luck. My palm had a permanent engraving of the wire-formed design of the spigot handle.

"You mind, Sir? I cans gives it a try, Sir," the first black man said, kindly.

I released the spigot handle. Attempting to explain my poor efforts and inspecting the deep-reddened pattern, I said, "Okay...I can't get it turned... I think it's stuck..."

"Thanks ye, Sir."

His massive, black hand swallowed the whole spigot, and with a simple turn, crushed the hidden rust that had built up on the inside that was keeping the water from coming out. Cool reddish water spit and sputtered from the spigot, followed by a smooth, cold flow of rusty, then clear water. Both men took their turns cupping their hands into rounded pale dippers and gulped large volumes of pure wetness.

I took it all in. The water ran down their wrists and elbows. One mover drew two hands full of water to his face and let it freely flow down his neck and below his shirt collar. As they drank, hums of delight and momentary worship vibrated onto the landscape.

"Jake!" Daddy suddenly yelled from behind me, launching me into a quick one-eighty.

"Yes?" I said, as if I'd broken some cardinal rule of society. "Yes, Sir?"

"Could you run next door to our neighbors and see if they have a phone book? Their name is Lee. Will you, please?" Daddy asked. He and the man continued walking past me. They never once looked at the spigot.

"Yes. Okay." I hesitated, looking at the black men still drinking. I made eye contact with one of the black men. He quickly turned away. I began to move around the driveway toward the neighbor's house. Abruptly, I stopped. "Daddy! Daddy!"

"Lee," he answered without me asking again.

I made one more glance at the well house. The men had turned the water off. They were using handkerchiefs to dry their hands and faces.

I trudged around the house, still thinking about the spigot incident. It made me remember my trip to Asheville with my grandparents. My grandmother and grandpa took me there during the holidays for shopping. We were in the Sears and Roebuck store. Telling my grandmother that I was thirsty, she led me down the back stairs of the store. We traveled down a couple of flights, and there, near the bottom of the steps in bright lighting was a water fountain with a freshly painted set of steps for kids like me. I walked up the steps and leaned over for the best drink of cold water.

It was rejuvenating. As I stood up to wipe my face from the splatter, I was face to face with a white sign with black block letters, firmly nailed to the concrete wall. It read: WHITE ONLY.

I had never seen one of the signs myself, but I had heard about them.

"What does this mean, Grandmother?" I asked.

"It means the black folks can't drink here, Jake," Grandmother explained.

"They can't? Why?"

"They're black, Jake." She smiled. "They're different from us."

Me and Grandmother studied each other's expressions and kept silent. It was awkward.

"Where do they drink when they get thirsty then?" I asked.

Tilting her body toward a darkened hallway behind the stairwell, she said, "Down there." A more regrettable tone drove her statement.

She took my hand to assist me down the steps and escorted me toward the dark corner of the stairwell. Suddenly, something inside my grandmother had caused her to take me there, to see it for myself. I advanced with her footsteps and held on tightly. As we rounded the corner, the other fountain became more noticeable, even in the shadows of the stairwell. The fountain was bent in several places from obvious impacts of some kind, rusted around the bottom. No steps. Above it, in large block letters, a sign read, COLORED.

Grandmother and me didn't speak until we had gotten completely out of Sears and back into Grandpa's station wagon and well down the road toward home. Nothing about the water fountains accompanied us on the highway.

4

My mind was preoccupied with the well-house experience, that I almost traipsed onto the edge of Highway 14, but quickly ceased my momentum, while glancing back at the kitchen window. No one yelled at me, so I looked up and down the road to see if it would be safe to walk parallel to it, if only for a few feet. A short chain-link fence surrounded the Lee's house. Cement blocks held the fence in place and tapered downward as the road dropped toward the Columbia end. There was a gate on the south side of the Lee's yard, where the family parked its cars. A '52 Impala and a '50 something-or-other sat in the sparsely rock-covered driveway. I didn't spot any signs of dogs or dog signs. I owned an innate fear of dogs, something that would haunt my youthful existence in Pelham.

I pulled the gate open and walked through, closing it behind me. The small white house had a metal awning extending over the cement front porch. There were a couple pieces of wrought iron furniture on the porch, rusting and in need of paint. One floor rug, crooked and exhausted, rested at the front door.

I knocked, peering to the right across the short chain-link fence toward the open front yard of the parsonage next door. A high-pitched sound of a dog bark trickled beneath the door, drawing my face back to the door.

Suddenly, the door opened. Standing at the door was a dark-headed boy, about my age.

"Hello," I said.

"Hello."

"I'm Jake. We moved in next-door...well, we're moving in today, spent the night last night, and my daddy wants to

know if you have a phone book. I think he wants to make a call about something."

"My name's Rocky," the boy said. "Let me see." He turned and started to shut the door, then shifted back toward me. "Want to come in while I look? But you'll have to be quiet. My mom works third. At the mill."

"Okay," I said. I eased into the small opening in the door. My eyes had to adjust to the darkness of the small house. All the curtains and blinds were shut solid. The only light was what was coming in through the door. I hung onto the door and kept it cracked. I could hear the steady roar of a floor fan.

Rocky vanished into another dark room. Finally, he reappeared into the doorway's light. "Here ya go," he said. He held out a kinda-thin, yellow book. "Keep it if you want to. We don't ever really use the phone book. We know everybody in Pelham."

"Okay. Thank you," I answered. I nervously sway slightly back and forth, still holding the door with the other hand. "I'll bring it back when my folks are through with it, though."

We both fidgeted. I filled my mouth with air. My cheeks swelled, and I blew it out like the exhaust of a small balloon. "Guess I better go."

"Okay. See ya later." I started to leave. "What grade you in?" Rocky asked. I paused. Both of us slipped into the slanted sunlight near the edge of the awning.

"Third, this coming year," I answered. I stepped down to the ground.

"Me too," Rocky said. He framed a smile.

"You going to Pelham?" Rocky asked.

Pointing, while hugging the phone book, I answered, "That school there, next door to my house."

"Me too. That means we'll be in the same class...and we get Miss Jenny. She's the best teacher in the whole school. Every kid has her, even my mom and dad had her," Rocky explained. "She tells the best stories."

“Good. That’ll be…good,” I said. The silence that lingered after Rocky’s last statement pushed me backwards, tripping on a partially buried stone. “Good,” I repeated, gaining balance. Nervous, I stepped carefully toward the gate. I could still hear the dog barking near the rear of the house, inside.

“Well, I’ll see ya later,” Rocky said.

“Okay, later,” I said. I opened the gate, closed it, and moved away from Rocky’s house toward the edge of Highway 14. My steps picked up pace. *Miss Jenny*? I darted quickly left and scampered past the Lee’s short front-yard fence.

For as far as I could see, up Highway 14, there was still no traffic. It was as clear as the early summer sky. Not a cloud or car in sight.

Once in my own yard, I sprinted down the white rock driveway, around the south corner of the rounded stonewall and toward the open basement door.

Daddy worked inside his office space. “I met Rocky,” I told him.

“Do what?” he asked. He wasn’t tuned-in to my excitement.

“I met this boy next door, our neighbor. He’s Rocky. He’s my age,” I added.

“You have a friend, already? That’s didn't take long.” Daddy said. He unpacked some boxes of books onto his new office shelves, one-by-sixes, built into the wall with nails and two-by-fours. Some of the shelves were painted, some weren’t, but were suitable.

“His name’s Rocky," I said. "His momma works third at the mill. He has a small dog. Me and him will be in the same class next year at the school...next door."

"Huh...don't say."

“Miss Jenny...we both gonna have her. She tells great stories...and teached Rocky's parents too.”

“Taught.”

“Taught.”

"What about that."

Daddy's books were in several boxes, strewn around the room. On the floor was a piece of old carpet, not quite the size of the small room. His desk had already been toted into the room. I suspected that the black men must have hauled the desk in. I wanted to step outside to see if the black men were still around. I took a little time to open boxes and hand the books to my daddy. Later in the summer, he would paint his desk black, and we'd have to unpack boxes again.

While helping him, I read all kinds of titles on the books' spines: *A Study in Revelation*, *Church Planting in the Last Days*, *The Tabernacle*, *Young's Concordance*, *The Amplified Bible*, and others. It was fascinating to see how authors would decide upon a title for their books. I wondered what I would call my book if I ever wrote one. Maybe, *My Life in Pelham* or something like that. A few songbooks and Bibles were scattered in amongst the study books.

The Bibles were all King James Version. My daddy stood strongly by the King James Version, or the KJV, some called it. Daddy would expound from the pulpit, "The King James

Version is the Bible that King James of England translated from the original Hebrew text. He had seventy of his brightest scholars to assist in the translation."

My daddy had worried what might happen if the Revised Standard Version should get a foothold in the church. Looking back, I believe he might have been right about that.

The first question to my daddy out of old Mr. Green's mouth--the chairman of the deacons and the key member of the pulpit committee-- was, "What version of the Bible do you read out of, Preacher?"

"The King James Version, Mr. Green," was Daddy's immediate-without-thinking reply.

Holding up a wrinkly, dusty book, I asked, "Daddy, whose book is this one?" It appeared old enough to be something special.

"Oh, that was given to me by Dr. Percy Ray at the Mississippi Revival Center. Dr. Ray had two copies. They were given to him by the late Dr. Finley Conner, the great revival preacher from West Virginia." Daddy went on to tell me the whole story of Finley Conner, the circuit ridin' preacher from West Virginia.

In church, my daddy often sang a song to the tune of "His Truth Is Marching On," called *The Circuit Ridin' Preacher*:

The circuit ridin' preacher used to ride across the land, with a rifle on his saddle and a Bible in his hand;
He told the mountain people all about the Promised Land,
As he went ridin' singin' down the trail.

Chorus:
Pow'r, pow'r, wonder-working pow'r,
In the blood, of the Lamb,
There is pow'r, pow'r, wonder-working pow'r,
In the precious blood of the Lamb.

The circuit ridin' preacher traveled through the mire and mud, told about the fiery furnace and of Noah and the flood; he preached the way to heaven was by water and the blood, as he went ridin', singin' down the trail.

Leaning, leaning, leaning on the everlasting arms. Leaning, leaning, leaning on the everlasting arms.

His rifle may be rusty, as it hangs upon the wall, And His Bible, old and dusty, may be never read at all, but until the resurrection, when we hear the final call, His truth will ride along.

Glory, glory, hallelujah,

Glory, glory, hallelujah,

Glory, glory, hallelujah,

His truth is marching on... his truth is marching on... his truth is marching on.

My daddy would sing the verses of the song, and the choir would back him up on the chorus each time through. Of course, Daddy would purposely slow down on the last verse to make the verse seem sadder. Softly in the background, the organist would play. The last three phrases of the chorus would fade out at the end until only a whisper remained as the final note to the song. People would cry thinking of the sacrifices that the circuit riding preacher had to make to get the message of God out to the world.

Over the years to come at Pelham, at the First Baptist Church in this small town in the South, I would hear many sermons from the books that me and my daddy unpacked that day in his home office. However, not one book title did I see in all the volumes that day on the topic of prejudice. It would have been a useful source for the events that lie ahead for my daddy's ministry and my days in a small Southern town of yesteryear.

5

Using rocks, Gabriel and Daniel were marking the perimeter for a large dog lot. Now that we had our own yard and house, it was Gabriel's hope to have a dog. We had never had a dog, and Gabriel had wished it for himself to be the sole owner of a four-legged beast.

"Daddy, you can trust me," Gabriel had said. "I'll feed it and water it. I'll even hunt it, if it *will* hunt." Gabriel had recounted these statements to Daddy on the several trips our family had taken down back and forth from the mountains. "Okay, Daddy? Please? Come on, Daddy!"

"Let's wait until we get to the parsonage to see what kind of yard it has...and," Daddy tried to say, but was interrupted by our premature joint-backseat celebrations.

"Yea! A dog!" Gabriel whispered, turning to us for empathetic smiles.

"We're getting a dog!" I chipped in.

"Let's call him Rover!" Daniel said, except babying it up with, "Wover."

"I never said that we're *getting* one," Daddy reminded us. "I only said if the yard were large enough for a dog, and if you three could actually take care of an animal."

"Adam," my momma yelled, "watch that shoulder. It's low." Momma could drive a car from the passenger seat long before England ever perfected it. "Keep to the center more, Adam."

Maintaining his I-just-got-a-new-church expression on his face, Dad said, "Lillian, leave the driving to me."

On the winding Highway 25 coming down the mountain, sharp curves and dangerous dips chartered the course.

Dead Man's Curve took our Roadmaster in a roller-coaster turn to the right, and Daniel piled on top of us to over-exaggerate the motion of the curve.

"Momma, make him get off!" I yelled.

"Daniel Bentley!" my daddy barked. That took care of that. Daniel stuck his tongue out at me.

Such street warning signs as, "Watch for Falling Rocks," "Low Shoulder," and "No Passing on Double Yellow Lines," marked the highway on the right side, and the other right side if we turned around to see out the back windshield.

What is the right and what is left? That was the question that was so confusing to me.

"If you're coming up the mountain, Jake," my momma explained, "the signs are on the right side of the road, *and* if you're coming down the mountain, they're also on the right side of the road."

"How can all the signs be on the right side?" I asked.

"It's all according to which way you're going, north or south," she added, to help clear up what was already a thick pot of mud in my convoluted mind.

When you add longitude and latitude into the mix of right and left, it becomes unbearable. "So, if we're going north, street signs are on the right, and if we're going south, street signs are on the right, right?" I asked once-and-for-all, to settle this puzzling issue.

"Right," Momma said.

"But, if we make all these turns on Highway 25, which takes us all kinds of directions, how can everything stay on the right side?" I almost panicked.

My daddy usually abstained from all discussions of daily relevance in our family. He allowed my momma to explain the unexplainable. It was Daddy's job to enforce the rules and preach, and sometimes to emphasize Momma's points. On some occasions, Momma would summon him for assistance if she needed him. He was like a principal or judge, the government, or God.

“Jake, why don’t you read a book? Didn’t you bring one?” Momma suggested.

“We’ve also gone east and west,” Gabriel said.

“What?” I asked. “East and west too?”

"How can we go east and west, north and south, up and down, and everything be on the *right side of the road*!" For a second, I lost it. My brain overloaded. My daddy knew how to settle my plight.

He said, "Jake, shut up and sit back!"

I did.

In the stillness of the moment, Daniel suddenly inserted “I’ve got to go, Mommy...Momm-ee.”

“Adam, Daniel’s gotta go,” Momma said.

“What? Why does he have to go when we’ve only been traveling such a little distance?” Daddy asked.

What human philosopher, psychologist, or pediatrician could ever answer the question of why kids *have to go* once they climb into the back seat of a family car for a trip? After years of deep deliberation, I now contend that the physical make up of a child contains a urinal reservoir--a small, secluded and undiscovered gland, if you will--that when triggered by the sounds and smells of a cluster of same kin--who confined to an automobile destined for a journey of more than a few miles--will exude extreme discomfort until its contents are dispensed.

Daddy continued, “Okay, tell him to hold on. We’ll stop next to the water shed.”

Why mention the word water?

“Mommy,” Daniel whined, “I don’t want to go at the water shed. I want a weel bathroom.”

“He doesn’t want to stop at the water shed, Adam. He wants a *real* bathroom,” Momma echoed. *Why was mediation necessary considering that the two sides were in talking distance of each other.*

“Well, if he needs to go bad enough, then he’ll go at the water shed. There are plenty of trees there," Daddy said.

"But, Adam..."

Daddy noticed in the mirror Daniel's face with its grimace and exaggerated contortions. "Nobody's gonna see him pee, Lillian." Daddy dropped the subject for us all.

Daniel wiggled and bellyached for the next four miles. He grabbed himself between the legs with both hands and twisted and convulsed in the back seat, occasionally kicking me on a twist or turn. He was the master of manipulation. His face reflected pitiful animations. He was writhing in pain. I never understood how he could go from happy-go-lucky to a have-to-go-liar in such a short amount of time.

"Momm-eee," Daniel virtually cried, "tell Daddy to hur-weee. It's coming out."

Everyone in the car knew that there was no urine within an arm's reach of Daniel's...

"Daniel! Shut up!" Daddy yelled. Daddy's patience was growing thin, and he knew that Daniel was looking for sympathy of some kind. "I've heard enough of your whining. Sit still; you can relieve yourself on the nearest pine at the water shed." Daddy's spirituality was being tried by Daniel's devilish deeds.

Then was Jesus led up of the spirit into the wilderness to be tempted of the devil. And when he had fasted forty days and forty nights. And when the tempter came to him, he said, If thou be the Son of God, command that these stones be made bread. But he answered and said, "It is written, Man shall not live by bread alone, but by every word that proceedeth out of the mouth of God.

"Daniel, you're a baby!" Gabriel whispered.

"Am not!" Daniel retaliated.

"Are so, whiny, little baby."

"Not either. I *do* have to go for real, Gabriel. I'm not kidding this time."

Doesn't that indicate that there were other times when Daniel lied about his bathroom emergencies?

I stuck my tongue out at Daniel and behind the front seat, kicked him back.

"Oww," he hollered, with relatively good dramatics.

Suddenly, the car began a gradual slowing and veered to the side of the road.

Grabbing the back top of the front seat with her left hand and holding onto the door rest, Momma said, "Adam, be careful...Adam?" Her mouth gaped opened.

Daddy didn't respond. He was in his discipline mode. He did not communicate to anything animate when he regressed to this point. It was a comfort zone he found impossible to forsake. He liked it there, often times grinning under his skin.

The car stopped. Putting his right arm atop Momma's on the seat, he turned and glared us in the eyes. "What is your problem, you three? Can't you see that we are trying to get to our new home? And you three can only fuss and complain. If I wasn't in a hurry, I would get out of this car, take my belt off, and whip each one of you good. Do you understand?" He paused there waiting for some type of response. "Say?"

"Adam, we need to get going..." Momma started to say. "The movers..."

"Lillian, leave this to me, please," he answered. He looked back at us, and we sat more erect. "So, do you hear me?"

Gabriel started the chain reaction of "Yes, sir's" and they reverberated across the back seat in chronological order, left to right, east to west, oldest to youngest, driest to wettest, altitude to latitude.

Daddy stared at us until our bottom lips kinda quivered. Then, he lifted his chin like he was looking at us through bifocals and inspected our faces. "Okay, Jake, take Daniel in the woods there." Pointing toward the nearest parcel of forestland, he added, "and let him pee."

"Adam, your language," Momma warned. When Daddy got upset, he would use some questionable language such as *pee*. This was pretty barebones bad for my daddy to say. Gabriel liked daddy to say off-colored words. Gabriel liked to repeat them some time later after Daddy would introduce the words to us as a family group.

I leaned across Daniel and reached for the door. I pushed it open and Daniel and me sauntered through the young summer grass toward the nearest pine tree. We rounded a few shoulder-high bushes and disappeared into the forest for relief.

Daniel dropped his britches and didn't aim for anything in particular. He just let it go wherever his body faced. A spray of errant fluids splashed upon dried leaves. After it became quiet, Daniel asked, "Jake, do you think there are any monsters in these woods?"

Where's his baby voice now?

"Of course, there are," I quickly said. "This is the Highway 25...forest of... *monsters place.*" I lowered my voice, growling, and trying to get him back for whining and almost beating me in foot racing.

"Really? Really?"

"Yep. See that bush over there?" I pointed at the dimmest growth of bushes I could find, since I had *two* free hands like he did. The bushes rattled against each other with a late afternoon gust. The sound effects were timely.

"Where?" he asked, pee-ing a zigzag pattern on the bark of the innocent tree he had chosen as a victim.

"Over there, near that dark place," I said, not flinching. Daniel almost peed on me when he rotated toward my direction.

"Yeah."

"That's where the monsters come in and out of the forest," I said. I taunted him, starting even to convince my own self what I was saying was true, "...and drag their victims in to eat." I decorated my story with a little more creepy voice, stepping back to dodge Daniel's unguided stream. "Hey, watch it!"

Almost at the same time I said those words, an abrupt breeze leveled a rotted tree limb from its heightened location above us to a short distance on the ground behind us, sending an echo reverberating between me and Daniel. *Cr-shk-thump!*

Immediately, Daniel's stream cut off. He stood upright, quiet, and shifted his zipper to the top of his britches, almost zipping part of himself in his haste. *Zippp*!

Without looking back at the pine or the forest or that tree, me and Daniel sprinted toward the black, 1950 Roadmaster at top speed, jumping a couple of low-lying bushes. We both crashed into the closed back door of the Buick, off-balanced and out of control.

For the first time, Daniel like to have beat me.

We both slid in, Daniel first and me next. I closed the car door. Daniel's shoulder touched mine as he leaned around me for a last look into the pee-trified forest of horror.

No one spoke for a few miles, until finally, I felt I had to say, "I'm thirsty."

Daddy pulled the rearview mirror down and glowered at me until I melted below the top of the front seat and out of sight like an overheated candle. As Macbeth said in Mr. William Shakespeare's play entitled *Macbeth*, "Out! Out brief candle!" I wished I could have reminded Daddy of the passage of scripture in Mark 9:41, where it reads, "For whosoever shall give you a cup of water to drink in my name, he shall not lose his reward." What an opportunity my daddy missed to gain a reward in heaven. When and if we get there, I'll remind him of that. I just thought it not necessary to mention it from the backseat of the Roadmaster.

After all, Moses spoke to the rock and water came forth. I thought, only for a milli-second, of mentioning to my daddy about that Biblical fact. Moses had millions of thirsty people following him, and he let *them* have some water. Not my daddy, though. If he had been Moses, archeologists today would be unearthing millions of dead Israelites who succumbed in the wretchedly scorched desert from lack of cool refreshing water that could have been procured with a simple word from God. Where's Moses when you need him?

I could have mentioned to my earthly father Jesus' first miracle at the wedding in Cana. When the governor of the feast ran out of wine, he came to Jesus. After having the men to fill the six large pots with water, Jesus turned the water into wine.

Water problems always ran in our family--excuse the pun. Running parallel to Highway 25 is the most tantalizing creek you've ever seen. Every time we ever had to stop beside that creek, the sound and feel of dashing and darting water inspired me, on the spot. It rushed and roared, especially after a series of rainy days, and drew my feet and hands directly into its heart. In their beds, the slippery mossy rocks rested. The creek dropped inches in some places and then would progressively rise so that it could take a sharp veer to the right or left--depending on whether or not you were traveling north or south-- in order to drop or turn again, twisting out of sight and sound. Laurel thickets contributed dark shadows of coolness.

On this day, with my being thirsty and my parents' needing to meet the movers in Pelham, South Caroline, our only option was to stop next to the creek. We had no other choice.

Our Roadmaster started steaming under the hood. Daddy got out of the car, lifted the hood, looked at the boiling steam that was escaping the radiator cap, and announced to all of us, who were squeezed into standing-room-only in the car, "The car is hot!" His voice echoed off the walls of rocks that lined the sides of the creek. "It's hot...hot...."

Daddy pulled his handkerchief out of his back pocket and attempted to touch the radiator cap. I think he knew better but was seeking some type of sympathy and response from my Momma.

"Adam, don't do that. You're gonna get burned," Momma said. She was holding my wriggling toddler sister, who was suffering from instant anxiety. "Adam! Be careful!"

Even in his voice, I could detect, behind that veneer of manly duty and protocol, an insecure individual in the presence of car trouble.

"Lillian, I'm just trying to get the cap off, to let off some steam," he explained around the lifted hood. Daddy and

Momma conversed around the hood at times like that. Momma, with her window down already--we never had air conditioning in our cars or houses back then-- leaned her head out the window as far as possible, giving timely advice to Daddy when she felt it was necessary to do so.

At times like that, I felt sorry for my daddy and momma. With active kids restlessly shifting around the car like cats on hot tin, the job of repairing our family's mode of transportation without any tools or expertise was overwhelming at best.

My daddy's knowledge of the automobile was limited to the operation of a radio, cigarette lighter, and the dipstick. He didn't smoke but could demonstrate the fierceness of a red coil of heat in a cigarette lighter. I liked it when he would use the lighter to burn a Kleenex or leaf. "Never play with fire, boys. It gets out of control quickly," he taught us. "This is a valuable lesson." Later on, Gabriel would ignite a fire with matches in the field behind the parsonage that would require a fire department to extinguish. Lesson unlearned.

Daddy stood leaning into the hood, steam still rising. Suddenly, he yelled to Momma. "Tell them boys to get out here and bring that Pepsi bottle."

Our family carried a sixteen-ounce soda bottle with us in the back floorboard of the Roadmaster Buick, just in case a bladder-related emergency should arise, mostly on long trips where an interstate highway should come into play. Of course, that didn't include Daniel, 'cause he always went in the bushes. He wasn't a soda bottle man.

"Go take the bottle to your dad, you three," Momma said.

"Has he got to go, Momma?" Jake asked.

"Jake, quit asking silly questions and get outside," Momma said, not happy with a steaming car and an anxious little girl in her lap.

We three slid outside. Daddy was waiting with orders for us. "Gabriel, you take this bottle to the creek," Daddy said.

"Fill it up to the top and then pass it to Jake. Jake, you pass it to Daniel."

Daddy took his handkerchief and twisted the radiator knob counterclockwise, and *spew*, the steam gave its last cough, with a single scattered spray. Daddy gave a petty yelp. Momma didn't respond. "Now, Gabriel, fill it up," Daddy said.

For the next twenty minutes, we passed the bottle up and down the creek bank below our Buick until my daddy filled the radiator. In the middle of the madness, as the bottle moved down the line, Daddy had time to lean into and underneath the hood. His face was flushed and sweat was streaming down his forehead and into his mouth. He spit it out. Daddy had one leg up on the bumper for support in order to tilt his large physical frame over the motor while remaining directly beneath the hood, as if he really could discern what he was looking at. Esther, my younger sister, eased from my momma's grip and toddled across the front seat, leaning herself on the steering wheel for balance. She pushed against her hands, trying to see what was going on outside. Suddenly, from the weight of her body, her hands slipped, landing her flatly onto the horn of the car. She lay there, her body's weight enough to blare the horn.

My daddy immediately jumped up and cracked his head on the underside of the hood, more specifically on the big metal hook that hung downward from the hood. In the next few moments, with the horn blaring inexorably into my daddy's ears, the scene exploded into an unpleasant one. Thankfully the horn blared long enough to drown out any unseemly words that our family was not supposed to be introduced to at that moment.

Once the radiator cooled and the hood was slammed shut, we all climbed back into the car, put our soda bottle under the front seat, and moved toward our destination in Pelham.. I smiled under my skin knowing that during the soda bottle transfer, I had dipped my hands into the crisp creek water for a quick drink of water. Even Jesus was thirsty at Jacob's well, and the Samaritan woman gave Him water.

From my perspective in the back seat, the only visible sign of our family emergency was a superficial trickle of blood that mixed with my daddy's sweat down into the collar of his Sunday white shirt

6

It took our family about a month to finally get all the boxes unpacked into the Pelham parsonage. In our bedroom, Gabriel and Daniel unpacked Gabriel's stuff together. Well, Daniel mostly watched. He was mesmerized with Gabriel's stuff. Gabriel's stuff wasn't any different from mine, but Gabriel kept his stuff so much more organized and personal than I did mine. He had stationery that our uncle in the Navy had sent him from overseas. It was still wrapped in the original cellophane like Gabriel had received it, but mine had already been opened, and Daniel and me had drawn all over it one day when we had gotten bored during a rainstorm.

Gabriel was different from me. He was brown headed and with slightly darker skin. He looked more like my daddy's side of the family. His face was splotched. My philosophical explanation for that was he ate too many mustard sandwiches.

My daddy had dark hair, and my momma had light brown hair. How we all ended up with blonde hair was a mystery. Daniel's hair was so blonde, that Bill Kimball, one of the deacons at our church, nicknamed Daniel *Cotton Top.*

In our bedroom, our double bed was pushed against the wall into a corner. We liked it that way because it cleared the rest of the room for whatever we wanted to do. We wrestled a lot when Momma wasn't around. Also, I liked to get my plastic army guys out of my soldier box and play with them on the floor. I had quite a collection of soldiers, all of them green, and could layout a battle plan that included a good four hundred or more stiffened combatants.

My grandparents and parents knew when they went to town, they could make me happy with another pack of plastic soldiers. The pack cost twenty-five cents at Woolworth's department store in Greenville. There were fifty green soldiers in a pack.

I really liked the tall maple tree in the backyard, because when me and my brothers weren't climbing it, I could setup a grand battle stand at its base. The roots made great mountains and hills and the grass, the greatest trees and bushes. One of my soldiers became my favorite, so I made him general. He commanded all my forces, and he knew he could come to me for instructions or therapy, if need be. We kept everything quite confidential between us two.

The reason I selected him was because he had an obvious flaw on his left cheek, a flaw I surmised he must've received in a heroic battle somewhere near his original manufacturing site. Upon careful inspection of each soldier--even though they were all supposed to be identical--I could note numerous differences. Sometimes, however, I could *not* find a difference, and I figured that those soldiers were just part of the package, not individually unique. *Anyone can be the same and do what they're asked, but it takes a real soldier to be different, to reach above and beyond the call of duty,* I told the troops one day when I had them in dress parade beneath the tree. I placed Ike, my favorite soldier, on a large rock above the other green-with-envy soldiers, as I made my speech. Then, I allowed Ike to speak. He was quite humbled by the whole ordeal, and I was surprised by his conclusion, when he gave a somewhat unexpected tribute to me. I smiled. It was subjective.

Of course, I looked over my shoulder to see if anyone was around. I didn't want to talk aloud to my soldiers if someone was watching me or was in hearing distance. One day, I didn't realize through an opened window, my daddy was listening to my speech. He didn't call me on it, but only commented as we were walking to the mailbox together, "This Ike must be very special. You need to introduce me to him someday."

I was mortified that he had overheard our conversation. I shifted behind my daddy as he moved closer to the mailbox.

He reached into the box and pulled the mail out, studying it. Then, turning back toward the house, he stopped next to me, still studying the mail. He breathed in, looked down at me, handing me a disposable piece of mail, and said in a deeper voice, “Carry on, soldier.” He went into the house.

I was careful after that day to keep my voice down when I played under the maple, and I always looked around to see if the coast was clear. Later, I would find a great battlefield on the school grounds, after school.

Ike’s greatest achievement was a battle against the Nicked-Arms. This was the most brutal army ever. Of all my years of collecting soldiers, I had never congregated a more wicked fighting force than the Nicked-Arms.

The Nicked-Arms came in a pack, all identical. The closer I inspected this company, the more each soldier looked alike. One thing that stood out about this force, and the fact they earned the name of the Nicked-Arms, was because each soldier’s right arm was nicked or cut, perhaps a fault of production or something. Usually when I would find a fault in a soldier, the fault turned out to benefit him in the whole system of military ranking. The Nicked-Arms couldn't fight past their innate faults.

Ike knew the challenge that lay before him on that June afternoon. He and I had talked for long minutes over the strategies we could possibly employ to combat this formidable militia.

Finally, Ike spoke, "Jake, it seems to me, Sir, that from my perspective here on top of Bolder Rock, the Nicked-Arms, which hitherto shall be referred to as, the NA's, have dispersed their forces into three battle groups. I could see, a little better if you'll lift me higher--which I did--the standees are assembled to the right flank, the kneelers to the center, and the proners are to the left flank."

Ike knew exactly where the troops were assembled. He studied the whole scene and would have immediately implemented the plan of attack, if it hadn't been for Momma calling me to lunch. Ike accompanied me to lunch in my shirt pocket. We didn't talk about war at lunch, but after my

last bite of salmon patty, I excused myself from the table and headed back to the battlefield. My unexpected burp announced the recommencement of the war.

Later on, when Daddy was painting his at-home office desk black, Daniel--to get even at me-- dropped one of my soldiers into Daddy's paint bucket. I fished the soldier out and let him dry on top of the well house. I thought once about throwing him away, since he had dried patchy and puny looking, but decided instead to make him the cook for my entire army. We called him Private Leroy.

"Let's send two regiments of grenade launchers to the right flank..." Ike began to command right away.

At the end of the battle, Ike's order for a surprise rear attack was brilliant. Not only did we destroy almost every NA, but we also captured over fifteen of their sharp shooters.

Ike was given another promotion that day and got the weekend off for R & R. He and some of his fellow officers went to church with me and made a mid-service exploration of a songbook rack in row three of the Pelham Baptist

Church. There were no casualties, but there were a few close calls. Daddy looked at me a couple of times during the operation, and I had to rescind the operation right before the altar call. All troops were safely returned to the soldier box immediately after the Sunday meal at another church family's home.

I don't know which soldier type I liked more. There were the soldiers that lay down to shoot, knelt to shoot, and stood up to shoot. The hand grenade throwers were okay, but they were apt to have their heads blown off for standing in that vulnerable stance for so long. The kneelers would kill more hand-grenaders--HG-- than any other combination of combatants. The bazooka boys were awesome. Taking out an entire platoon was no problem for a BB--bazooka boys. Ike was a commanding officer. He stood erect with one hand empty--the other directing the troops.

I have to admit that the BB's, of all the soldiers, inspired me to get more directly involved in the battles, when I received, from Santa, my first BB gun one Christmas. By springtime, Daddy took me to replenish my BB supply and I saved three boxes of BB's. In one war, the biggest of Ike's career, I stood by the maple, and took a standing position, and in a calculated maneuver, shot one by one, the entire brigade of enemy soldiers. I missed six times from a range of four feet. It was the only war where I actually had to bury soldiers on the battlefield. There were fresh graves all over the place. Three soldiers were missing in action and two were impossible to identify without their heads attached. Pvt. Leroy made leftovers that night.

Ike died in 1959. He was dismembered when Brutus, our distant neighbor's brown boxer bulldog chewed him up into five separate pieces. I had a complete military funeral for him. To this day, he is still buried under a large rock at the foot of the maple. I buried him three feet deep. Bolder Rock is his marker. "A soldier who was my personal friend," I eulogized.

Because of Ike's gruesome departure from this earth, Brutus became my archenemy in Pelham. I hated him and he me. He attacked me every time he saw me, every time. For some reason, which I could not figure out, and still can't to this day, I was a continuing target for Brutus. My brothers or one or two of my friends could be around, and it wouldn't make a spit of difference to Brutus; he would chase me.

One day Gabriel, Rocky, and me were playing in the backyard. Rocky was hitting us some grounders with a baseball and bat, when suddenly Brutus appeared around the curved corner of our cement wall. "He stood there a while watching us play," Gabriel would tell me later. I didn't see Brutus at all.

I believe there was something that connected me and Brutus, irrespective of our different species. In Brutus' eyes, he was an animal, and I was an animal toy. Brutus' prime purpose for me was --after torturing and belittling me in front of every friend and family member I knew, to eventually kill me. He wanted to kill me.

On that day, Brutus stood there and watched us field a few ground balls, and then, as soon as I spotted him and Rocky yelled, Brutus began the pursuit. I wasn't the only kid who feared this gruesome creature. He was massive for a dog. He was a brown bulldog. His chest muscles reacted to his every move like a weight lifter trying to impress the judges. His mouth was perfect for a New York Bronx fighter, who had had every jaw muscle loosened by too many direct punches. His legs were powerful, and his front right paw was pure white. Of course, his tail was gone. I don't think I ever heard him bark. Perhaps he was dumb. I would never have told him that to his snout.

I highly respected him. He was always on the job, gave me his best chases, and never turned down an opportunity to scare the squaw-goozees out of me. His owners, the Lees, three houses down, not the Lees next door, but their cousins, never knew where he was and figured, I'm sure, he was in the neighborhood somewhere playing with small children. They were right on that part. I was the child with whom Brutus was playing. Wasn't I the fortunate child? Why couldn't the Lees have bought him a large toy with a bell in it? No, I had to be the ding dong!

Rocky yelled, "Brutus!"

A bat was dropped, two gloves tossed into the air, a ball bounded into the paved driveway of the school, and all three of us sprinted toward the well house. We knew that if we could somehow get on top of the well house, we would be out of Brutus' reach.

"Hurry, Jake!" Gabriel screamed. "To the well house!"

Well, since I was the slowest of the community runners, I had last place on the top of the well house, if I should make it alive, that is. Of course, Brutus loved these moments because he would measure his paces. I knew he could have killed me at any moment of his or my life, but he wanted--more like a cat's contingency plan than a dog's--to make every encounter theatrical and romantic. So, he allowed

Rocky and Gabriel to secure their places atop the well house, and then as I was being assisted up onto the well house by the other two survivors, Brutus would secure a mouthful of my pants leg and began to tug against my pullers.

No, Brutus couldn't bark, but he could growl like no other dog on earth. His growl stirred the marrow inside my leg bones into a percussion-like jell, closer to a Jamaican serenade sound than anything I have ever felt or heard. It was terrifying enough to relive the sound on numerous occasions in my sleep. He was a prominent contributor to many of my yellow circles at night.

Rocky and Gabriel pulled and pulled. I couldn't let go. I was already crying and that was bait for Brutus' appetite. He loved my tears. They were food for his soul. For Brutus to hear me cry, while I was running from him or hiding from him or thinking I might have seen him, was like throwing lighter fluid on a hot cigarette.

"Pull!" I yelled.

"We are," Gabriel said. "Don't let go!"

Like I was going to let go. I didn't even look down. I could feel his hot breath, and every once in awhile, to feed his ego, Brutus would shake me and growl even louder.

Rocky comforted me with, "He's not going to hurt you!"

Tell that to the dog, 'cause you're not going to convince me of that.

"Daddy! Daddy!" Gabriel called.

For some reason, Brutus knew my daddy. I don't know if they had met in another life or if my daddy had thrown something at Brutus when he had passed through the yard at an earlier date. I do know whenever Gabriel would yell for Daddy, Brutus would take one last vigorous shake and let go, only if we were near the parsonage.

Again, he let go.

I slid up onto the well house and sat down. My face was dirty and black from lying down on the well house roof, and my pants leg was ripped open, my lily-white leg exposed.

Brutus turned and trotted around the dull curved corner of the stone wall and out of sight. I can never get rid of that image of Brutus' behind telling me goodbye.

"You okay?" Gabriel asked me in his older brother voice. I liked it when Gabriel would be concerned over me. I think Daniel and me contested over Gabriel's attention even more than we foot raced each other.

Rocky and Gabriel jumped down off the well house, dusted their britches off, and headed to the backyard. I went into the house to tell my Momma about my latest scrape with Brutus. She was very compassionate but warned me about soiling my clothes.

"We don't have much money, Jake," Momma said. "I know Brutus did this to you, but please be easy on your clothes. Your dad is working very hard as a pastor and may have to take on a part time job just to get us by. Do you know what one pair of new pants cost nowadays?"

Sitting on the bed, still shaking, I answered, "No ma'am, I don't."

"I bought these two weeks ago," she said pointing to the ones Brutus had just shredded, "at J C Penney's for three dollars. That's a lot of money, Jake. Please be careful, will you?"

Feeling my Momma's heart and knowing she was a good woman, I said, "Yes, ma'am, I will."

I headed back outside to see what my big brother and best friend were up to, stopping at every corner of the house to look for Brutus.

7

The first time I ever saw him was on a Monday, in June. We hadn't lived in Pelham long and the hot, humid days had introduced themselves to me in an intimate way. My clothes stuck to my skin.

It was that same June, I think, that I sweated for the first time. I remember running into the house and into my Momma's room to tell her about my sweat. I knew she would want to know. I had played around the yard, running and chasing an old baseball. Then, I realized it had happened.

“Momma, I sweated! Look!” I said, pointing to the drop that was barely heavy enough to trickle on its own without a little prodding from me. I tilted my head forward, trying to feel the sweat drop moving from beneath my hairline, down my forehead. “Look at it. That’s something, ain't it?”

"Isn't it, Jake."

"Isn't it, Momma?"

"Well, wait now,” she said, her hands busy folding a washrag that she had dropped from my sudden entry. “Let me take a look at it, Jake.”

She moved to me and tilted my head a little more into the light from her bedroom window. “You’re right, Jake. There it is, as big as any sweat drop I’ve ever seen. Yep, I see it.”

I stood up, still not straightening my head, but holding on to the life of that very first drop of sweat I had well earned, in that month of June.

Momma had a way of tenderizing any moment with her voice and eyes. She could tip her head ever-so-slightly and purr like a kitten. She would caress my face like a new summer tomato. It's the same attention all six of us kids yearned for, and sometimes competed for. But don't get me wrong; please don't. That same pleasing lady, who we called Momma, if prompted by our iniquities, could be rapidly transformed into a vehement potion of discipline, completely contrary to the compassionate caregiver of whom we were accustomed.

One boring day behind the parsonage, Gabriel came up with the brilliant idea of spitting on a silk worm crawling across our driveway. Carefully checking both ways with his eyes, Gabriel primed his mouth with an ample volume of saliva, and posturing his lips and cheeks just so, expectorated a perfect shot of spit, one of Gabriel's renowned skills, directly onto the forehead of the silkworm.

"You got him, Gabriel," Daniel yelled.

"Shut up, you idiot!" Gabriel whispered. "Momma's gonna hear you and then---"

"She'll kill us!" I chided in.

Two things that Momma had forbidden us to ever do was to call adults by their first names without saying mister, mizzes, or miss, and to spit on a human being. Gabriel had spit on our neighbor's kid in the mountains one day when we lived there, and Momma found out about it. After a lengthy lecture on that day, Momma proceeded to take her hickory switch and leave a roadmap of regret all over Gabriel's legs. Since that experience, I had seen Gabriel literally force-swallow spit I knew he had intended to contribute to Mother Earth's topsoil. Momma's wrath had spoken deeply to Gabriel's conscience and spit glands.

The silkworm attempted to inch itself across our driveway but had been halted by Gabriel's spitball. At school, Gabriel was the only boy in his grade that could spit all the way from the dumpster to the corner of the cafeteria building.

"Soak it, Jake!" Daniel whispered. The silkworm goo-ed forwards, extending a sliming web in his plump shadow.

I was the world's worst expectorator. A finite spray I could generate, but the bulk of my spit always drooled down my chin, onto my shoe tops, weak and slobbery.

"Okay," I said.

For a few seconds, I held my saliva and then blew out my spit, in a spray, dribble, and drool.

Gabriel laughed. "You're one crappy spitter, Jake."

"It's all over your chin," Daniel said. Gabriel and Daniel gawked at me. "Show him how to do it, Gabriel. Do it again."

Gabriel started his face-wriggling motion, calling up all his saliva glands into action, preparing to finish the silkworm off, which had stalled under the first gluey spit barrage. Gabriel slightly tilted his head back to load all his fluid in his mouth into one final spit of death for the stalled silkworm. Gabriel was milking his throat and mouth, concentrating extra seconds to generate the killer spit. His mouth was full and running over.

Out of the blue, Momma's voice interrupted our fun with, "What y'all doing back here?" She was rounding the north end of the parsonage and moving at a steady pace. Gabriel had way-too-much spit to swallow. He began to slosh it side to side in his mouth but there was little room for sloshing. His face was tight like a balloon ready to bust. "What's going on here?" Growing impatient and not getting pertinent information, she added, "Do I have to ask you that question again?"

Me and Daniel were waiting for Gabriel to respond since he was the oldest. However, he just stood there looking at Momma while she looked at him. He looked like he wanted to vomit. I could tell this wasn't the first time he had sweated.

"Gabriel, what's that in your mouth?" I think Momma thought she had caught us with chewing tobacco. We had experimented before with rabbit tobacco that grew in the field behind the house.

Gabriel tried to smile, and saliva began to ooze from his tight lips, now quivering. His eyes were watering; he was fighting off a cough.

"Open your mouth, Gabriel, and show me what's in there!" Momma said.

"He can't---" Daniel began to say.

"Daniel, be quiet, I'm not talking to you," Momma barked. "Open it now, Gabriel," Momma demanded. She swiveled her head to search the backyard for the closest bush, from which she probably felt she should pluck a hickory switch. We all recognized that look of hers, and I could see her look was un-damming Gabriel's face. Spit was commencing to pour down his chin and onto his shirt, wetting it like a baby's bib from a bottle with a cracked nipple. Gabriel mimicked a garden fountain with clogged spray holes.

Momma's eyes followed Gabriel's river of spit down his shirt-front until her eyes made contact with the poor silkworm, halted in a pool of Gabriel's saliva at his feet. She knelt down and studied the worm. Standing back up, she dug deep into Gabriel's eyes and asked, "What has this creature done to you to deserve such treatment?"

Here comes the lecture.

Momma stood, and we three took a half step backwards, sensing the impending moral communication.

She obliged with, "God created all of us, great and small, from the pauper to the king," she spoke. Her hands were like wild birds. Our countenances melted on our facial bones like over-heated candles. "When God had finished His creation," Momma continued, "He said it was good. We as Children of God must treat *all things* with respect, whether it is a soaring eagle from the heights of the bluest sky or a meager silkworm, etching its way across the face of mother earth."

Through my years of hearing preaching, I would never listen to a single man behind the pulpit who could out-orate my momma. For a woman preacher, she was Billy Graham's competitor. When she got wound up, there was no stopping her, until she completely emptied her soul of all its profound poetic conscience into our more-than-attentive ears.

"And Gabriel," Momma continued, "you and I have been through this discussion before..."

Momma took extra time to retell the story of the boy in the mountains on which Gabriel had expectorated. She recounted the lecture and the switching, to which Gabriel slurped some excess slobber escaping his mouth and tried to grin. The voluminous pressure was indirectly producing obvious discomfort to Gabe's soul.

"So, now I want you boys to hear me, and hear me well," Momma said.

Here comes the climax and the invitation.

"In the future," Momma preached, "I had best never catch *anyone of you* spitting on *anything...ever...*and especially, I had best *never* find out that you have even thought of spitting on another human being. That is the lowest of low insults in the human race! There is no one who should be spit upon, especially in the face...*never*!"

There was a moment of silence, where I could tell Momma was trying to conjure up her form of discipline for us. Her sharp eyes scoured the backyard; she was thinking at the same time. It was almost a spiritual silence. What Daniel soon would extemporaneously spout into the sultry summer air proved to me that it was indeed a spiritual silence.

Daniel said, "'cept the Devil, Momma!"

Momma ceased any movement. "What, Daniel? What was that?" Momma asked.

"The Devil himself. We can spit in *His* face, can't we, Momma? If we see Him, we can't spit on Him, huh?"

Momma was quite taken aback by Daniel's beyond-his-years answer. She looked down at him and into his jumpy eyes, knowing he had somehow realized who had caused us all to sin and get in trouble in the first place. Me and Gabriel observed closely as we thought perhaps Cotton Top may have gotten us out of a heap of trouble. Momma's face swelled out into a pleasing smile. We all sighed quietly, relieved. She knelt down at Daniel's feet like she had for the silkworm earlier, and said, "Yes, Daniel. If you *ever* see the Devil, I want you to spit right in his face." She paused before standing up, kissed Daniel on the forehead, and then, taking a few steps away from us, not even attempting to retrieve a hickory switch, rotated and said, “And if you *don’t* spit in His face, I’ll switch all three of you good.”

Momma disappeared around the corner of the house, but then stepped back into view to announce, “One day, you boys will look up to see that silkworm flying over your heads arrayed in beautiful wings. You best be glad he can’t spit.”

Gabriel threw up on the ground, away from the silkworm.

Momma walked into the house loudly singing the first stanza of *At the Cross.* I can still hear her sweet voice. “A’las and did my Savior bleed and did my Sovereign die; would He devote that sacred head, for such a *worm* as I?” She never mentioned spitting again.

On a following Monday in June, Emmett’s A-model automobile pulled up in our driveway. I could hear his car running and it fascinated me, that strange *clickety-clack, rattle-lee pomp* sound. It sputtered and spit and then stopped running. His A-model resembled a woman’s chalk-gray Easter Sunday morning hat, adorned with an extra-tire-with-yellow-spokes bow decorating its side.

His name was Emmett, pronounced *M-it.* He was our church custodian; he wasn't *right.* What I mean by that is, "He's not all there." That's what one of the kids in my church told me.

Several of the older boys in the community teased Emmett quite a bit. They asked him to shake a leg, or to dance a jig, or to walk the centerline on Highway 14. On occasion, Emmett would walk the centerline to amuse the boys. He would also lift his leg and shake it; I've seen him dance the jig, which was a dance move, composed of a mixture of Elvis, Fred Astaire, and Bozo the Clown.

One thing that the boys usually ended up taunting Emmett with was "Walk the dam, Emmett!" It was a bad joke that carried back to earlier in the century when Emmett's dad had challenged the dam, only to fall to his death in the violent waters of the Enoree below the bridge. "Walk the dam, Emmett!" The death of Emmett's dad was said to be an accident, but others suspected that Emmett's dad had committed suicide when he had realized that his son was in actuality retarded. Emmett had a severe fear of water. He would not walk in the shadow of the Enoree.

Mr. Buford Jackson was the one who told my daddy, "It definitely was a suicide, Preacher."

When Emmett would hear the boys or others in Pelham challenge him to walk the dam, he would shake his head *no*, and then immediately leave in his A-model. That's one reason why most people didn't tease him to walk the dam. They liked having Emmett around to poke fun at.

In my heart, I believed that Emmett was too bright to walk the dam and often thought if Emmett's father would have lived long enough to see his son grow up, he would have been proud of Emmett.

Emmett lived north, past Pelham School, past the giant swing set and hedge-covered ditch, below Mr. Rose's white house. Emmett's back yard connected to the lower playground at the school, across the ditch. On occasions, school kids would gather at the school side of the ditch and make comments about the back of Emmett's barn and house. Every time my family would pass Emmett's house on the way to town, I would see Emmett's A-model, parked under the barn opening. Emmett always backed his A-model inside, so he could simply pull straight out if he needed to go some where, which couldn't be too many places, because his only occupations were to clean the church weekly and cut people's yards in the summer, if they needed him to.

Emmett wore a dirty-but-dressy rimmed hat with a feather in it. I supposed he had two of those hats, 'cause he would wear an identical one on Sundays, 'cept it was spotlessly clean and the feather was less ragged. A bulky red handkerchief, which he used frequently on hot summer days, hung from the large pocket of his bib overalls. Out of his right back pocket hung his outsized black wallet, connected to his belt by a droopy, dull silver chain. Emmett always, Sunday or any other day, wore his brown working boots, tied all the way up to the top hooks. On Sundays, they were shined immaculately.

“Is yo daddy hea’?” he asked me.

“Yes, Emmett,” I answered. Everybody in Pelham called Emmett by his first name. No one ever said Sir or Mister to him or even Mister Longstreet, no matter how much older he was. He was Emmett to everyone; he preferred that.

“Cud-ja go’n fetch ‘im fer me?” he asked.

"Is there something wrong?"

"Naw...I need to talk to 'im."

“I’ll be right back, Emmett,” I said. I turned away from Emmett to find Daddy, who I remembered being in his home office. From Daddy's earlier practice session, I could still hear the trumpet solo in my ears. *His eye is on the sparrow.*

I knocked on his office door. He always asked us to knock in case he might be praying to God or something. I guess he didn’t want us to interfere with any serious conversations between him and God. I could understand that.

"Come in," Daddy answered.

I opened the door. Daddy was sitting on a low couch beneath the small window that allowed us to see the ground level of the side yard near the blunt stone wall along the driveway. "What do you need, Jake?" he asked.

"Emmett is here. He's outside next to his car."

"What does he want? Did he say?"

"No. He just said that he wanted to see you," I answered.

"Okay, tell him I'm on my way." I stood aloof. "Go ahead. Don't make him wait," Daddy said.

"Okay."

I headed back through the cool, dark garage and stepped into the glaring sunlight that was beginning to bend the leaves. "Daddy said he'll be right here, Emmett," I said. "He's on his way. He was in his study room."

"Okay. That's fine, Jeck. Thank ye."

I hesitated. I couldn't believe that Emmett knew my name. My name from his lips sounded different, a kinda new different. I liked it. Emmett had both hands by his sides. His left hand, nearest me, was rough, with black crud under his fingernails. He fidgeted, briefly tugging on his left pants leg.

"Want me ta shake ma leg fer ya, Jeck? I will." Emmett said. He wanted to do a one-man show for me.

"No."

Emmett had been asked to be church custodian when he was only seventeen years old. His momma, a widow since her husband's alleged suicidal death, had asked the deacons if it would be possible that Emmett could learn to clean the church, since he was not going to be able, mentally and socially, to do most other jobs in town.

At the deacon's meeting, to vote whether or not to hire Emmett, Mr. Green, the chairman of the deacons spoke up. "God is no respecter of persons. He loves us all... and Emmett has been one of our best kids around Pelham Baptist Church. Sure, he hasn't been able to do some things because of his...well, his mental learning abilities, but he has always had a smile, and his momma says he's a hard worker around their place. I recommend that we hire Emmett on a temporary basis, and then permanent if he shows us he can do the job."

The deacons had voted eleven to one to hire Emmett. The one vote against Emmett was a young deacon in his first year, Buford Jackson, who commented, "Emmett's not capable of keeping the church clean. He don't have a mind to do it."

Springing out of the back screen-door, my daddy said, "Emmett!" Daddy walked patiently toward us. "I had to wash my hands before I shook your hand. I've got my hands dirty fightin' the Devil this mornin'." Daddy walked toward Emmett with his hand out. They shook. Daddy had no idea about the fingernails, I guess.

Emmett grinned. His teeth were murky and tarnished. Behind those teeth, he laughed a pulsating grunt that drug across his throat like a deep wash tub.

Daddy asked, "What can I do for you, Emmett?"

“I tho’t, Paster, if’n yuh wish fer me to, I’d cut yuh grass fer yuh, if’n yuh need me ta,” Emmett said, shyly. A left-over grunt slipped from his throat.

“Well, Emmett,” Daddy began, “I don’t have a mower of my own and don’t see how I could ever afford one. We didn’t need one in the mountains with our small yard.”

“Yes, Paster,” Emmett agreed. For the first time, I saw Emmett’s whole smile. It opened tentatively but expanded warmly. It was cavity infested and yellowish. His genuine nature was written into his hearty smile. I tried not to be noticed, leaning over and taking a direct look into his mouth.

“Well, let’s see,” Daddy said. “What do you regularly charge, to cut a yard, Emmett?”

I could tell that Daddy was trying to dicker, but he was also trying to be kind.

Daddy and Emmett's conversation was broken temporarily by the rumble of an airplane passing overhead and its subsequent shadow that rolled across our yard and through us. Emmett paused, took his hat off, and looked directly up at the plane. He plainly said, “Now, I’m not God…or nothin’, Paster, but if’n I was…Him, I’d knock all o’ those planes…out of thuh skies.”

With that abrupt statement, my daddy and me suddenly gained a new insight into Emmett’s rambling and scrambled mind. Daddy looked at me to make sure I didn't respond. I didn't. From a distance, and to the average eye, Emmett appeared normal; however, once he commenced to speak, the distortion of his pattern of thought was clearly exposed.

“Fer a yard as big as your’n, Paster, I ken cut it fer two dollars or two dollars-fifty, if that be okay wi yuh, Sir?” Emmett answered. "I cut grass gud."

"That's what I hear, Emmett. You come highly recommended."

"Yes, sir, Paster."

“Well, when can you begin? It don’t really need it *too* bad now, but whenever you want to begin, you can,” Daddy said.

“I tho’t, if’n it’s okay wi you, Paster, that I mite run to thuh house and bring my mower down now, and cut yo grass fer ya," Emmett said. His excitement showed. He tugged briefly on his pants leg. Emmett's speech design was inconsistent. He could say some words almost correctly and others not, sometimes repeating the same word differently the second time around. "My house jus' up the highway. I be back in no time flat. I ken jus' hop right on it...lickety-split." His eyes blinked dryly.

"Yes, Emmett," Daddy said, "why don't you do that. I do believe our yard needs a good cuttin'." Daddy smiled, offering his hand to Emmett again.

Reaching to his rear pocket, Emmett pulled his handkerchief and wiped his right hand. They shook. "Gettin' the Devil off," Emmett said. He grunted at his own joke.

Emmett turned and moved to his A-model, still grunting. He opened the metal door. It cringed loudly. He sat high in the driver's seat and began the starting process, a low, long groan-groan-groan sound, until finally, something made contact and the running noise engaged. Emmett began to pull forward, and as smoothly as any other driver could do in a more modern vehicle, Emmett rolled his four plump, bicycle-looking tires across the graveled driveway and putted around the stonewall curve. Not one rock moved from its prior spot on the driveway along Emmett's path. He could slap drive that A-model.

I ran around the north side of the house, past the back porch and into the front yard and eyed Emmett plodding up Highway 14 toward his house.

"Is that Emmett?" Daniel suddenly asked, sliding in beside me.

"Yep. He's gonna cut our grass starting today. Starting in a few minutes," I answered.

"Our grass? He is?" Daniel asked.

"He's gone to get his mower."

"Emmett cuts a lot of grass, don't he, Jake?" Daniel asked.

We were both still watching up the highway, even though the sputter-mobile had disappeared. "Yep, he sure does."

“Hey, Daniel, let’s go swing,” I announced, looking down at Daniel’s cotton top.

“Really?”

“Yep. Go ask Momma if we can go, and hurry,” I said.

I knew to send Daniel. He was quicker than Wells Fargo. I also knew I could get a head start toward the swing set while he was gone. I purposely stood at the edge of school's side road, knowing in order to beat Daniel across the school lot to the swing set, I would have to start running once Daniel’s shadow appeared at the back door. My clue would be the squeaking of the screen door. My ears keenly listened for the squeak.

I heard the squeak and took off without breaking stride. Keeping my body in a direct line with the playground, I ran with all my muscles and might. If I had of had a pair of them P.F. Flyers I saw on my Grandmother’s television set commercial, I would have set the grass on fire. I kept my head straight ahead and focused on the swing set at the end and to the front of the schoolhouse. Like Lassie, I jumped two big rocks that were in my path. Taking longer strides as I reached the other loop of the school's side road, I jumped the curb and made a mad dash toward the first swing. I knew if I reached it first, I could sit down and yell, "I won!" To this point, however, Daniel hadn't passed me, and I was only a few steps away. Finally, I was there. Being off-balance and practically missing the seat with my behind, I almost fell. I settled in and turned to see Daniel, who I was assured, would be right on my tail; but there was no Daniel. I won?

I stood back up and searched the yard where I had just sprinted in a mad dash. I even looked behind me, thinking that Daniel's improving speed may have caused him to pass me and win. Frustrated, I began to trudge toward the parsonage. It took me a good four minutes to backtrack the same path I had just blazed. Arriving in the side yard, out of breath still, I stopped and listened. *What happened to that boy!*

I was confounded to look up and see Daniel was sitting on the back porch, on a green metal swing, made for two adults, or three or four kids, as long as they weren't fat like Ellen Fox. She was a redheaded girl that would later be in my junior Sunday school class.

Daniel suddenly commented. "Momma said not to go to the playground. Dinner's almost ready." He said it a little lightly, as if he had and was enjoying every miserable step I had run like an idiot across the school's front yard. "We're having fish sticks and potato patties."

Still standing in the yard, I asked, "Why didn't you yell at me?" Glaring up the four steps leading up the screen door, I questioned him. "Say?"

"I don't know."

"Yes, you do. Why?" I asked; I recognized Daniel was ignoring my question. "Tell me." I was getting madder by the minute, and he knew it, and wallowed in it. "You better tell me now."

"I don't know," he whined. "I just didn't."

I opened the screen door, and like a lion tamer, entered the back porch. Daniel was sitting on the edge of the seat and pushing it back and forth with his legs. He was staring outside, through the screen, intentionally ignoring me. I could tell.

"You're gonna be sorry for that!" I shouted, letting my anger take over. "You wait!"

Daniel refused to look at me. He only wrinkled his forehead and smiled inside. I could tell. He was trying not to smile, holding it inside.

I pushed him, just a little, to get his attention. He fell off the seat onto the porch floor, on purpose. He began to act like he was dying. Crying, he rolled over, grabbing his elbow. With each second, he increased his volume and the width of his mouth, pivoting his head toward the kitchen door. He rolled his eyes onto it.

"I didn't push you that hard, cry baby. You know it," I said with a partially plead in my voice. "Don't cry so loud."

“Yes, you did, Jake. You pushed me hard, and you’re not supposed to push me ‘cause I’m littler that you, Momma told us,” Daniel added, with no visible tears.

In the middle of our conversation, Daniel quit crying and jumped up, dry-eyed and quiet. I even helped him up. We both had heard the distant rackety sound of Emmett’s A-model. I moved through the screen door with Daniel on my heels. We scrambled into the yard and paused beneath a large tree at the side of our yard. From our perspective in the yard, we could see Emmett’s car as plain as day.

It turned down the hill and into our drive. Emmett shut the chunking sound; he stepped out. He never used his running boards on the side of his A-model. Once, I stood on the passenger side running boards when Emmett was cutting our grass. He didn’t see me, but I don’t think he would have minded anyhow. I would have loved to ride standing on those boards.

Emmett had his mower hanging out of his car from a rumble seat kinda place in the back of his gray vehicle. He picked the mower up, and reaching inside the rumble seat compartment, pulled out an oily rag and began to wipe his mower. He opened a couple of holes in the engine's top and wiped off some excess dirt from around the shell of the mower. He stepped behind the mower and began the stiff push up the hill toward the front yard. With each step, the rotating blades of the reel push mower shaved the tops off the dry standing grass blades. Daniel and me walked behind Emmett at a car length, noticing the sliced leaves helplessly flipping in the air in front of Emmett's pants legs.

"I'm cuttin' thuh yard," he said. He never looked at us.

Abruptly, Momma came to the door and yelled. "Boys! Dinner!" When Momma yelled those words, we knew that meant to get to the table as quickly as possible. Daniel and me ran up the steps and through the back door. We both stepped back between the threshold at the same time, as we heard Emmett's pace.

That day, at our noon dinner, our family was serenaded the entire meal by a reel push mower that began near our house like an active bee hive, trimming in and around the low-sittin' hedges, and then progressively getting farther away, rolled north and south in straight lines until two of the mower's wheels rolled within inches of the outside white border line of Highway 14.

8

Daniel and me never mentioned my solo race that I had run to the schoolyard swing set by myself before dinner on that day Emmett cut the grass. For some reason, our minds were completely erased of that argument. However, every once in a while, I would feel cheated by a strange feeling, any time Daniel and me would race to anything. I always took one extra step at the *ready, set, go!* to make things even.

The summer before my third-grade year, Rocky, Gabriel, and me took our first trip to the Enoree River in the woods below the house. When we asked Daddy in his home office if we could go to the river with Rocky, he agreed to let us go. “Don’t get *in* the river or too near the bank, boys,” was his last comment to us before we left the basement. “Rocky," Daddy said, "you keep an eye on these two. They don’t like water that much. They take a bath every Saturday whether they need it or not, but that’s about as close as they get to water,” Daddy said. He smiled. Rocky smiled back.

We walked through the back yard between the open field of briars and varied-sized scattered trees, and the school. A semi-bare, red-clay bank sloped downward at a manageable angle to the big field on which teachers would allow their kids, mostly boys, to have recess. Along the path to the river, to the left of the playground, a large walnut-shell shaped hill hauntingly lay. “Made by a bulldozer years ago,” is the way Rocky explained it and his daddy explained it to him. Its grotesque appearance was made more the eerie by the alternating angles of the sun throughout the day and into the late afternoon. Sparsely covered by wiry grasses and shallow bushes, the hill seemed out of place in South Carolina. Caves and caverns were direct results of nature's contrary behavior. At a distance, it appeared to be a giant rhino, picking its wide head up from a muddy Asian river. Rocky called the hill the *twilight zone*. I didn't find out about that hill in a personal way until the fourth grade.

Past the open field and the twilight zone was the Enoree River's tree line. The river was outlined with large and medium-sized trees like a green and brown wall of caution to passers-by. Trailing Rocky, we eased through the woods. Rocky had told us that he had been to the river many times before. He knew exactly when to duck and step over things. I didn't and received a few limbs and leaves in my face, not to mention one stealthy stumble I made behind the other two boys.

Rocky explained, "The kids at school can't come down here during school. If you do, you have to go to Mrs. Duncan, the principal, and you don't want to do that." Rocky stopped walking. "She's got a paddle---three feet long, and she swings it like a man."

Gabriel and me didn't say anything back. We were too busy listening to the rolling river behind some thick trees and vines. I leaned forward to get a better listen. The river was not as big as the main channel of the Enoree River that roared only a short walking distance away at the foot of Pelham.

Three inlets fed into the Enoree River directly above the church. All three inlets propelled water through the Enoree Dam, momentarily slowing the water's progress before dumping all of it into the chasm below the Highway 14 Bridge. The dam reminded me of my dad, who often held back much stress, dividing it from its confusion, and then presenting it in other formats. Standing on the bridge could give anyone a thorough misting from the steady and frightening crash of the cascading falls. Waters from the three inlets united, surging against the backside of the aging dam, swirling, becoming one river, until they were coerced through Enoree Dam's three rounded holes, where once again, the three waters divided to plunge into the huge basin below the bridge. Once the water crashed, it settled down past the bridge, moving more submissively past the south side of Pelham along the banks, touching Blountville.

"Any fish n' her?" Gabriel asked Rocky.

"My uncle caught fifteen or so one day right above the dam, but they ain't no fish right here, I don't think. But we ain't never fished it."

"I'd like to see for myself," Gabriel said. "My grandpa's coming down next week from the mountains. I hope he brings his fishing poles."

"How deep is it?" I asked.

"In some places, you can walk right across it, and it comes up to your knee..." Rocky said. He paused. Gabriel and me listened. "In other places, you can step into a death hole."

"What's that?" I asked.

"A death hole is a deep hole in the water that has no bottom---" Rocky said.

"Huh? No bottom?" Gabriel asked. "No---"

"Pudge McPhils is our best swimmer in Pelham. He's in the sixth grade. He swam into a death hole and told us there was no bottom. He said he found nothing but black and darkness."

"Black?" I asked.

"Black," Rocky said.

Reaching out his right hand, Rocky touched a long vine, about the size of a wooden tennis racket handle. He pulled it, and we could see it had already been separated from its root at the bottom; it swung freely. "Here's where it gets fun. All you have to do is hold onto this vine and get a good run and swing all the way across the river," Rocky explained.

Backing into me, Gabriel said, "Show us, Rocky." I almost stumbled again.

"Yeah," I added. I moved back more to give Gabriel more room.

"Okay, let me step into the path here," Rocky said. He moved into a clear line of visible wear in the grass, like a worn scar along the green river bank. From what I could tell, with the sun flickering in and out of the canopy of trees, there appeared to be a large rock on the other side of the bank. Clumps of laurel thickets decorated the opposite bank.

"What about that rock?" I asked, pointing.

"Don't land on that rock," Rocky said. "That's a killer. Just ask Ray Lawrence. He'll tell you what it feels like. We had to fish him out of the river with a long limb. His arm was broke."

Rocky backed up. "See you on the other side." He began his short run to the riverbank. As he ran, he slid his hands up the vine; he jumped and left the ground. He tucked his feet beneath him and floated into the air, across the flowing river, and released the vine. His feet stayed tucked as he passed the rock and he disappeared into some taller grasses.

Gabriel and me watched.

After a few short seconds, Rocky stood up. He looked okay to me. He made one swipe across the knees of his pants and said, "Who's next?"

Rocky climbed and stood upon the rock like an Olympic champion.

Gabriel walked to where the vine still wiggled jerkily from Rocky's ride and grabbed it. He stepped back onto the path, and without hesitation, ran, slid his hands upward, retracted his legs, soared, and cleared the rock. He dusted himself off and rose beside Rocky on the rock. Two down, one to go. Gabriel rode the vine way too easily for a first-timer.

I hated heights...especially heights over moving water...especially moving water that was running toward a rushing river...below which were death holes that were bottomless...and into which Pudge McPhils swam in total darkness...and Ray Lawrence fell and almost drowned...and at the foot of which is a dam that could rejoin my body parts...then separate me again into three other parts and then reunite all my pieces through one of three violent openings in the dam and pummel me into a thunderous splash of death under the bridge.

"Get the vine, Jake!" Rocky shouted. "Grab it now before it stops over the river."

"What? Huh?" I asked myself out loud. "Over the *river*? Over the river?"

"Grab the vine!" Rocky yelled. "We need it to get back across the river!"

I ran toward the vine, forgetting about the river. The vine jerked and wriggled out of control. At first, it slapped me on the cheek. I looked up the vine as I wrestled it, noticing it extended from a limb high above me. I had no other option but to hug it like a large disagreeable boa constrictor. The weight of the vine and its nervous reactions to Gabriel's 9.75 routine jerked me forward. I leaned back as leverage and did my best, grappling against gravity and nature. My feet dug in along the path. The river laughed at me the whole time, making me more determined to hang on for dear life. As long as my feet were on terra firma, I had hope of surviving the ordeal. Hesitantly, I glanced across the river, and Rocky and Gabriel were still on the rock, watching my drama unfold. I clung to the vine. Its laughed deafened me.

The tips of my feet hung over the edge of my side of the riverbank. I held on. The vine gave one last squirm, shaking me, but I didn't let go. I felt so triumphant standing there, almost leaning out over the river. I had conquered the rampant, unconquerable vine. I had single-handedly arrested a tragedy in the making. I had satisfied the task that could potentially save the lives of my two comrades. *I should have brought Ike.* He would have loved to see this feat of courage. Mission accomplished.

"Now," Rocky said, "it's your turn to swing across."

Still leaning, I looked directly down at the river and plum-near passed out. The river was moving, and I was standing still. Those two separate reactions were not agreeing with me at all. For a few seconds, I couldn't tell if I was moving north or if the river was moving south--I would get the same sensation later when Sears would install the first escalators. My eyes lifted, and I could see Rocky and Gabriel. They looked like two statues on a hill far away. I began to hum a hymn we sang often in church.

On a hill far away, stood an old rugged cross, the emblem of suffering and shame. And I love that old cross, where the dearest and best for a world of lost sinners was slain… so I'll cherish the old rugged cross---"

"Jake, did you hear Rocky?" Gabriel asked. "Jake? It's your turn!"

I heard Gabriel's voice. I began to pull away from the river and tugged the vine along with me. The vine had calmed into submission, but periodically it hissed into my nearest ear. I backed up on the path and gazed across the river once more at the Olympians on their victory stand.

"Okay, now run and jump," Rocky said. His voice mixed with the river's, creating a gargling and distorted sound, like *O-clay, nowg run gland ja-glump.*

Something inside me said, "You're dumb if you *run gland ja-glump.*"

But I knew that I must jump if I was going to fit in, if I was going to make any kind of positive impression amongst my new friends in Pelham. This was my opportunity to make it. I pulled back, took a deep breath, and suddenly and gladly, was interrupted by a loud wavy sound.

"Rock-ee! Rock-ee! Get up here *now*!"

Rocky's mom was yelling for him. She was notorious for being impatient. Rocky suffered a lot from his parents' whims and impulsive actions, and he knew his mother meant business.

Rocky panicked. "Jake, pass me the vine. Quick! Hurry!"

I pulled the vine back and propelled it directly toward the other side. Rocky reached out from the rock and grabbed the vine. Without running at all, but simply climbing aboard--because the rock was higher than my side of the river bank--Rocky coasted across the Enoree River and hit the ground a-runnin'. He never looked back, but yelled, "See y'all later!"

I swung the vine to Gabriel who repeated the ride. Together, we figured how to secure the vine's end to the same root where Rocky had found it earlier; we moved back through the tree line between the river and the parsonage. We passed twilight zone, studying it as we dared not stop, and continued for the house. Neither of us talked about the river. Gabriel did ask, however, "Was you gonna jump?"

"Of course, I was...I had to stop the vine first." I was, of course, lying right through my separated and tarnished teeth.

"You did kick that vine's butt, Jake."

I suddenly felt pretty tough. I caught up with Gabriel to walk stride to stride with my big brother, who was shorter than me, but then, tripped on some thick grass, falling to one knee. Gabriel never looked back. I caught up with him again before we reached the back yard.

Daniel was looking out the bedroom window and saw us coming. He disappeared from the window like an apparition in *Macbeth*, and then reappeared out of the basement like a cotton-topped bullet from a wide rectangular barrel.

“Where y’all been?” Daniel asked. “To the river? Did you go to the river?”

If there had been medical conveniences like ADD or ADHD or whatever back in the 50's, Daniel would have been the ideal patient. He was always moving, like the river. He never stood still. If he could flip or tumble, he would. Or, if he could run, he would. Or, if he could jump or climb, he would. To Daniel, there was never a normal way to do anything. He had to do things the motion way.

“Yes, Daniel," Gabriel answered. "Daddy said we could go to the river, but don’t you *ever* go to the river. Never!” Gabriel demanded like a father. “It’s very dangerous.”

Spinning in step, jumping while we walked, Daniel asked, “It is? Like what?”

Trying to get in on the scare-the-little-kid-into-not-doing-something strategy, I added, “Like deep holes called holes of death." *Hey, it scared me, and I was in the <u>third</u> grade.*

"Death?" Daniel asked, only picking out one word of my response.

"Yes," I said.

"And don't go there," Gabriel finished up.

"Why can't I?" he asked. "Why not? You went," he whined. He double stepped to keep up, and then ran around me to Gabriel's side, like a puppy looking for a biscuit.

Gabriel stopped. He looked down at Daniel. "Because if you go to the river ---Daddy will beat you black and blue and then me and Jake will beat you too." Gabriel stared at Daniel, pushing his threats through Daniel's skewed outer layer.

Daniel looked up at me to see if I was going to amen Gabriel's sermon.

"That's right!"

Daniel didn't say anything else about the river that day.

Gabriel began walking again. We both followed in his diminutive shadow.

9

Daddy's only brother Joe came down to stay the week with us. For some reason, his mother and father--my grandpa and grandma on my daddy's side--were out of town, and Joe needed a place to hang out for a few days. My daddy decided, I suppose along with Momma's approval, that Joe would stay with us for a whole week.

Now, there was one snag in this scenario: Joe was a *chain smoker*--no he did not smoke chains! But he would be residing temporarily in the Pelham First Baptist Church parsonage. Some people in Pelham placed the same amount of significance to the sanctity of the parsonage as Italian Catholics placed on the Pontiff's palace in Rome, Italy. Well, after all, I called my dad *father* on occasions.

Now, we didn't drink or smoke or cuss or beat each other up, but we were just a family that had the same kinds of problems, as did the Lee's or the Moxley's or the Jacksons or the Brown's. Boy, some of them people *really* had problems too, which kept my daddy's daily calendar filled with producing solutions, especially for the Browns.

Momma told my daddy Joe would have to understand he would have to smoke his cigarettes outside and near the back of the parsonage so no one would see him. The problem with that recommendation was Joe was a *chain* smoker. Joe would be better off having smoked on the porch than to have to tramp up the basement steps forty times a day. A chain smoker, over-exerting himself, could become a prospective heart-attack victim.

However, Joe agreed and marched up and down the steps all week.

On Thursday of that week, the day after Wednesday evening prayer service at our church, Daddy and Momma went away for the day to attend an all-day camp meeting in a nearby town. Since Uncle Joe was staying in our house, my parents felt comfortable enough to leave us with him for the day.

About midday, after our parents had exited, Joe suddenly came up with what he thought was an innovative idea. He moved to the basement door on one of his chain reactions and stopped. He said, "You three...follow me."

Well, since he had wrestled us in the grass earlier in the week, I figured we were going to wrestle some more. The only thing we had done with Joe while he was at our house was to wrestle; however, one day we did sit in the front yard and watch three black boys pass by. Joe tried to get us to yell out *nigger* when the black boys were in front of the parsonage, but we were afraid to. Behind the billowing white clouds of cigarette smoke, he laughed at us.

After we followed him downstairs, Joe led us around the house and up the curved driveway, until we reached the level ground of the front yard. We took a sharp left turn and moved right up next to the brick wall of the house. Daddy's small office window was near our feet. At this vantage point, we were concealed from a view of the highway. Joe lined us all three up against the wall, like we were being presented before a firing squad, and in a way, we were; we just didn't know it yet. He took a pack of cigarettes out of his shirt pocket. There was a camel on the front of the pack. Joe didn't have a filter on his cigarette; "I smoke 'em straight up," he told us later.

Strangely enough, Joe took out four cigarettes. I first thought he was going to do a smoking trick, you know, blowing smoke rings, blowing smoke out his nose, swallowing smoke and bringing it up later in the day, and so on. But he didn't.

He gave each of us a cigarette.

"You boys want to smoke?" he asked.

Gabriel looked at me and Daniel like we were co-conspirators in crime. “Uncle Joe... we’re going to get in trouble for playing with cigarettes,” Gabriel said, semi-passionately. “Daddy don’t let us play with cigarettes.”

“No, you’re not going to get into trouble,” Joe said. “I’m not going to tell him, are y’all?”

Gabriel shook his head no, and we did too.

“Well, then. Let’s try to smoke one. It won’t hurt you to smoke one little cigarette, now will it?” Joe asked.

We didn't answer, although we wanted to.

None of us knew how to hold a cigarette. We hadn’t seen anything in magazines or on the television set to help us with this situation. Anyhow, we didn’t even have a television set in our house. Well, actually, there weren’t many people who *did* have a television set in their houses, and my daddy preached against television sets pretty hard anyway.

Daniel tried to look through his cigarette like it was a looking glass.

I held mine in the palm of my hand and examined it as if it were loaded dynamite.

Gabriel copied Joe's technique and looked just like a shriveled-up little Joe standing there against the south brick wall of our house, atop the blunted curved stone wall around the driveway. At a quick glance, Gabriel resembled James Dean in *Rebel without a Cause.* Gabriel's rolled-up britches legs and tight white t-shirt magically placed him in the Dean persona. All Gabriel needed was his own pack of cigarettes rolled-up in his sleeve, slicked-back hair--since Daddy kept our hair buzzed off or in flat tops--and some black penny loafers. He was already short like James Dean. A leather jacket would have helped to accessorize.

"Now, put your cigarette in your mouth," Joe demanded.

We were shocked.

"Hurry. Put it in your mouth like this!" he said. He demonstrated by making his cigarette-into-his-mouth move look as awkward as he knew ours would be, to make us feel like it was something we could do without feeling dumb.

Daniel was first. The cigarette went between Daniel's lips like a bear's leg into a tight trap. He couldn't keep the cigarette from jumping around on his lips. Eventually, he had to secure it with his hands again. Daniel sneezed.

I was next. I was surprised at first. It wasn't that bad. It was like putting a spongy, light-weight, tasteless pencil into your mouth. I didn't mind. Daniel was looking around me at Gabriel to compare notes.

Gabriel was cool and comfortable with the whole thing. He even put the cigarette between his fingers, however, the wrong two fingers and backwards, and then pulled it in and out of his mouth a few times for show. He giggled. Two times he blew out fake smoke. I got choked on mine; it wasn't even lit.

Joe pulled out a box of matches from his pants pocket. I recognized the matches. They were Momma's from her kitchen drawer. We weren't allowed to touch them. He struck one match and lit his own cigarette. He blew out smoke while blowing out the match at the same time. I felt like we should applaud at that moment, but we just stood there.

"Now," Joe said, sending smoke out of a rounded hole between his lips' left side, "let's light yours."

Gabriel put his cigarette in again and leaned forward. An additional giggle followed.

Joe continued, instructing behind a screen of smoke assembling around his face like Moses' snowy white hair in the book of Exodus. "Now, here's what I want you to do. We're going to have a contest. We're going to see who can smoke their cigarette the fastest."

Well, that's all he had to say, 'cause his sentence had the word *fastest* in it, and that was enough to light us all up. We were ready.

Joe explained, "When I light your cigarette, you can begin to suck in as fast as you can. I want you to suck in until your cigarette is gone, completely gone. Do you understand?"

Gabriel responded, speaking with his cigarette hanging from his lips like...well, like James Dean. “Yeah,” “Me first, Joe.”

Joe kept explaining the rules of the contest while he lit each one of us.

We sucked. Boy, did we suck.

For fifteen or twenty seconds, we sucked.

Suddenly, and without warning, the world went pale. Gabriel spit his cigarette directly out into the air and began to cough. I could not breathe. I was making teakettle sounds, wheezing and wispy. Daniel began to cry. Snot oozed from his nose.

Within seconds, three Camel cigarettes were burning away on the ground at Joe’s feet. Joe wasted little time in sucking his cigarette. Across his face was an incredible sneer. We were all gagging and struggling to breathe. Joe wallowed in his admiration of the moment.

Joe spoke. "Go into the house and eat one of your mother's leftover biscuits. It'll help you swallow and breathe."

With those words of wisdom, we sprinted, while gagging, across the front yard and around and into the back screen-door. We opened the oven and grabbed a cold biscuit from beneath the tinfoil covering. We ate and swallowed, ate and swallowed, until we were outside seated on the back steps, chewing our last bits of baked batter.

After a few bites, I began to feel a little better, but then... *puke.* Everything I had eaten came up, cloudy and brown. The aftertaste of biscuits and smoke settled on the wide and sensitive taste buds like a pee-stained, wet smoking blanket. My eyes and nose watered.

Gabriel's yellow face became clammy and quiet. He looked at me with a desperate expression, as if he was drowning in the river and I couldn't reach him. Suddenly, he lunged onto the grass on both hands and knees like a mad dog, staring at the ground, head lowered, barking. He paused there for a few seconds. He resembled our dog Pearl, hovering over her dish into which Momma, on occasion, would slip leftover fried squash, which affected Pearl in a negative way. Abruptly, Gabriel's back bowed like an angry cat, convulsing in its center, and his head thrusts outward, spewing violently with biscuit ash and smoke, a volcanic vomit.

After the expulsion, Gabriel rolled over in the grass away from the smell and lay still on his back looking up at the pastel, blue sky. His face was set in a cold stare like a dead man.

Daniel had curled up against the steps, holding his stomach, crying; his thumb was close to his lips.

Once we three had completed our varied reactions to the smoke, regaining our color, Joe emerged. He walked in front of us, clearing his throat to get our attention, and said, emphatically, like we were in a grand banquet hall somewhere, "Don't you ever smoke. Smoking is a bad habit." Uncle Joe stood like a drill sergeant at ease, but firm.

"Once you start," Joe said, "you can't quit. You need to grow up like your daddy, who is clean and does what God asks him to do. You don't want to smoke like me. Do you understand?"

We sat and lay still, contemplating Joe's words.

For some reason, of all the messages my daddy had ever preached, on the cross, on doing the right things, on Noah and the flood, on Jonah and the whale, on Adam and Eve, on Joseph and Mary, I had never experienced a message as personally powerful and applicable as I did from his chain-smoking brother, my Uncle Joe. Joe would have made an effective surgeon general.

For the rest of my life, I would never smoke a cigarette; even in my teen years, I easily turned them down, often accepting the cigarette, only to crush it with my hand. What preaching! Amen!

10

A preacher's life is not easy. Most people judge a preacher by what they see on Sunday. They figure he only has to preach a couple of times on the Lord's day, about thirty-to-forty minutes at a clip, and visit a handful of sick people in hospitals and at home. Other than that, he might have to bury or marry, but that's only on rare occasions.

"And he gets paid that much money for that?" is a typical reaction and attitude that preacher's kids hear from church members and others.

A preacher carries with him as his every day and night luggage all the problems and concerns of his church members. A preacher has a twenty-four hour responsibility. While he's working on getting sermons prepared for Sunday morning, which could take as much time as several hours for each sermon, he has to be open to his members' phone calls and emergencies. He has to balance his schedule with church problems and business matters that might arise during the week, not to mention running his own household effectively, like Timothy says in the New Testament. Nothing comes easy for a preacher. *One that ruleth well his own house, having his children in subjection with all gravity.*

The week after Uncle Joe left, our family was sitting down for our evening supper. My mother had fried salmon patties and mashed potatoes. Traditionally, we sat around the table the same way. Daddy sat at the head of the table, Gabriel the oldest to his left, and continuing around the table in this order of oldest to youngest. Momma always sat on Daddy's right with the youngest child, usually in a highchair, sitting to her right.

My momma's sitting down signaled the meal was ready to be eaten. At this point, we would all await Daddy's prayer. He would alert us to his upcoming prayer with the words,

"Let us pray." The words to Daddy's prayer were not always identical, but did carry with them the same pattern, including the basics in our family and church life.

It was something like, *Our heavenly Father, we thank you for this food we are about to eat. Bless it to the nourishment of our bodies and our bodies to your service. Bless the hands that prepared it and our church; use each of us for your glory and honor, in Jesus name we pray, Amen.*

If there were other pressing issues in our lives, his prayer would reflect those issues, too.

On this night, the phone rang down the hallway during our meal. Daddy left the table to answer it. I could hear Daddy talking. The echo carried his words to our table, not clear enough to hear, but clear enough to understand the tone of the conversation.

"Oh, I'm sorry about that, Bonnie," was the clearest sentence I could make out. I knew that Bonnie had a family in our church. Her husband was not saved; he didn't attend our church. Bonnie had a boy named Eli and a girl named

Melissa. They were twins and were both Gabriel's age. "I'll be right there."

Daddy went to his bedroom and stayed there a few minutes. Momma left the table, and I could hear them talking. Gabriel moved around to Momma's seat and made sure Carol was okay in her highchair.

"What's wrong?" Momma asked Daddy.

After that question, I could tell Daddy toned his conversation down on purpose. It was one of those the-children-can-hear-us moments.

Shortly, Daddy came through the kitchen, Sunday suit on and hat in his hand. Momma followed him out the back screen-door. Again, they whispered for a little while. Daddy left and Momma reentered.

Gabriel switched seats, and Momma sat down in her chair.

"What is it, Momma?" Gabriel asked.

Momma's eyes were welling up with tears. She sat quiet until a couple of the tears escaped and trailed down her cheeks. She used her napkin to wipe her face.

"Bonnie's husband's been in a bad car wreck. It's not a good situation," she said.

The truth was that Bonnie's husband was thrown from the wrecked car, up into the air, and into the side of a tree. Gabriel made an off-colored comment about the dead, and Momma corrected him at once. "Gabriel, you had best not ever offend the dead again!"

I couldn't understand how the dead would be offended, I mean, since they are already dead and all.

Daddy had preached on dying with Christ. Galatians 2:20, says, "I am crucified with Christ, nevertheless I live in Him, yet not I, but Christ who liveth in me; and the life which I now live in the flesh, I live by the faith of the Son of God who loved me and gave himself for me."

I think that's what kept me from getting saved until I was ten years old. I didn't want to die with Christ. It seemed to me that since one of us had already died, the other one could die posthumously.

A few weeks after the funeral of Bonnie's husband, Daddy invited an evangelist from Tennessee to come and be in a revival meeting in Pelham. We were going to have a one-week revival campaign. That meant that there were going to be revival posters to put up all over the community. We boys rode with Daddy all through Pelham and Blountville and up into Pleasant Grove to hang revival posters in all kinds of business establishments and on telephone poles. Daddy stopped and bought me and my brothers an ice cream at the store in Greer.

Understand we called every power pole a telephone pole, only because we saw with our very own eyes a man from the telephone company climb a pole in front of the parsonage to repair our phone. After that, there was no use trying to convince us that the tall, skinny, brown pole was anything but a telephone pole.

One of the kids in our community said telephone poles were made out of *nigger* pines. My daddy said if he ever heard us saying a word like that, he would wash our mouths out with soap. We received the soap punishment eventually, but never for saying the N word.

I would have given anything to put the telephone man's belt and spikes on to climb that telephone pole like he did. And all the time, I knew I was a-skeered of heights. I had never heard a sound that worked as hard as did that sound of the man climbing the pole. The wide leather strap holding the man onto the pole whined and groaned as he inched upward. The steel leg supports clanged above my head like an elevated horse shoe game. After getting to the top of the pole, he set himself up a little workstation and hung there in space, in a seated position, with no cares in the world. He even stopped working long enough to make a phone call and chat for a while. And you know that I didn't take my eyes off him the whole time. I don't think I even closed my mouth, 'cause I was too preoccupied with his occupation. I'm so glad a bird didn't fly over while I was watching him.

Bartholomew Keller was the evangelist from Tennessee. He was a larger-than-life character. He was red headed, freckle-faced, and quite hefty. Because his head and belly were so big, he walked with his arms kinda behind him. He swayed side to side when he walked, and his eyes were bug eyes, bulging out more when he wanted to be funny, and he could do that quite naturally.

He would sit down at the upright piano in our house and sing endlessly. He sang one song after another. One song was *Bill Grogan's Goat* that I still sing and play today.

Bill Grogan's goat was feeling fine
He ate three shirts right off the line;
Bill got a stick, gave him a whack,
And tied him to the railroad track.
The whistle blew, the train drew nigh,
Bill Grogan's goat was sure to die;
He gave an awful cough with an awful pain,

Coughed up the shirts, flagged down the train.

I loved the way Evangelist Bartholomew Keller played the piano with his bulky fingers. He would spread them out in a non-piano-playing style, sometimes using three or four fingers, depending on the speed of the song, resembling a dexterous one-finger typist.

He always moved one leg up and down with the rhythm of the song.

With no motels within miles of Pelham, Brother Billy--as he was known by us and my daddy--stayed with us in the parsonage during the revival meeting. That meant, of course, that me, Gabriel, and Daniel had to sleep other places besides our bedroom, so I slept on the floor in the living room. Don't ask me why, but I loved to sleep with a quilt on top of the heating vents in the floor. When the furnace would come on, I felt that I had my own privately heated room. I never once wet the bed while sleeping on the floor. I can't explain it.

While Brother Keller was at our parsonage in revival meeting, he would also baby sit us if Momma and Daddy had to go somewhere. One of the things he loved to do for his own entertainment was to chase me and my brothers throughout the house with his belt. He really did hit us with it, while laughing at the top of his voice. My brothers and me panicked a lot of times and would hide in some really weird places inside the house. We took this belt-chasing thing very seriously.

One time, when the tires of Momma and Daddy's car couldn't have been much more than air temperature, as they had just pulled out on Highway 14, Brother Keller yelled, "I'm giving you boys two minutes to hide and then I'm coming after you. Do not go outside the house, or I will find you, and you won't be glad about that either."

In a way, we were totally terrified and intimidated by Bartholomew Keller, but in a way, we loved the attention he gave us. I guess we were like the little boy who received multiple beatings from his drunken dad. The little boy later on told someone, “Sure, the beatings hurt, but at least I feel he’s paying me some attention.”

Daniel always secluded himself in the small closet in Momma’s room. He hid there, horrified in the darkness, until the game was well over. He was never found. He knew how to hide among Momma’s light-colored stuff in the closet, and with his cotton top, he was impossible to find. However, Daniel did find some things while he was in the closet. Some of those things he could recognize, but some of those things none of us had ever seen before. It wasn’t until we were teenagers that we discovered the significance of those fluffy feminine products.

Daniel told us once, “I found some more of those long, flat cotton bandages in a box in Momma’s closet.”

“Not anything like the cotton bandages I’ve ever seen,” I added.

Gabriel hid in many places and was found sometimes and sometimes not. This was good training for him later when he would travel as a teen to Vietnam with the United States Air Force.

I hid beneath the kitchen table, and Brother Keller found me. I hid under the sink, and Brother Keller found me. He found me almost every time. It hurt when he hit me with the belt. When he laughed, it hurt even more. For some strange reason, the more he laughed, the more we just took it as a game and went on. It still hurt.

Finally, I was desperate for the ultimate and safe place to hide, the greatest place on earth to hide. I set my mind on going where no one had ever gone before. Then, I thought of the small door past the kitchen door, the door to the attic.

I raced to the door. I opened it. The sunlight that had partly lit the attic before, when Gabriel and me had opened the door on the first day that we moved to Pelham, was gone. The day was late. The sun was getting awfully tired and was thinking about sleep. Stepping into the attic stairwell, I shut the door behind me. The attic's personality sprung to life. I noticed it, especially since I was standing on the bottom step, engulfed in the increasing dankness.

I knew my time was short, since Brother Keller was counting down the seconds in the living room, aloud. “20, 19, 18...”

I looked up the attic steps. The wind was cutting through the gable vent, sweeping part of the floor dust into my hair and face, and with a little unbridled imagination, sounded like mourning bumble bees. I began the climb, and with each step up, felt the soft popping of the stair boards beneath my feet.

Several old boxes greeted me at the top. They were dust-covered and stale. One separate box, sitting in the far corner, where the darkness congregated, looked especially old. I moved toward that box, since it seemed to hold the secret of my escape. I squatted next to the box, turned to face the gable vent, and sensed that I was totally invisible for the first time in the Brother Keller hunt. Sitting beside the ancient box, in the cover of darkness, I could not be discerned. My color and shape were dissolved into the shadows.

Moments passed. I could hear the large movements of Brother Keller. He stirred around in his sneaky ways, making noises along his hunt, searching for all of us. I heard no screaming or belting, and then, the attic door... *opened.*

Brother Keller could have walked directly up the steps, but he purposely moved as slowly and as quietly as he could. While climbing, he made all kinds of scary noises. *Oooo... yah yah yah... I will kill you...you're going to die, little Jake...oww.* He slapped one of the top steps with his belt and a pop of dust beveled upward like a splash of fine saw-mill shavings. Arriving level with the attic floor, Brother Keller twisted, and his silhouette filled the gable vent and more. His silhouette was large and intimidating. Studying the darkness, he could not see me. He could not detect me in the shadows. I had no color, no shape. For all intents and purposes, I was just another box, sitting quietly along the naked rafter boards. A smell of insulation burnt my nostrils.

After a couple of minutes, he gave up. Huffing and puffing, he quickly but cautiously exited the attic, and after a few more minutes of intense searching, announced, “I give up. Everybody to the living room!”

I didn’t want anyone to know where I had hid, so I moved down the steps without a sound. I opened the door and let my eyes adjust to the fading late afternoon light. Like a cat near a mouse, I tippy-toed toward the living room and slipped in.

Daniel and Gabriel were already on the couch. Brother Keller was sitting at the upright piano. I sat on my hands next to Daniel.

Brother Keller spoke. “You little rascals. You all fooled me this time. Congratulations. Where did everyone hide? I looked over the entire house.”

“I hid in ...” Daniel started to say. Gabriel whispered to him in his ear. Daniel stopped mid-sentence.

"I hid in the basement," Gabriel lied.

"I hid in my bedroom," I lied.

"I hid in the attic," Daniel lied. He had learned well.

"You did not!" I said. "I did!"

"You did?" Daniel asked, shocked that I would mess his lie up. "You hid in the attic, Jake? By yourself?"

"Yes..." I said. "Hm...huh."

Brother Keller turned around to directly face us. His round eyes enlarged as he thought about what we had just slipped into his ears. He responded. "Oh, you are all trying to confuse me, ain't you? Well, I'm not falling for it. I know for a fact that no one was in the attic, because I went all the way to the top and there was no one there, so that proves that you're *all* lying. I'm ashamed of you three," he said. In a semi-joking way, with a smile on his face, he added, "You three are pretty good kids...good sports. I like playing games with you."

Then, he turned around toward the piano, and began to introduce a solo he sang at the house and at church all week:

"I will not be a stranger when I get to that city, I'm acquainted with folks over there," his voice was clear as a bell and ten times as loud. What volume! His red head tilted back as he sang toward the ceiling of the parsonage, "Through the years, through the tears, they have gone one by one, but they'll wait at the gate, until my race is run..." Brother Bartholomew Keller was a unique character, a one-in-a-million personality that shows up on God's planet very rarely. Of all the people that would pass through the parsonage for revivals, weddings, Bible conferences, vacation Bible schools, or funerals, the Reverend Bartholomew Keller from Tennessee made the most impact on us three boys' minds and lives. His voice still echoes in my memory:

"I will not be a stranger when I get to that city; I'm acquainted with folks over there!"

11

Many of those summer days after Brother Keller vanished out of Pelham were spent with my brothers, making new friends and acquaintances. We explored several of Pelham's secret places and killed the summer days with tall stories, out-of-the-blue chases, and baseball.

I loved baseball. From the first time I ever held one in my hand, I knew there was something special about it. It was complete. The perfect white sphere--albeit, having to run, field, and hit a baseball atop the red clay of the foothills of South Carolina, it would be quite a while before I would actually hold a *white* one in my hand--with the tight-stitched, almost-figure-eight design caught my fancy and seized it forever.

We first played baseball in the backyard of the parsonage. Rocky was the really great player; he could hit anything you threw at him. I discovered his secret. His dad was an umpire for the Pelham few who would brave the climb from the Pelham Bridge up the hill to the ball field. The Pelham ball field was in actuality a cow pasture, fenced in by a couple strands of barbed wire on scattered shaky posts that semi-circled behind home plate, bordered by a crude backstop structure, homemade.

Rocky's dad would send Rocky down Highway 14 to Stuart's Store for all of Mr. Stuart's bottle caps. The store was only four houses and one block-building garage down from the parsonage. That would make it three houses and one garage down from Rocky's house. When everybody would get their bottled soda drinks at Stuart's Store, the caps from their drink-tops fell into a metal box and stayed there until Mr. Stuart would empty them into a larger paper bag. He saved the bag every month for Mr. Lee.

If you've ever tried to hit a bottle cap using a shortened shovel handle as a bat--a bottle cap thrown fairly hard from about thirty-to-forty feet away--then you know the type of target that Rocky tried to hit for practice. The few times I ever got to take a swing at the darting and dipping bottle caps were quite intimidating. As soon as the cap would leave the pitcher's hand, it had a mind all its own, going one way and then the other, suddenly dropping in midair, then curving off in another direction. It made me have to keep my eye on the cap until it literally hit the bat or else sped by, untouched, or dropped out of sight to the ground.

Rocky could hit a high percentage of caps with little effort, probably the reason he grew up to be a famous ballplayer. His dad was not content that Rocky could hit a few. He wanted him to be able to hit each and every cap. I would hear him yelling at Rocky in their backyard. His language was pretty rough too. Rocky didn't cry though. I think I would have cried.

Rocky told me once that he could tell the difference in the caps and could sometimes read the writing on the cap while it was in the air.

"Dr. Pepper caps are the easiest ones to hit. There's some kind of rubber lining or something on the inside of the cap that makes it heavier. I can tell it's a DP cap as soon as it leaves my dad's hand."

I sure couldn't tell the difference. All the caps looked like silver mosquitoes on a dive-bomb mission to me.

Rocky's mother is the person who got me, Gabriel, and Daniel on the same baseball team. Daniel was a good pitcher. He could hurl the baseball. Gabriel was a hind catcher, and I played shortstop.

In one game, me and my brothers pulled a triple play. The bases were loaded and Daniel was pitching. The batter hit the ball to me at shortstop. I touched second base, out one. I threw it to Gabriel who tagged the runner rounding third, out two, and Gabriel threw it back to me, and I tagged the batter who had tried to take second, out three. It was a triple play. However, Daniel only threw the ball to the batter and always thought that he had something to do with it.

One day, in the back yard of the parsonage, a few of us organized a baseball game, except we used a rubber baseball Stanley Keller's mother had bought him up at the McCleskey-Todd drug store in Greer. The ball was dark red and hard to see in the evenings. Luckily, on this day, we were playing on a bright summer morning.

My brother Gabriel was pitching, and the rest of us were scattered about the yard in all kinds of baseball postures, waiting for Ralph Henderson to hit. The rule under which we played was that each of us would get a turn to swing at ten pitches. Tommy Blackmon was the hind catcher and always *was* the hind catcher.

Once Tommy squatted down in the catcher position, he never came up. If the ball went past him, somebody else had to leave their place on the field and retrieve it. To put it mildly, Tommy was fat. He really couldn't play any other position on the field. If he stood in one place too long, his legs would hurt. No one ever made fun of Tommy's weight in public, but when Tommy wasn't around, a few boys in our community laughed an awful lot at something I never could hear. I felt in my heart it might have been about Tommy being fat.

He did eat a lot. When Momma would make half-sandwiches for the kids who played ball, she would always ask me, "Is Tommy playing today?" She never told me why she would ask that, but I noticed, if I hung around the kitchen and watched her work long enough, she would make five or six spare half-sandwiches with extra peanut butter and jelly on them.

Rocky yelled from shortstop, "Throw the ball harder, Gabriel. Anybody can hit that!"

Gabriel acted like he didn't hear Rocky but he did throw the next pitch harder. Before Gabriel would let the pitch go, all of us would make this *eh-eh-eh-eh-eh-eh swing batter* noise that sounded like a gatlin gun on the *Rin Tin Tin* television show on Saturday mornings.

Ralph would never swing. He would just stand there acting like he was gonna hit a grand slam, but he *never* would swing. Why we always fell into his trap, I'll never know, but every time it was the same old story.

"Swing, Ralph! Swing!" I yelled from right field.

Someone else yelled, "Come on, Ralph. If you ain't gonna swing, then let somebody else have a turn!"

Ralph just stood there. Any major league pitcher would have been intimidated to face Ralph. His expression was grimaced, and with his knees slightly bent, he focused his eyes to look the part. But he never swung the bat. Never.

Ralph explained to me after one of his fifty-pitch, no-swinging escapades in the backyard, "When I don't swing, I put pressure on the pitcher. He has to walk me every time." I tried to explain to Ralph that intertwined with the four balls

that was required to walk him, the pitcher also had thrown forty-six strikes he hadn't swung at.

Gabriel had argued, "But we agreed to get only ten pitches, Ralph!"

Ralph retorted, "Not if I don't swing at 'em."

"But we didn't say ten pitches if you swing at 'em...we just said ten pitches," Stanley added in. "Ain't that right, yall?"

All of us pitched our varied reactions. *Yeah. Right. Yeah, that's what we said.*

Again, this time, I could tell everyone, including Gabriel, was getting really impatient. Gabriel had begun to fill his cheeks with extra puffs of air, making him appear like he had a toothache on both sides of his face, grinding his teeth at the same time. He was mad.

"Give him a hard one, Gabriel!" Rocky said. "Knock him back from the plate!"

"Yeah. A hard one," I echoed. "Up and in one time!"

Gabriel bent over at the waist, as if Tommy was giving him a pitching signal, like Yogi Berra would give Whitey Ford on the Saturday game of the week, but from where we were all standing, you couldn't see anything between Tommy's legs, except more leg.

Once Gabriel stood to pitch, he gave a glance at first base, to keep the runner--and there wasn't a runner--close to the bag, made of one side of a Tide detergent box, Tide side up.

Gabriel glared again at Tommy's mitt, and then, picked up his leg like Juan Marichal from the San Francisco Giants, and let his pitch fly. To re-enact a real Major League game, all we needed was Pee Wee Reece doing the color commentary. Gabriel came off the mound with fire in his eyes, and the pitch smoked toward home plate. With all Gabriel's good intentions, the ball bounced slightly behind the plate in front of Tommy Blackmon and disappeared.

Everyone stood straight up and tried to eye the dark-colored rubber ball from each vantage point, all of us wondering who would have to make the trip to recover the ball in the weeds behind Tommy. Tommy didn't move. Ralph finally made a motion in the batter's box. He leaned back and looked toward the fence that separated the parsonage yard and Rocky's back yard. It was only a quick look, because Ralph then looked back at his bat and studied the writing on it. He was in love with his Rocky Calavitto bat.

At first, no one moved or spoke or had a clue where the ball had vanished to.

"You got it, Tommy?" Rocky asked, trotting toward home plate.

"No," Tommy answered, looking in his mitt, not moving. "No."

"You see it, Ralph?" Gabriel asked, also moving.

"No," Ralph answered. "It hit the ground," he said, pointing at the ground at his feet.

Me, Daniel, and Stanley joined the others to look for the rubber ball.

All of us, besides Tommy, who stayed squatted behind the plate, and Ralph, who had already begun to take his bat and glove and head toward home, scanned the fence area. Ralph had seen his tenth pitch for the day. We looked under every twig and searched any possible nook and cranny in the yard and around the bottoms of the trees and bushes, and no ball was to be found.

Finally, Tommy got up from his squat and helped us. Still, no ball.

Daniel was playing around behind all of us when he yelled, “There it is!” Then, he grabbed his mouth with both hands and tried not to laugh or throw up; I couldn’t tell which.

“Where?” Gabriel asked, looking where Daniel was pointing.

“Huh?” Rocky commented, still not seeing the ball.

“There,” Daniel finally shrieked. “In Tommy’s…Tommy’s butt.”

All of us, at the same time, looked at Tommy's butt, and there, pillowed snugly between Tommy's butt cheeks, was the rubber ball. Because of him being fat, the ball had suddenly disappeared into Tommy's portly posterior. We would have never found it had Tommy not bent over to help us look for the ball. And there it was, wedged.

At first, we all stared. Tommy didn't move. He couldn't feel the ball himself.

A little thrown back by the situation, Tommy muttered, "No, it's not. I don't feel it!"

We all tried not to laugh. We didn't really want to hurt Tommy's feelings, but the ball was jammed into Tommy's butt. Tommy tried his best to look beneath his legs but couldn't see past a part of him that always hung in the way. He couldn't reach the ball with either of his hands.

At last, Stanley said, "In his butt. The ball is in his butt!"

About to cry, Tommy pleaded, "Somebody's got to get it out then!"

"Huh?" Stanley muttered.

"I'm not touching it," Rocky grimaced. "Eww."

"Me either," Gabriel groaned.

"Nasty, oh shew...nasty," Daniel added.

"It's your ball, Stanley," Rocky said.

"That's right, Stanley; it's your ball. You get it," Tommy whined.

The whole thing reminded me of the lepers in the Bible, who others could not touch, unless they wanted to die with the same disease.

Tommy was afraid to stand up. He was still bent over with his hands on his thighs to hold him in that position. Actually, he was in a pretty good umpire position. In his case, however, it wasn't as easy as screaming, "You're out!" to get the ball dislodged.

Without any discussion about Tommy's plight, we all began nervously to move about, picking up our gloves and bats. Daniel stood there behind Tommy gawking at the ball. At least Daniel was finally concentrating on something for more than three minutes. His teacher would have been proud of him.

Suddenly, Daniel yelled. "It's out! The ball fell out!"

Immediately, we all dropped our stuff and ran toward Tommy to see for ourselves. He was beginning to straighten like a patient recovering from back surgery. He turned to see the rubber ball lying on the ground behind him.

"It just fell out!" Daniel cried. "Just fell out. I was staring at it, and it...out."

All of us stood around the ball as if it was a sacred stone from the wilderness adventures of the Children of Israel or a rare giant-rhino egg...well, that would be rare wouldn't it.

Tommy smiled. His smile steadily moved us all to giggle, then to laugh. All the bottled-up feelings we had held about Tommy's being fat released into the summer air and we laughed and laughed for what seemed like a summer. Tommy laughed too. All of us ended up sprawled out and rolling around on the ground, surrounding the rubber ball, but not touching it, and laughing about the story. Everyone added new anecdotes. We laughed all the way up to sandwich time.

Tommy ate more sandwiches that day than any other day. It was no problem, though, because he got to eat all Ralph's sandwiches, the same Ralph who had left us high and dry in the hunt for the missing rubber ball.

The ball lay in that same spot on the ground, untouched, until one day when Brutus picked it up on his way through my yard. He deserved it, too. I think he must have buried it somewhere in the woods.

Later, in the fall during school, when Miss Jenny would tell us a story about Brer Rabbit, all alone, I would burst out laughing at a quite tedious part of the story, remembering the rubber ball stuck in Tommy's behind. I didn't get in trouble, but Miss Jenny did ask me why I was laughing.

Embarrassed, I answered, "...Because Brer Fox made me think of something from last summer, that's all."

12

On Saturday evenings, when the sun was setting, things at the parsonage would begin to change. There were no unnecessary movements in and around the parsonage, no yelling, no running in the house, and no loud playing. It was time to get ready for church on Sunday.

Daddy would barricade himself in his home office in prayer and Bible study. No one was allowed to go near the office.

"Your father needs to spend time with God, kids," Momma would explain to us.

Momma spent part of her Saturday laying clothes out for Sunday School and church. We were always early to church. Most other church members arrived right on time or else a few minutes late, with the exception of Emmett.

The sewing-machine rhythm of Emmett's A-model was a signal that Sunday morning had arrive. To unlock the doors of Pelham Baptist Church and get everything warmed up or cooled down, Emmett traveled down Highway 14.

As was my routine in the summer months, I got up early before anyone else on each morning to check the Major League Baseball standings in the newspaper. I was a die-hard Detroit Tiger fan. I didn't know anyone personally on Detroit's team, but with a passion I followed everything the Tigers did.

Emmett's A-model usually passed by our house while I was reading the paper on the small front porch. From its weekly Saturday washing, his car shimmered. Emmett always waved with his hand. I waved back. I could see Emmett sitting high in his front seat, smiling his ragged smile. He had on his Sunday coat over his bibbed overalls. His striped tie was partially hidden by the bib. Directly atop his head, his Sunday hat sat, straight and level.

I perched on the brick steps, spreading the paper out until I found the sports page. My eyes searched the page until I located the American League standings. With educated interest, I took note of the league leaders in homeruns, batting averages, and stolen bases. In the '50's, there were only two standings, the American and National Leagues. Only two teams ever made it to the World Series, and that made the pennant race exciting. There were no wild card teams and no six or more divisions. It wasn't a watered-down enterprise to get to the World Series, where everyone has a chance to get there. It was the best two teams over the long haul that played in the big show's grand finale.

Of course, the Yankees, Gabriel's favorite team, were always in the playoffs. With Mickey Mantle, Roger Maris, Yogi Berra, Whitey Ford, Tony Kubek, Bobby Richardson, and others, the Yankees were a formidable force in the American League.

However, I liked the Tigers. Al Kaline was my favorite player. He was fast and could hit off any of those Yankee pitchers. If the Tigers were playing, whenever I was near a television set on Saturdays around lunchtime, I would turn on the *Game of the Week*. No one could hold a bat like Dick McAuliffe or clutch hit like Norm Cash. Dizzy Dean and Pee Wee Reece were the ideal play-by-play commentators. I didn't tell Gabriel I also followed with interest the home run derby between Roger Maris and Mickey Mantle.

My daddy would not allow me to read the sports page on Sundays, but I didn't tell him that that's what I was doing. By the time he and Momma were up, I would have the newspaper neatly refolded and on the kitchen table. It went unread, as far as everyone was concerned, until after the morning church service.

On Saturday nights, Momma would make sure we all had our baths. It was quite an undertaking, especially after

Carol and Becky were finally added to the family to make six kids.

Clothes were laid all over the place for the next day. The girls always wore those frilly dresses that puffed out from the effects of extra-stiff slips and thin white socks that folded down like silk pillowcases. The latches on their shoes were impossible to fasten. As if wrapping a Christmas gift, Momma would tie big bows on the backs of my sisters' dresses.

Me, Gabriel, and Daniel mostly wore ties and coats. Momma was pretty determined to make sure we looked like her *little preachers* when we were at church. We wore wide-brimmed hats with broad, colorfully-striped bands, and white shoes with black soles. We favored one of the *Motown* singing groups of the '60's, the *Four Tops*, but probably with one sister, we more favored *Gladys Night and the Pips.*

"To show reverence to God, we must dress up when we go to His house on Sunday," Momma said to us. I guess it had to be said quite often to help us get over the uncomfortable confines of those Sunday suits. Even though I wore a clip-on tie, it felt like a noose around my neck. On some hot days, I could hardly breathe.

I loved to go to church, especially to see Mrs. Bonnie. She was beautiful. All the boys secretly eyed her. Her voice and face were fashioned by God at his most talented moment. She could sing like a robin, and like warm, running bath water, her smile relaxed all of us. Mrs. Bonnie was the leader of the children's Sunday School opening.

A little, white, plastic church, a little smaller than a Pic 'N Pay shoebox, always sat on the old communion table near the Sunday School-opening podium. Whenever kids would have a birthday, they would walk forward to put their birthday offering into the small slit on top of the white plastic church. No one ever emptied the plastic church except at Christmas time each year. The plastic church could hold over one hundred dollars in coins. Us church kids sent that money to an orphanage for black children in Africa. The plastic church offering was a tradition at Pelham Baptist Church and had been for generations.

Us kids had to stay in the children's Sunday School opening until we were thirteen years old, and then we went in with the old people in the main church. After that...death. It was downhill from there.

On one Sunday morning, when Mrs. Bonnie was on vacation and the substitute was sick, all of us kids had to go into the main church with the old people during Sunday School. There were people in there as old as thirty up to over a hundred years old. It was like walking into a funeral home, 'cept the dead were singing hymns and dozing off, more like Zombie Baptist Church.

I told my church-friend Grant, "This is like a Halloween place. If this is what happens to you when you get thirteen, I'm glad I'm only going on nine."

"You're getting close to thirteen, Jake," Grant said.

"I'm not going all the way to thirteen, I promise."

I liked Sunday School because of the class I went to. It was the primary boy's class, and Mr. Buford Jackson was our teacher. He was a pretty important person in Pelham. Even though he was younger than nine of my daddy’s eleven deacons at the church, he had worked very hard to rise to Assistant Chairman under Mr. Elijah Green's watch. Mr. Jackson lived across the bridge in Blountville. His house was right above the Enoree River Bridge, where the river's waters crashed and swirled, and like the blunt stone wall in our driveway, curved around Mr. Jackson's property, turning south past Blountville.

Mr. Jackson carried the biggest, blackest Bible I ever saw. He walked with it right over his heart on Sundays, like he was somehow trying to hide something big beneath its cover. His black hair was slicked back on both sides, and he had this little wild slice of hair that fell back on his forehead like a pig’s tail. He had a Hollywood gangster face with brown piercing eyes and a dulled chin, but pleasant most of the time, especially on Sunday mornings. His trademark was his rattlesnake-skin boots, dyed red. “No one within five hundred miles has a pair like these babies,” he often bragged to my daddy, when our family was over at the Jackson’s house or they at ours. “I had them custom colored, Adam, by a boot maker in Texas.”

Rattlesnake-skin-boots, dyed red. I had that phrase memorized.

There were about nine boys in our Sunday School class, and sometimes Mr. Jackson would take us on three or four trips during the year. We went to the Pete's Drive-in hamburger place in Greer, to the Lyman Lake to fish or to swim, and to the farmer’s market in town to pick out a watermelon to feast on.

On one trip to Pete's, Rocky and Gabriel got me tickled in the backseat of Mr. Jackson’s clean used car. Rocky and Gabriel were clowning around. Mr. Jackson had parked his car beneath the long awning, attached to the drive-in eating establishment. We three decided to eat in the back seat. I was devouring my jumbo hamburger plate and almost had it completely eaten. I had actually taken the time to chew most of it. Guzzling my strawberry malt down my goozle pushed the food down more quickly. My shake had shoved my fries, slaw, and burger to my stomach opening, when Rocky and Gabriel's horseplay suddenly got to me. I began to laugh, and laughed so hard that my food became lodged in my digestive path, shutting off my air supply to my throat. This abrupt reaction sent my stomach muscles into a chaotic thrusting motion. Momentarily, I threw up, vomited my entire jumbo, fries, malt, and slaw directly into the back floorboard of Mr. Jackson's new car, onto his new floor carpet. There was so much throw-up that I had to use my nose and mouth to get it all out, even my eyes, it felt like. That's the first time I ever saw the temper side of Mr. Jackson.

Since he was an independent used car dealer, he didn't take a liking to my upchucking in his vehicle. I suppose I would have felt the same way, but hopefully, I would not have reacted the same way.

One of the boys went to get Mr. Jackson who was trying to sell the proprietor a new car while we all were taking a lunch break. When Mr. Jackson saw the thick, pinkish-brown pool in the left side of the floorboard, he hollered, "Who did this?"

Rocky, Grabriel, and me sat still; only my face was puke-covered, still dripping.

Rocky and Gabriel choked on one last snicker, fading out slowly, and then pointed innocently toward me. In a flash, Mr. Jackson reached across Gabriel and grabbed my left arm. With his tense grip, he heaved me promptly from the car, across Gabriel's lap. Mr. Jackson looked around the area for something. Still clutching me, he barked, "Take your nasty butt over to that spigot and wash yourself off." Jostling me, he added, "You little bastard!"

That was a new one to me...*bastard.* I had heard the word in my daddy's sermons before. He used it when he would preach about being a child of God. He said, "If you are not saved, saved by the power of the blood of the Lamb, then you are a *bastard* and not a real child of God. God only chastens those who are His children. God don't go around whooping up on the devil's kids."

I didn't find out until later from Rocky that he thought a bastard was some kid that didn't have a father or who had a father that wasn't his real father, like Lanny Wilson. Lanny lived with his mother alone, without a father. "Lanny's a bastard," Rocky had whispered to me once.

When Mr. Jackson called me a kid without a father, I felt really bad, especially the way he said it. I had never suspected such animosity lurked inside my Sunday School teacher's heart. Later on, Gabriel explained that maybe Mr. Jackson was just upset like Daddy was when he had hit his head on the hood-hook by the side of Highway 25, when the '55 Chevy ran hot.

Mr. Jackson disappeared into the Pete's Drive-in and came back in a few minutes with this lanky black boy, who was carrying some rags and a bucket. "Get out! The-rest-of--you-boys, get out of the back seat," Mr. Jackson yelled. He was still mad about the bastard throwing up, I could tell. This is one bastard that had enough sense to stay back away from the car. Mr. Jackson commenced to pull the other boys out.

Near the side of the hamburger joint, I quietly rinsed my lunch off of me, glancing every once in a while, toward the goings-on near the backseat of the car.

The black boy, dressed all in white, was working hard to scrub my puke off the floor of Mr. Jackson's new car. The boy's drive-in hat was sideways on his sweaty head. Mr. Jackson stood over the boy's shoulder inspecting every inch of the cleaning job. And I thought he yelled at me?

Suddenly exploding, Mr. Jackson's words began to vomit forth. “I said get it clean!” he yelled at the black boy. Thrusting the black boy to the side, Mr. Jackson reached around him and mumbled just loud enough for me to hear, as I neared the rear door, soaked, “You niggers are all the same. Looks like I'll have to do it myself!”

Black people were alien to me. I just couldn't put my finger on it, but I had never had any type of connection with them. I had only seen them from a distance and was led to believe by kinfolk and acquaintances that black people were a subservient race and quite the ignorant bunch and didn't have the ability to learn.

I had heard some grown men talking one day in front of Mr. Moxley's general store, when Daddy had sent me down from the church to get some drinks. "They all look the same; have you ever noticed it? You can't tell one nigger from another."

Eddie McPherson had told me later in the school year on the playground monkey bars, "That's why they don't go to our school." Pausing, he added, "My pa says their brains are way too small. You can't learn 'em nothing new. Pa calls 'em gorillas." Eddie laughed and climbed down.

Mr. Jackson's forehead curl began to straighten with all the humidity and sweat that had accumulated around his face, trickling off his curved chin. The back seat, on that mid-summer day, was unbearable. All the shade inside the car had vanished. In its place was Mr. Jackson's anger and stifling, humid hot air. He was alone in the car. His bitterness and my soggy puke were his only company.

The black boy took his hat off and wiped his skint head with his forearm. His face was frozen like an inkblot on white paper. Not showing any breathing in his chest, he stood stoic, like a coal statue, with his hands motionless at his sides. The bucket was sitting next to his tattered shoes. Turning around, I could see the fear in his face, depressed. Stretching around Mr. Jackson without touching him, the boy's body spoke language, indicating he would like to try cleaning the car again.

In the back seat, now lying prostrate and scrubbing ferociously, Mr. Jackson groaned his frustrations with phrases, some of which I couldn't interpret, some that don't deserve repeating, and some filled with references to race, color, national origin, and children of unwed mothers.

Finally, he climbed out of the car. Standing completely drenched in sweat--really, it was the first quintessential sweat suit I had ever seen--Mr. Jackson spun around. He was ill-feeling and mean. Pushing the dirty rags into the black boy's arms and pointing down at the bucket without looking at it himself, Mr. Jackson ordered. "Make sure you get these back to Mr. Patelli, and don't drop 'em. Now, get out of my face...I'm tired of looking at you!"

After a few minutes, we were all relocated in the car again and on our way back to Pelham. The car was quiet during that trip, except for the constant hum of the air, speeding past our open windows. Mr. Jackson kept glaring at me through his mirror, while my eyes darted nervously away from his, in the backseat of a car that smelled like a bastard with bad breath.

13

Mr. Jackson always stood to teach us the Bible in Sunday School. He spoke with assurance and sometimes would break into a preacher's posture, his fiery eyes gluing us to his lesson. He never said *nigger* in any lesson. His leg propped up on a chair he kept near his podium; he rotated one red rattlesnake-skin cowboy boot on the chair and then the other, back and forth throughout the lesson, like a reptilian exhibition on a metal pedestal.

"If you have a birthday next week, remember to bring that offering for the church," he would say, closing the class session.

Once Sunday School was finished, and Mr. Jackson prayed his dismissing prayer about forgiveness and love, we all moved into the main church building for the morning worship service. This is when Daddy took over.

He could order a service that was powerful. The song leader, Mr. Dillard, stood up and announced the morning hymn. Everyone stood, and the piano and organ lifted us into the right key as one voice. Dwynelle Dill and Eva Greer were the two finest pianist and organist I would ever hear. As a preacher's kid, I had every hymn memorized by the time I was in second grade. I never looked at a book. This gave me more time to study my environment. I could see everyone in his or her spiritual attire and attitudes. I tried to sing and move my head around, so everyone could tell I already knew the words. On occasion, I would catch a well-meaning adult eye, through which would pass my young form of worship, and in return, I'd receive a smile.

If we sang *Count Your Blessings*, which has four verses, I could sing every word, not missing a one. I liked *The Old Rugged Cross*, *Amazing Grace*, and *Rock of Ages* the best.

I liked to hear the men sing *Just A Little Talk with Jesus*, because of the bass part in the chorus. I liked to hear the women sing, *In the Garden*, because of the soprano-alto duet in the verses.

I liked to hear the older people sing the third verse of *Amazing Grace*. They sang, "Through many dangers toils and snares, I've already come. 'Tis grace has brought us safe thus far, and grace will lead us home."

The funniest thing about church was when Mr. Santell would stand up to read the minutes and the financial report from the last business meeting. His voice was so dull and mechanical, it sounded like our antique phonograph player at the parsonage.

The phonograph was broken, or at least the needle was. Gabriel and me figured out a way to make it play. We made a cone out of a sheet of notebook paper and put a straight pin through the narrowest part of the cone. By placing the pin in the record groove, we could get a sound to come through the cone that sounded like Mr. Santell talking through his nose.

Closing out his business meeting report, Mr. Santell would say, “Balance on hand,” and then I knew he was fixin’ to sit down. It would be years later I would realize the importance and meaning of the word *expenditures*. “Greek to me,” I thought when he'd say it.

I loved the special singing, trios, solos, choir, quartets, instrumentals, and especially the piano-organ offertories. We had incredible musicians.

But I loved the revivals.

I was saved in a revival meeting.

We had a wild revival meeting one summer, and yes, you guessed it, Evangelist Bartholomew Keller was in town. He was a Holy Ghost preacher. His mammoth yet graceful persona glided across the platform like an Olympic ice skater, periodically stopping at the pulpit to find his place in his notes and taking a pause to catch his breath. Then he kept preaching, lifting his leg into the air, leaning backwards to throw his words up into the rafters of our church building, and loosening his string tie, held together by a shiny cowboy buckle. He preached hard for two weeks, and I was at every sermon. One sermon was "When Lefty Let Fatty Have It." Great sermon and funny! People were getting saved all over the place. While he was in town, the pool hall closed, men quit drinking booze, harlots confessed and joined the choir, gambling tables were folded up and put in the closets, and kids were getting straightened out and being nice to their folks.

On the final Friday night meeting, Pelham Baptist Church was full. It was standing-room-only. When my daddy introduced the evangelist, Reverend Keller moved to the piano and began to sing *I Will Not Be a Stranger.* I loved to hear him sing that song. While he sang, three or four ladies began to raise their hands and handkerchiefs, praising the Lord, my momma included. It was a song about heaven, and people who'd lost loved ones to death cried and praised when the evangelist sang it.

When Momma decided to shout in church, it meant we all got involved; it was a family affair. Timing and cooperation were essential ingredients. Because there were six children, Momma had to pass the youngest down the row to free her hands for shouting. She was a two-handed shouter. She would stand up and look at the ceiling to shout--not the same way she would look at the ceiling before she spanked me with a hickory switch. She cried hot tears of praise for minutes and lifted both hands to the heavens. Sometimes, she would remain standing after the song was over and talk to God aloud. Momma's sudden praise-a-thon would frighten the youngest in our family, until the youngest cried. Me, Gabriel, and Daniel were used to it. We didn't even have to sit with Momma any more in church, so it was more up to Carol or Becky to take care of Esther during the shouting moments, while Esther cried and sometimes screamed.

"Help yo'self, honey," Daddy would say to my Momma. I've even heard him say the same thing to other people in the church. "Help yo'self, honey!"

The most sacred moment of any service was when Mr. Elijah Green, the chairman of the deacons would rise to his feet, with the help of his wife and daughter-in-law, and hang onto the pew in front of him in order to testify. When most people testified, everybody else listened, amen'd, or didn't listen, but when Mr. Elijah Green testified, *everybody* listened, no questions asked. It was as if Moses himself, or Noah, or Michael the archangel was speaking. Mr. Green's white hair flowed back from his forehead, thick and heavenly. His voice was raspy and ancient, and his eyes roamed over the entire congregation. You could feel them when they touched you. There was a collective sigh of relief, when he finally said his peace, and then was helped back into the pew with no apparent injuries. He always began with, "Let the redeemed of the Lord say so." Most people said, "Amen," or else breathed out all the trapped oxygen they had arrested in their lungs, once Mr. Green stood initially.

On that Friday night, Bartholomew Keller preached on hell, and was it ever hot.

He made me feel like I was swinging across the opened flames of hell, holding onto a rotten corn stalk. He told about the fire, the worms, the torment, the devil, the gnashing, the smoke, the separation from God, and eternity. I thought about his message long and hard. Finally, it was time for the invitation, the time when the evangelist or preacher asked for decisions to be made for God.

I was almost ready to go to the front and get saved. I thought of how I would do it, if I did decide to do it. I could see that there were about six or seven people on my church row who were standing between me and the church aisle, down which I would need to walk in order to get saved. It seemed embarrassing I would have to step on people's shoes or ask them to *excuse me* just to get to the aisle to get to the altar to have someone tell me how to get saved--not have to go to hell with all them harlots and people.

By the time Mr. Dillard had led us to the third verse of *Just As I Am*, I had pretty much talked myself out of getting saved that night. I figured since I was a preacher's kid, God would have to take that into consideration before chunking me into hell with Cain and Festus. And besides that, I gave my offering every week in Sunday School, and I didn't even get mad when a grown man--who wore alligator-skin cowboy boots--said I didn't have a father.

But then, on the fourth verse, near the end of the service, the church went totally black, no lights, and total darkness.

Little did anyone know in Pelham, a few hundred feet past the bridge, through Blountville at the corner of Blountville Road and Highway 14, a drunk had lost control of his car and clipped a telephone pole, the one that held up the power that kept our church lit up with light bulbs.

At first, I thought I was not only lost and condemned to spend eternity in hell with Pharoah and Jezebel, but I had suddenly lost my sight. I couldn't see a thing inside Pelham Baptist Church, powerless. *I'm blind too,* I thought, *and our church don't believe in healing like the other church up the road.*

It's one thing to believe you might go to hell if you don't get saved, but it's another thing to think that thought while you're standing in a completely dark church building during the invitation time. Add to that a lady, standing only a couple of pews behind me, who yelled at the top of her voice, "I don't want to go to hell!"

That scared the kuh-gee-bees out of me. It was the first time in my life I had ever *felt* like I was in hell. I could hear the screaming, taste the darkness, and smell eternity. I didn't hesitate. Somehow, I managed to get past all the people on my pew. I don't remember ever touching them. I'm sure, in hindsight, I must have trampled each person considerably, but there were no repercussions after the fact.

To help with the darkness, some of our deacons and other men went to their cars and brought back flashlights.

Mr. Dillard kept leading the invitational song in the dark, despite the organ's abrupt silence. Church kept right on going.

And so did I. I moved down the aisle and met my daddy at the altar. He took a flashlight and his Bible, and he showed me in his Bible how to get saved. It was grand.

That night, when we got home to the parsonage, I sat on the living room couch in front of the upright piano and talked to God for the first time. It was good. He did a lot of listening as I set out to tell Him how proud I was to be in His family. He didn't say much back to me directly, but I could tell He was pleased as punch with everything that I had to say. In my own heart, I heard Him say, "Welcome to the family, Jake!"

I fell asleep on the couch, sleeping late the next day, and woke up. Dry.

14

It wasn't long until Momma had to take a job in the public. She became a shoe salesman in Greenville at the Buster Brown Shoe Store on Main Street. She was gone quite a lot for long periods of time.

Momma was to begin work on a Monday. A few days before her new job, Daddy and her drove toward the Enoree Bridge, hanging a right on Pickett Road. Pickett Road crossed an inlet of the Enoree River and rolled out into the black section of Pelham. Most of Pelham's black families lived along this narrow, winding lane, poorly paved and bumpy with potholes. The houses were sparsely erected in the woods and some in open spaces.

Not many white Pelham people ever traveled this deserted road, except on certain occasions, like when Mr. Jackson would bring us out to look at the blacks and their shabby houses. “That house there... the one between those two nigger pines... that house is right behind the parsonage where you live, boys, if you come straight across Enoree River behind the school.”

He enjoyed playing practical jokes on black people. Once, he saw a black man walking on the side of Pickett Road. We were in the car. Mr. Jackson turned his car off just in time to make it backfire, resembling a shot gun blast. When the black man dove into the nearest ditch, Mr. Jackson laughed for the remainder of the trip up Pickett Road and back to the north crossing of Enoree River to Highway 14. "We scared that black boy, didn't we!" he said.

It failed to humor me. Daddy either.

Daddy and Momma had decided to hire a housekeeper and babysitter, all in one, from Pickett Road. Someone at our church had recommended Mattie Robinson. We had never met her, of course.

It was rainy the day Aunt Mattie--a name we affectionately called her--came to the parsonage. Daddy and Momma came through the basement door and behind them walked the most pleasant lady, solid black, barefooted, and sweet as honey.

“Why, my, Missuh Adam, you has some fine chil’lun, hee’ur,” she smiled. She had every tooth but one, near the right front. Her smile was so warm that the rainy day stayed outside, and the snuggly sunlight moved with her, inside.

“Not all the time, Mattie," Daddy said. "Sometimes, they’re gonna need tending to,” he added out loud so that we all could hear the rules for us.

“Why, they all pre’shus, Sir, jus’ pre-shus!” she praised. Her hands were folded respectively in front of her.

Sometimes she talked with her eyes closed, like she was seeing another place.

Gaining our undivided attentions, Daddy said, “You kids, listen.” Daddy paused to collect his thoughts. “Miss Mattie here is going to supervise you while Momma’s working. On some days, I’ll be in my home office studying. If Miss Mattie needs me, all she has to do is walk down the basement steps and fetch me. You know what will happen if I have to leave my study for your misbehavior.”

The whole time he lectured, I couldn’t take my eyes off this remarkable woman, created in a different time and place. Her eyes were warmly alluring. Her rounded face was genuine, and her head was covered with a colorful kerchief, wrapped tightly and tied in the back of her head, completely covering her hair. She wore a long flowing cotton dress, with an apron, its silhouette imprinted deeply into the front of the dress. Her shoulders were draped with a soft, black shawl. She was barefooted. Her feet were rounded on top, and smooth. A few days later on another rainy day, when she had fallen asleep in the basement atop Daddy's folded, green gospel tent, I studied the bottom of her feet, which were thick, light-colored, and as tough as any piece of leather, yet as tender as a Momma's love on top.

"And that's what I expect," Daddy continued, "of each of you. Do you understand?"

We all six answered *Yes, Sir* in unison, like a Sunday morning children's choir.

"Do you have anything to add to that, Miss Mattie?" Daddy asked.

Mattie Robinson was embarrassed to have to speak so formally in front of us. She turned her body away from us and said, "No, Sir, Missuh Adam. You says it jes' right."

Even Daddy was taken aback by her shyness. "Mattie?" he asked, not knowing why.

"Sorry, Sir," she whispered from her other side. As large as she was, she moved like a kindergarten child.

After a few introductions and a thorough explanation of routines, Aunt Mattie was driven back to Pickett Road in the back of our 1950 black Roadmaster Buick.

Once school started after Labor Day, Aunt Mattie became a fixture at our house, Monday through Thursday. We knew she would be there when we walked through the parsonage door.

However, whenever Momma worked Saturdays or whenever Daddy and Momma had to go to a church meeting of some kind, Mrs. Black sat with us. Usually my sisters would stay at someone else's house, if Mrs. Black came over.

Mrs. Black was a lady from our church. She was very short, had one good arm and one almost arm, with the end part missing. The arm stopped at the wrist and made a perfect nub, a rounded weapon. Mrs. Black knew how to use that nub too. She had a limping leg, opposite her shortened arm. That combination caused her to toddle as she walked. She lived in a two-room apartment beside the Moxley's general store.

She always wore her oversized, button-down-the-front gray sweater with big pockets in the front at the bottom. Her mouth was twisted, and she was toothless, making her speech distorted. Her short-muffed hair added to her curious appearance. She walked anywhere she went, unless Daddy and Momma picked her up or took her home in the Buick. In her hand at all times was her long, black flashlight. It was longer than her bad arm. She went nowhere without it.

Coming up Highway 14 from the bridge, she would hold her flashlight in her left hand with her pocketbook draped over her nubbed arm. She was quite a curious sight as she moved through the community.

Of course, there were many stories about Mrs. Black. Not many people believed any of those horrid stories, but kids loved to spread them around and make light of her. She was the topic of many a bad joke and scary tale.

When we were told Mrs. Black would be going to sit with us, we tried to be very careful. She was as quiet as a mouse in the parsonage and could suddenly appear in the doorway without warning...and she was the biggest tattletale I ever knew, excluding Daniel. She looked for anything to blame us for, some of which was more than we deserved.

"Daniel, quit dat runnnin' in the hallway!" she yelled one night while Daddy and Momma were gone to church. The family daughters were at a friend's house, except for Esther who accompanied our parents to church.

"I'm not runnin'!" Daniel yelled back. That's what we were telling Daniel to say.

Gabriel and me were at the other end of the hallway, encouraging Daniel to keep runnin'. "Keep going. See if you can go faster, Daniel!" Gabriel whispered. "Hurry!"

Daniel was eating it up. He was almost dancing with his quick feet down the hallway, flowing across the narrow wooden floor like a ballet dancer. His socked feet sizzled.

"Daniel!" Mrs. Black yelled again, "If I come in dare and tatch you runnin', I'm gonna tell yore daddy, you hear me?"

Gabriel and me broke out in a stifled laugh, grinning at Daniel and motioning for him to keep it up. For some reason, we would never think of consequences until it was too late.

"Daniel!"

Before this incident with Mrs. Black, we had never been hit in the head with the nub. We had no idea what it was like. Some kids later told us Mrs. Black's nub was registered at the police department in Greer.

Gabriel and me rolled like combat soldiers into our room and left Daniel in the hallway to face Mrs. Black's punishment. We figured she could never bend down to find us, with her physical limitations.

Suddenly, the hallway got quiet. No noise.

Gabriel and me lay still. Our heartbeats could be heard against the wooden floor beneath our chests. We were still uncontrollably expectorating giggles.

"What happened?" Gabriel asked. "Did you see anything?"

"No."

The longer we lay there under the bed, the more the silence made our minds imagine.

"Go see about Daniel. You don't think it's true about her, do you?" Gabriel asked, sounding very unsure. "Huh?"

I wasn't the one to ask. I was less sure than he probably was. "You go."

Gabriel said quietly, "Daniel?"

We both lay still again. Without warning, the lights in the hallway went out. There was no sound. I had never heard soundlessness so loud before.

"Daniel? Is that you?" Gabriel asked again.

Then, like in a summer thunderstorm, our bedroom lights went out. We were both under the bed in total darkness.

Were those stories about her murdering kids with her nub true? Did she really finish them off with her black flashlight and then drag their bodies to the dam, before throwing them off into the whirlpool of foam below? Did she secretly sneak up on you in the dark and then grab...?

"Oh, God, help us!" Gabriel yelled to the top of his voice. "Please!"

I screamed right into the wood finish as if it were a flat microphone. My mouth was wide open, lying on top of the floor. I was almost out of control, kicking my legs into the under-pending of the bed. Gabriel kept his prayer hot and loud. There was no sign of Daniel.

Suddenly, a bright light came from beside the bed, down low. It was shining right in our eyes. We both quit screaming, and I ceased to drool on the floor. Gabriel had his hands folded under his chin, like a child praying before bedtime.

"Boat of you... tum out!" Mrs. Black's voice reverberated. "Tum out." Her voice was powerful, enclosed.

Gabriel slid out first, pulling a few bits of dust piles from below our bed. I came out immediately behind Gabriel's sock bottoms. Once out, we were forced back against the wall by the light's energy. No one touched us, but we naturally backed into the wall. When we felt it, we leaned there, finally feeling something we thought would hold us up for a while.

The unexpected appearance of the flashlight had us totally blinded. I tried to look through the brightness but couldn't see past the frontline of glare. I was actually afraid to see what was behind the flashlight. I found comfort in staring directly into the light. Now, I *wished* to be blind.

Then, I heard Mrs. Black's voice. It wasn't coming from behind the flashlight, but to our right sides. How could she hold a flashlight in our faces and her voice be coming from the right side of the bedroom? The bedroom lights came on, and there stood Mrs. Black with her good hand near the light switch. Daniel peeped around the far end of the flashlight. He was holding it with two hands, grinning.

She asked, in an eerie voice, "You two learnt yore lessin' yet? Huh?"

"Yes, Ma'am," I answered first, still blind.

"Yes," Gabriel quickly followed.

"You two was makin' Daniel git in trubble, and dat's not rite," she sputtered. "I want you to 'pologize, now."

Daniel hadn't taken the time to turn off the flashlight. He stood in front of us like a hired henchman, glaring at us across the flashlight's long barrel, ready to fire it at her command. His expression was sickening, stark and haughty. He was an official member of the *nub club.*

"I'm not apologizing to anybody!" Gabriel suddenly yelled out. I couldn't believe his reaction. How could he taunt God's haunting creations?

Mrs. Black's good hand dropped like a lead hammer. She hobbled across the floor to face Gabriel. "Yes, you will, Gabe!" she snarled. No one had ever called Gabriel a shortened version of his name before. He was stunned. I saw the same scene in saloon fight on *Gunsmoke.*

Like a lightning strike, Mrs. Black popped Gabe on the top of his head with her nub. Gabe's feet and legs slipped outward beneath him, and he sat down on the floor, stunned. Even with my recovering eyesight, I could tell he didn't look healthy. He was speechless, gawking into space. His head moved side to side before he whined,

"Sorry...Daniel."

Immediately I sat down beside him and said, "I'm sorry too, Daniel." It didn't take a rocket scientist to detect I was next in line for the nub.

Mrs. Black put her nub back in its holster. It was loaded, still smoking.

I cried on general principles. I was actually sobbing. My shirt was already soaked from our twenty-thousand-leagues-under-the-bed experience.

Daniel finally turned off the flashlight and handed it back to its rightful owner. She hobbled between Daniel and us and took it from his hand, like the changing of the guard in London. She tapped Daniel lightly on the head with her good tender hand. He smiled at her, then directly at me, trailing her out of the room and down the hallway like a puppy after its first successful trick at a dog show.

Gabe rubbed his crown as if he was checking for a soft spot. I sniffled. We both sat there until we couldn't feel Gabe's pain no more. Then, both of us got up and walked into the kitchen for Mrs. Black's cheese toast. It was the first time she didn't tell our parents on us. It still hurt.

15

School started on a Tuesday.

Pelham School, even though a ghost town for three hot months, resurrected into a vibrant institution on the first day of school.

Buses began to pull up at the school around seven in the morning, gearing down the decline beside the parsonage, emptying brightly clad students onto the front steps and through the double doors, held open by Mrs. Duncan and an assisting teacher. The buses then grunted and churned up the other side of the curved school driveway to Highway 14 and departed north toward the high school in up-town Greer.

Me, Gabriel, and Daniel tried to get to school by seven thirty, so we could watch "The Three Stooges" or "Popeye the Sailor" on the school television set. All the kids were grouped around the front of the television in the school cafeteria. We sat, scattered around the floor, awaiting the eight o'clock bell for the day to begin.

The double doors of the school opened up into the main indoor hallway with the cafeteria on the left and the office on the right, Mrs. Duncan's office. Mrs. Duncan was the principal and the sixth-grade teacher. She pulled double duty.

Past her office door, a few feet farther, was a door that led outdoors to a cement walkway, under a covering that extended from the school's flat roof, supported by steel poles every few feet. Along this sidewalk, on the right side, were the classrooms, beginning with sixth grade and continuing in chronological order to the end of the outside walkway to the first grade, the last room, on the far end of the building. Kids would enter the first and travel down this sidewalk over a sluggish six-year journey just to be bussed up the road to the junior high school. Some kids took longer than six years to soak up their primary education.

When the eight o'clock bell rang, Gabriel led me and Daniel to our rooms. First, he dropped his notebook and pencil pack to a desk in his fourth-grade room, leaving us outside dodging traffic, under the covering. Next, me and Gabriel escorted Daniel to first grade, at the end of the building, where Daniel would study for two years. Then, Gabriel took me to the third-grade classroom. Gabriel left for the fourth grade.

Ain't it interesting to think how a person feels about his grade, or place in life, and how it is the most important thing to him at that specific moment. Daniel wasn't thinking about fourth grade and me either. I was glad to be in the third, and the chalk and the thin bulletin-board walls that separated me from Gabriel's classroom and his one-hundred-eighty-day world in that room with those particular people, did not enter into my emotional priorities.

Of course, Daniel wasn't thinking about fourth; he was thinking about the first grade, for two consecutive years.

As the door closed behind me, I could tell there was something different about this room. The smell of waxed floors, fresh potpourri, and Ivory soap coated my nostrils.

For a second, I stood stationary, looking around at this wonderfully warm room, all decorated with words and pictures and smiles. Miss Jenny was surveying the room, kneeling beside each child and making that first contact into the child's heart. Every kid in the room had already heard about this loving teacher, even me.

"Jake!" Rocky Lee yelled. "Over here!"

Rocky was sitting near the middle of the classroom beside Ray Lawrence and Lanny Wilson, the bastard. I wondered to myself if one third-grade class could hold two bastards.

I slipped down the near aisle and sat behind Rocky. He turned around.

"Where's Gabriel?"

"He's in fourth."

"I know. He has Miss Campbell. He's in trouble!" Rocky explained.

"He is?"

I hadn't heard much about Miss Campbell.

"Miss Campbell is new. She's mean," Rocky added. "Makes you do a lot of homework, I heard."

"Who told you that?" I asked.

"Clanton Butler." He paused. "Well, he didn't tell me. I heard him telling somebody else. "

Rocky nor I spoke or moved when he finished that statement, which included that name. Clanton Butler was the oldest boy in Pelham School. He was supposed to be in the eighth grade but had flunked two times--first and fourth grades--and was now in the sixth grade, only because he was too tall to fit into a fifth-grade desk. He was the school and neighborhood bully and had whooped all the bigger boys in Pelham. His name was synonymous with terror and torture.

He was the fastest, biggest, and toughest boy in Pelham School, and everybody knew it, or else *he'd show 'em.*

Wanting to see what the name sounded like on my lips, I asked more quietly, "Clanton Butler?"

"Yeah. I overheard him telling another sixth grader," Rocky continued. "If anybody knows about Miss Campbell, Clanton Butler does."

Clanton Butler's nickname, which no one dared to say to his face, was *Rooster*. He was a fighter, like a fighting cock, or rooster, and could run faster than any other boy in school. I wondered why the name rooster had anything to do with speed, though, I didn't understand, except that a rooster could fly. Pelham had a few cock fighters, but since it was against the law to gamble on chickens, most people stayed away from cock fighting.

My Uncle Gene was a cock fighter. I had seen him leave home on Friday after work with a trailer full of cock pens and come back from the low land either penniless or with a wad of *moo-lah* in his wallet. He either made a lot of money or else lost it all. There was no happy medium in cock fighting.

My Uncle Gene had a couple of champion roosters. He had a rooster named Hoss. I saw Hoss one day. He was sitting in his cage in the mountains at my uncle's farm. All the other roosters' cages were scattered around Hoss' larger cage in the middle of the yard. Hoss was pampered. His photo had appeared on two occasions on the national cock-fighting magazine. My Uncle Gene had every monthly copy of the rooster magazine from 1952-1957 in his workshop below his apartment. He must have had a million issues. The magazines told a fighter how to train, feed, and fight his cocks. My uncle had become pretty good at it.

Strange enough, though, I asked my uncle on one of my hot summer days, of all the many roosters he ever owned or fought for money, which rooster impressed him the most. He proceeded to tell me an unusual tale about his favorite rooster. We were sitting under the large oak tree in the front yard of the parsonage. Here's the way he told it:

Well, I was burning trash in the fifty-five gallon can near my house one day and this rooster walked up. He was scraggly and poor. He had feathers missing and looked sickly. I watched him for a couple of days. He never left to go anywhere else. He just hung around and pecked in our yard. I wanted to make sure no one had a claim to him. I figured I could use him to train my <u>*good*</u> *roosters. Finally, I caught him, tied his legs together, and carried him in the back of the truck over to the farm.*

I tried to feed him, to make him fatter, but he didn't gain much weight. He didn't like being cooped up in a cage, either. His freedom meant more to him than a healthy diet and exercise or prestige.

So, I put him on some fighting gloves and set him loose against Hoss and the others. He got beat up pretty bad. I figured then, I'd take him to my next fight and put him in a match with some cock that might put him out of his misery, and then I'd bet my money against him. Which I did.

I took him to the big fight in the low part of the state. I left early on a Friday evening after work with seven of my best fighters. Hoss was going with me to defend his regional title…no problem for him. Before he would leave the ring, Hoss always killed his opponents, except for one cock from Georgia, who a few months earlier had to wobble off with some help from his trainer after a vicious attack from Hoss.

The other six cocks that I took with me were young, up-and-coming fighters. I was definitely puttin' my money on five of 'em, but not on you-know-who though.

After Hoss had defended his title at the big fight, and four of the five up-and-comers had made me a little spare change, I untied Scraggly's legs; yes, I named him Scraggly. I matched him up with that same giant rooster from Georgia, who Hoss had defeated earlier in the summer. The rooster's named was Bulldog. He was large-chested and proven and still reeling from his summer whooping. His only defeat had come at the spurs of Hoss. Bulldog was scarred and had a bad attitude, especially against scraggly looking cocks that didn't belong in the same ring with him, insulted.

The referee signaled a start to the fight. I had already made my journey around the circular ring to bet against Scraggly. I put it all on the line against him. Before he would die, this scraggly cock was going to make me some big money.

Bulldog did a double take when he saw Scraggly. I think he was a little taken back by the appearance of this undernourished weakling. Scraggly seemed to be enjoying his freedom inside the ring--stretching, struttin', almost crowin'--and hadn't even noticed the monstrous cock approaching him. Bulldog hit Scraggly with a whopper of a stroke against the head and Scraggly went down, only temporarily.

Staggering side to side, and wondering what he had done to offend this ogre, Scraggly scooted away from him toward the rounded side of the ring. For a second, and only for a second, I felt sorry for Scraggly. He seemed to be looking for me, for some outside help. I couldn't help him, 'cause I had bet all I had against him.

Bulldog didn't waste any time. I think he must have known that Scraggly had traveled in the same trailer with Hoss; he could smell and taste it. With all the energy he could collect, Bulldog came at Scraggly. His spurs were lightning quick and sure. He battered and tore Scraggly up one side and down the other. Scraggly took it all, without retaliation, still looking for an escape.

Then, it happened. It was incredible.

Suddenly, while Scraggly was lying in his own warm blood, he shook his head, scrambled to his feet, and tore in to Bulldog. Scraggly's legs were robotic and precise considering his weakened physical condition. He put one spur deep into Bulldog's chest and ripped it open. Bulldog was stunned. He couldn't move. He was beside himself.

While Bulldog was bent over slightly inspecting his reddened chest, a powerfully and precisely placed spur landed directly in the side of bulldog's head; he lost an eye with that attack.

Bulldog had backed Scraggly into a rounded corner, and Scraggly adored his freedom too much to die. He was willing to give anything to have his freedom. He was like the early American Patriots in the Revolutionary War. Poor old Bulldog hadn't paid enough attention in history class. Perhaps someone should have informed him, long before he was lifted from the ring, lifeless.

I saw it with my own eyes, or else I would have never believed it if someone had told me.

I lost almost all my money on Scraggly. I went home penniless. The odds were stacked against Scraggly. He emptied my wallet that day...but he filled my heart.

On the way back home to the mountains, I wrapped up Scraggly's wounds and put some medicine on 'em. He rode in the trailer with Hoss, and when we got back to the farm, I fixed Scraggly a special place...which was anywhere at the farm he wanted to strut his stuff. He spent the last days of his life walking past all the cages and crowing his freedom. Sometimes he would fly to the top of Hoss' cage, and after regaining his breath, would crow. The echo of that crow could be heard all the way to Georgia. He was the cock of the roost.

When my Uncle Gene told that story, I realized he had learned a lesson in that experience with his chickens and about life. I know I did.

"Now, class, I want you to know that we are going to have a good time this year in the third grade, and you are going to learn a lot," Miss Jenny said.

She stood in front of the class with her glasses on a string around her neck and her graying hair pinned in a bun to the back of her head. Her face was bright and drew me in. She was dainty and light on her feet. I could tell she was getting energy from her students.

She spent the third-grade year telling us many stories. With her gestures and facial expressions, she captured my imagination. In my third-grade year, I was inspired to teach when I grew up.

"Now, I hope you have learned a lot this morning already," Miss Jenny said, "but now we are going to recess. We will line up at the door to go outside. As you know, the boys can go down the bank to play, but the girls will need to stay up on the hill with me."

This is what me and Rocky had been waiting for, to get outside and see the *hut.*

"Okay, boys, you may go," Miss Jenny said. We sprinted from our straight line onto the hill and down it to the lower playground. Every boy in Pelham School played within the shadows of the twilight zone but never paid it attention, until it was time to go there, mostly after school.

"Rocky, where's the hut?" I asked.

"Over there. It's not a hut yet. It will be in a few days," Rocky told me.

"Huh?"

"It takes a few days to build it."

Every year, after Mr. Peters would cut the hay on the lower field, after it had grown all summer long, the sixth-grade boys would use the hay to build a hut. Poles and strings were left over from the year before, so after tying poles together in the shape of a large room, the boys only had to gather up the hay and fasten it onto the poles with string.

A large quilt or covering was draped across the doorway of the hut and only sixth grade boys could enter, unless a lower grade boy was accompanied into the hut by a sixth-grade boy. That very rarely happened.

Since the hut was not being built yet, our minds were distracted by the other playground noises. We raced across the open field to the baseball diamond, crudely arranged at the edge of the woods. We ended up sitting down around second base, talking about third grade and the river.

"Are you ever going over the river, Jake?" Rocky asked.

I wished he hadn't, because Ray and the bastard were sitting right beside us.

"Yeah, I know I will," I answered.

"You never swung the river, Jake?" Lanny asked.

"Not yet. I will though...soon," I said.

Ray, who needed to be fished out of the inlet, said, "It's not that hard. You just pick your legs up and let the vine do the work."

Yeah, that's easy for you to say, Ray, since you were fished out of the Enoree. I tried to let this conversation evaporate with the mid-morning September sun, but it wouldn't go away fast enough.

"So, are you going to try after school today?" Lanny asked.

"Who me?" I finally asked. "Me?"

"Yes, you," Rocky filled in. "When are you gonna swing?"

"Today? Did you say today?" I hesitated. "I don't know if my family is going to be here today." *That'll shut 'em up. Case closed.*

"Yes, they are," Rocky inserted. "Gabriel and another fourth grader said they was goin with us too... so, if Gabriel is goin', I guess you can go, huh?"

Oh, boy!

I stammered. "Guess you're right about that...guess so."

About that time, a little too late to save me, Miss Jenny held her hand up, at the top of the hill, signaling recess was over. We all jumped up and sprinted again, trying to be the first in line. Of course, I wasn't.

That day, after school, I tried to find a hiding place at the house. Should'a gone to the attic.

16

I found a corner in the basement to hide, almost behind Daddy's study.

Nobody will find me here.

I went there early after school. It didn't matter to me how long I had to stay there, I didn't want to have to swing across Enoree River with the possibility of becoming part of Enoree underwater buffet or part of the deadly depth in a death hole.

I'll stay in the basement forever, if I have to.

"I know he has to be in here somewhere," Gabriel's voice sounded.

"How do you know?" Rocky asked.

There were seven of them, three third graders, three fourth graders, and a sixth grader. It wasn't Clanton Butler, thank goodness. Seven's such a good number, so perfect, holy, and uh lucky. *Seems like the seven boys would be satisfied with their good fortune and move on*!

My daddy always preached that the number seven represented perfection because the world was created in seven days and the Israelites marched around Jericho for seven days and something else in the Bible, I can't remember.

As best as I could tell from their voices, the boys were Rocky, Ray, Lanny--third graders, Gabriel, Tommy, Fred--fourth graders, and Pudge McFills--sixth grader.

Oh no, Pudge McFills. Please, Lord, don't let them find me.

All seven of them stood at the bottom of the basement steps talking, kinda quiet like, since Daddy was in his study, spending time with God.

"Why do you think he came in here, Gabriel?" Rocky asked.

“’Cause he ain’t been upstairs since school was out, and he don’t like to go outside by himself without his soldiers."

“Soldiers?” Pudge asked, surprised.

Pointing toward the back yard, Gabriel said, “Yeah, he plays army a lot under the tree out there."

Suddenly, Lanny, the other bastard, fell against a folded chair that rested next to the stairs. The chair hit the cement floor with a bang, echoing off the floor and walls like a crashing plane that Emmett would like to knock out of the sky.

“Hurry, let’s get outside,” Gabriel whispered. “Quick... Daddy...” He gestured toward Daddy’s study door. "Daddy..."

But it was too late. Daddy opened the door immediately. “What’s going on here?” he asked.

“Hey, Preacher,” Rocky said, awkwardly. “How are you, Sir?”

“Fine, Rocky. What you boys doing? Going somewhere?” Daddy asked. He looked Pudge over, who was bigger than the rest of the other boys, even wider than Clanton Butler.

“We," Ray inserted, "...we thought we might wander toward the Enoree, sir, and we are looking for Jake. He said he wanted to go with us today.”

“I see. He likes the river, you say?” Daddy asked.

“Yes. He told us today he was going to...” Lanny started to say but was interrupted with a slight kick on the leg from Rocky.

“Say what?” Dad asked.

Rocky finished Lanny's statement, "...that he was going to go with us."

“Well, if he wants to go that bad, it seems he wouldn’t be hiding right over there in that corner behind my study, does it?” Daddy said. He smiled, pointing exactly where I was crouching.

“Jake? Are you over there?” Gabriel asked.

"Jake?" Lanny echoed.

“Yes,” I said, defeated. I stood up, dusting my knees off.

“Come on, Jake!" Rocky said. "We’re going to the river. Hurry, ‘cause it’s gonna get dark on us if we don’t hurry. We're not going without you."

How thoughtful!

“Let’s go!” Pudge said. He turned and walked out of the basement with everyone behind him. I delayed, hoping they would keep walking and not notice me lagging behind, beneath the steps.

Suddenly, Rocky’s head peeped around the brick wall. “Jake!”

“Coming!” I muttered. I climbed out of the red clay piled behind a small block wall in the basement, thought bad things about my daddy for just a second, and then ambled outside into the afternoon light. My eyes didn’t want to adjust. I thought of faking blindness, but I remembered getting saved and didn’t.

Pudge led us like a team of eight, and I felt like I was behind the eight ball. We tromped into the field, past the hill, and to the tree line.

Beginning to show his seniority in the group, Pudge said, “Nobody’s going before me!” I had no qualms with letting him go first, or even going in *my* place, if it would make him happy. Nobody argued with Pudge anyhow. Everyone was quite willing to cross the river after Pudge; after all, Pudge had swum into the middle of a dark hole, a hole of death, and lived to tell it.

Pudge grabbed the vine and without hesitation--and in the perfect form--swung directly over the river's inlet and past the rock. He then stood upon the rock, like Peter on the day of Pentecost.

Everyone took their turn in food-chain order; of course, that would mean I would be at the bottom. I was. I was even below bastard number one.

Lanny swung across, and the vine dangled his release at my side of the river. I thought for a moment of letting the vine go and running back home and hiding in the attic, because without a vine, *no one* could come home. That moment melted with the other boys’ warnings.

“Grab it, Jake! Don’t let it go into the river!” Rocky yelled.

“You better not, you little coon!” Pudge barked. I knew what he really wanted to call me.

That’s all I needed to hear. My whole body reacted to his voice like an order from Ike. I instantly secured the vine. The river swooshed and sloshed below me, trying to get me to look at it, but I didn't.

“What? What’s wrong?” Pudge suddenly screamed. However, he wasn’t talking to me. He was talking to one of the boys on the other side. “Are you okay? What kind of snake was it? How long?”

I couldn’t see who he was talking to or what specifically they were talking about.

Pudge continued, “Gabriel, are you dying?”

Gabriel?

“Jake, come here, hurry!” Pudge yelled, in an uncharacteristically sympathetic voice. “Get over here and help Gabriel...*now*!”

I didn't stop to think about the river. I pulled the vine, held on, and pushed across the river like a trapeze artist from Barnum and Bailey Circus. I gained strength from somewhere. My landing was superb, flawless. Pudge even grabbed me when I landed to make sure I didn't fall, and Lanny seized the vine to keep it from leaving us abandoned on the rock, alone.

"Gabriel?" I asked. I felt like The Lone Ranger without Tonto. "Gabriel?" Hoping I could somehow help him, I touched him on the shoulder. My mind raced, attempting to recall the several steps in removing as much of the snake's poison as possible. I knew it would mean sucking the blood with my mouth, but to save my brother's life, I'd do it.

Suddenly, Gabriel jumped up, and began to laugh. All seven of the boys joined in, laughing.

"We tricked you, Jake," Gabriel said. "To get you to jump...and you did! You jumped! It was Pudge's idea, and it worked." All the boys looked at Pudge.

“Way to go, Jake,” Pudge said. Then, Pudge turned, saying, “Let’s go, everybody. Let’s go play some ball in your backyard, Rocky.”

“Okay, good idea,” Gabriel said.

Without hesitation, in the same order of the food chain in which they initially crossed the river, they all swung back across. From Pudge to the bastard, they swung and disappeared into the tree line, running. I didn’t own the same motivation that earlier had propelled me across the rolling river, and I didn’t wish to expose my weaker self by asking for help. The vine hung lethargically over the river, gyrating and taunting. I stood on the rock by myself wondering why they had played such a cruel trick on me. I also wondered what I was doing alone on the rock, on the opposite side of the Enoree River from my house, with no way to fetch the vine, deathly still across the rustling river water.

I could hear their voices in the distance. At first, they ran. Then I could tell they paused by the twilight zone, perhaps for a wild story from Pudge. I could then vaguely hear them while they gathered equipment and chose sides for the ball game. For some reason, the riverbed absorbed some of the sounds and made it less hurtful. I knew I couldn't go back across the Enoree by myself. The passionate energy that had lifted me onto the vine had suddenly left in somebody's back pocket.

I had no other choice if I was going to get home. The day was soon to be over. The options in front of me were nullified, the river churning its threats below the useless vine. I pivoted around behind me toward a thinning in another tree line. Gabriel and Rocky had warned me before *not* to go through the tree line. "That's the back of Pickett Road," Rocky had said. "Don't go through those trees."

Having no other choice, if I wanted to get home, I began the trek, pushing tree limbs aside, and eased into an open field of thick but empty corn stalks. The rows were lined up with the river's flow. I found my own path in and out of the stalks, trying to get through to the nearest person who could help me get home before dark. Stalk leaves scraped me as I walked. With each step, the beats of my heart intensified. There were no visible or audible signs of life in the field.

Suddenly, I stopped. A sound of lightning-quick running feet captured my attention. Whoever it was running wasted no time in getting where he or she was going. Leaning into the next row, I saw my first glance of this kid barreling down a long row of loose red clay. When he saw me, he stopped too.

There he was. I was within feet of him, and he was within feet of me. He was black, and I was white. We both froze in the heat. Neither knew what to do. There was no Southern protocol available to either of us, no Pickett Road possible, practical precedent to resource.

For what seemed like days, but was only stretched seconds, him and me stood there.

"Hello," I tried to say, a late summer fly tormenting my eye.

The black boy hung his head like he was breaking a forbidden law in looking at me.

"My name is Jake. Who are you?" I asked him.

He made no sound. Just stood there, head down. Then, he spoke, quietly.

"Josiah, Sa."

"You live here?" I asked him.

"In dat house, ober dare," he said. He pointed shyly past the cornfield.

I looked in that direction and could finally see his house. It was the one Mr. Jackson had made fun of and told us about. It was leaning one way and then another at the same time. A clump of river rocks and some thinly spread cement held it up. The windows were wide open, and frazzled rags blew in and out with the breeze like S.O.S. flags. I could see no door.

I talked. "I got to get back home, across the river, and I can't." I looked back at the river to make a reference point.

"Ober dare, yah says?" he asked. He tilted his head sideways, studying the tree line.

"Yes, I need to get back across the river. You know anybody that can help me do that?" I asked. I tried to look more at Josiah's face, even though he was avoiding my eyes. His face plummeted.

"Yes, Sir, I does believe I cans he'p you, Sa," he said, like I was his boss or something. "Wants me to sho' you how, Sa?"

"Yes, yes I do. Is it okay with your folks?"

He didn't react to that question, but sheepishly stepped around me, making sure not to bump me. After a couple of steps, he paused until I started walking. He began to lead me toward the river.

While we were walking, I asked, "Josiah, where do you go to school? I don't see no school anywhere."

"I don'ts go, Sa," he whispered. "I can'ts read."

"You can't read?" I asked, quietly.

"No, Sa, can'ts read, but Miss Berthley, she be teechin' readin' me some."

The tree line parted much easier this time. I followed Josiah through it, straight to the river bank. He stopped to listen. His head still drooped.

Gesturing toward the vine, I said, "I need that vine there, over the river."

"You wants me to fetch that vine fo ya, Sa?" Josiah asked me, his head facing the ground.

"If you can. I'm afraid to swing across the river. My brother is not afraid, but I am. He left me on this side and went back home, him and some boys from school," I explained, dying out on the word *school*, since I remembered that Josiah didn't have one.

"Gives me a minute, Missuh Jeck, Sa," he said. *At least he said my name, kinda.*

He reached into the other vines that were fallen on the ground near the rock. He pulled one of 'em up like a fireman getting his fire hose. He fashioned a hook-like shape on the end of his vine and threw it out. It lassoed the river vine, reeling it to him. He seized it with his hand.

Josiah was barefooted and hadn't winced one time from the sharp briars and rocks as we explored his path through the woods. He glided across the ground like he was walking on water. His too-short pants were ragged at the ends and he had no shirt on. His dark skin was shiny and glistening in the partial sunlight in the woods.

His black hand held the vine out to me.

"Hee-uh, Missuh Jeck, Sa," he said. He sounded like the shoeshine boy in Greenville, near Momma's shoe store job. One day in the summertime, he shined Daddy, Gabriel, Daniel, and my shoes. Daddy gave him a quarter for each one of us.

"I still don't know if I can…I'm afraid of the river," I told him. I was kinda shy about sharing my fears with a stranger.

Breaking his cheeks into an impromptu smile, and speaking a little lighter tone, he said, "Yo' scay'd of da crick? Say, yo scay'd o' da crick, Missuh Jeck?"

“Yeah, I am, Josiah…so what? And it's not a creek, it's a river!” I said, feeling he was making fun of me. “So?” *He called it a creek?*

“Day ain’t no *so* to it…yo scay’d o’ da crick, brotha. Lawdy muh-sy, yo gotta lic dat crick, Missuh Jeck… lic it.” He danced a couple of steps, then stopping, giggled.

“Huh?” I asked. I was mesmerized with Josiah’s rhythmical language, his confidence in this tension-packed situation. He called the river a creek. He reminded me of the black keys on our upright piano, rising above the white ones, adding the sharps and flats to a composer’s symphony. Somehow I had opened up a can of music inside him. “Can you help me, or not?”

“Hee-uh, Missuh Jeck, Sa…” For some reason, we were relaxed, breaking some code of ethics or something, and it wasn't as bad as we had been told.

Without thinking first, I said, “Don’t call me *sir* no more!" I paused; his head dropped again. "That’s the last time you call me that!” I demanded, frustrated by Josiah’s subservient reactions and humble words. Looking down at Josiah's closed right hand, I asked, “What is that?” I felt like Mr. Jackson, a little bit, commanding.

He rotated his hand, palm up and opened it slowly. In the palm of his hand was a small rock. I studied it. It was shaped like an anvil, a blacksmith’s anvil. While we had been talking, Josiah had taken it from his pants pocket. I had seen an anvil before at my grandpa’s farm. He used it to shape horseshoes and to hammer things on.

I asked again, “What is it?”

“It’sa cur-idge stone, Missuh Jeck...I’ll lends it to you, to give you cur-idge to cross da crick,” he said, holding it out for me to hold. “Take it. It yo’s now.”

“Why? What does it do?”

“Wid dis in yo pockit, yo cans swings all de days ‘cross de crick hee-uh, and yo be’s fine...jus’ fine...God, He take care o’ you, Missuh Jeck." His voice sung; he could express himself better with a sing-song cadence. “My papa, he gives it to me fo’ cur-idge, and yo needs it now, Sa.”

“This stone will keep me from getting hurt?” I wondered to him aloud.

“Yes. Take it...and go, before it get dark, Missuh Jeck,” Josiah said, now, for the first time, looking me straight in the eyes. I could see his sincerity, pushing itself past his fear. He was taking a chance talking to me. Inside of Josiah was a proud person, who through his secluded history was content with his place along the side of Pelham’s Pickett Road, and a river he called a creek.

I placed the stone in my pants pocket. I took the vine from behind Josiah where he had secured it with a loose vine. I stood upon the rock and leapt forward. Like a swashbuckler in the pirate movies, I swung onboard the mother ship safely, although with a tumble, heading home.

Josiah turned toward the thin place in the opposite tree line. He was dancing his way across the briars and rocks.

“Wait!” I suddenly yelled. “Josiah...how old are you?”

“Eh-uht.”

“Eight? Hey, so am I. We’re the same age, Josiah…me and you,” I said. The river kept moving, not even pausing between us, both of us within feet of the tree lines on our respective sides. I wondered who was more nibble, the river or Josiah.

Josiah began to turn again.

“Wait!” I yelled again. “I need to know. Where did this stone come from?”

“My Pappa…he finds it…at de Enoree, below de dam…whens he was a fishin’ in da riva…he say he believes it be somebody’s lost soul. A lost soul…in de Enoree, Missuh Jeck.”

“Okay. Thank you. I’ll see you later, Josiah. Thank you for the stone. I’ll get it back to you when I finish with it. It sure works,” I said.

Josiah smiled, disappearing through the trees.

I moved through my tree line, past the hill, the field, and into the parsonage's backyard, feeling brave and confident. I was as strong as an anvil and was the possessor of a lost soul in my pocket. Supper was good that night. I kept one hand on my fork and one on my anvil. Gabriel didn't ask me how I got home, and I was glad. At least, I wasn't breaking Momma's etiquette rules.

In my mind, I could see how Josiah had turned my apprehension into a song. He was singing at the *crick* when a song wasn't in sight. He played his tune off the riverbank like a chorister at Carnegie Hall.

Momma called me down for humming at the supper table.

"You shouldn't hum at the supper table, Jake. Remember your etiquette," she said.

Call me Jeck, Mother.

I smiled at her with my mouth full, stealthily humming behind my face.

17

Gabriel was a daredevil. I don't know if it was because he was the eldest son in a family of six children--and he felt it his calling to cross the boundaries of common sense in order to challenge the impossible--or because he was short for his age and had something to prove to the rest of us, or what...but he took chances for money...small change.

Because Theodore West dared him to do it for a dime, Gabriel rode his new Christmas bicycle off our rounded stone wall and onto the rock driveway one day.

Well, back in the 1950's, boys didn't know how to ride a bicycle off river stone walls. The fifties were the cruising days for bicycles. Bicycles were heavy, with padded soft seats, passenger ride-along accommodations on the back, tooting horns, large fenders, front-and-back wheel shocks, fancy baskets for carrying stuff, wide mirrors, rubber handle-bar covers with colorful plastic streamers, and white, wide-walled tires. Those bikes were made for slow cruising, not jumping up or off anything, especially a river-stone wall five feet high.

"You heard me, Gabriel...ten cent for riding off the wall," Theodore said.

Gabriel answered, "You *promise* you'll give me the dime?"

"Don't do it, Gabriel," I said. To the contrary, I knew he would, so I tried to get a head start on talking him out of it. Once Gabriel set his mind to doing something, it was almost impossible to help him change his mind, except for hog-tying him before he got up out of bed.

Standing near the top of the wall, looking down, Rocky asked, "You really gonna do it, Gabriel?" No answer.

"Really?"

Gabriel glanced at the wall, not intimidated, and thought about the money, focused. “Show me the dime,” Gabriel said to Theodore.

“Okay,” Theodore said. Theodore reached into his pocket and pulled it out.

There it was, a dime, sparkling new and shiny, with a lady’s image on the front.

That’s all Gabriel needed to see. When partnered with a dare, money was hypnotizing to him. He gawked at the dime again and the mesmerizing effect of the mirrored glare from the sun’s reflection off the dime’s sides cemented Gabriel’s commitment to the dare. The dime was whispering...*off the wall...off the wall...off the wall, you total idiot!*

Gabriel stood up and put his hand out to Theodore. Rocky, Daniel, and me were the witnesses. We stood in honor and horror of the agreement. Theodore rose and took Gabriel’s hand. They shook.

The dare was now official. Gabriel went around to the garage to get his bicycle.

(My poem I wrote on notebook paper in school)

Gabe on his bike,

off the wall with a fall,

plunging down on the ground,

a dime for a narrow mind,

going south, right on his mouth.

- Jake

The rest of us moved to the boundary of the stone wall, and rationale stopped us near the periphery. Daniel put his toes over the edge and looked down at the configuration of rocks, dirt, rocks, and red clay near the wall's foundation. Did I mention rocks?

"Is Gabriel really going to do it, Jake?" Daniel whispered.

"Yes...I think so...I think he is."

"Will he die?" Daniel asked.

"I don't think so...hope not."

"Me too," Daniel breathed.

Gabriel pushed his bicycle past the foundation and around the stone wall, until he and his bike were front yard level, and then making the turn, wheeled it to the rear of the side porch on the south side of the parsonage. He backed the bike against the brick wall and faced the stonewall cliff. Theodore and the rest of us stood between Gabriel and the end of the earth, leaving enough space between us for a bicycle to pass with a gullible rider, being controlled by the root of all evil.

Daddy preached a lot about money, *the root of all evil.* It had amazed me that our family was not entirely exempt from sinning, because we never had enough of that root of all evil in our bank account to make any appreciable difference.

Daddy preached, "It's not money, but the *love* of money that is the root of all evil!"

How could you love it, when you never saw it? I wondered.

"You promise, Theo?" Gabriel asked Theodore one last time to make sure.

“Gabriel, you don’t have to do this---” I started, but Gabriel’s bike wheels were already rolling forward and toward the top of the stone wall--I believe if Gabriel had had a barrel, he would have gone off the Enoree Dam for a quarter. We all watched, as his bicycle’s speed increased slowly. Cruising gradually toward the end, he maintained just enough speed to keep the bike balanced, so that he wouldn’t fall off left or right onto the grass and get his pants soiled. Gabriel knew Momma wouldn’t like that.

Suddenly, his front wheel rolled off, seemingly in slow motion, right off the end, down the wall, followed in suit by the rest of the bike, back over front until Gabriel was face first in dirt, rocks, and red clay. His bike rested on top of him, burying him deeper into mother earth’s womb.

At first, he did not move much. Then, he pushed himself up, and noticing the flow of blood from his mouth, turned and walked quite steadily toward the basement door. We all followed him, stepping around the red trail that he left behind. I felt like Hansel, avoiding breadcrumbs.

Gabriel walked into the bathroom and began to wash his face with water in the sink. Momma noticed the trail of blood though the house and rushed to his side.

“Adam... Adam! Come here!” she yelled from the top of the stairs, toward Daddy’s study.

“What?” Daddy asked from his partially opened door. “What is it, Lillian?”

“Hurry, Gabriel has busted his mouth somehow...it’s bleeding.” She finished as Daddy appeared at the bottom of the stairs. “He’s bleeding!”

Daddy ran up the steps, skipping every other step. All of us boys were in the kitchen hallway, waiting to see the outcome from Adam and Lillian, the trauma team.

They washed and inspected the wounds in and around Gabriel’s mouth and face, pulling parts of teeth and dabbing cuts and abrasions with iodine and warm water. Gabriel never winced, or at least we never heard him wincing.

“Why did you do something so stupid, son!” Daddy preached. “If you had used some common sense, you wouldn’t be in this condition. You've gone and knocked a tooth out and broke another one. Why? Why did you do this? Answer me, Gabriel James!"

"I on't o," Gabriel sounded out. He talked like a dental patient trying to answer a dentist's questions, whose mouth and jaw muscles are shot full of Novacaine, and whose mouth is packed full of dentist and assistant's hands, cotton swabs, suction tubes, and mirrors. "'Heo is 'ivin' ee uh ime," Gabriel said, head down, mouth still dripping blood.

"What? You did this for money?" Daddy scowled. "You rode your new bicycle off the stone wall because you wanted to get some money?"

For a minute, I thought Daddy was going to keep repeating the same question in several different ways, a rhetorical device that ministers use to emphasize a truth while preaching.

Momma inserted, "Adam...Gabriel meant well, I'm sure--"

"Lillian."

All of us had now gotten our heads around the bathroom door and could see the father-mother-son trio around the blood-stained sink. Gabriel spotted us with his peripheral vision. More specifically, he saw Theodore West.
Gabriel lifted his head, focusing his eyes on Theodore. He asked, "'Ere's 'eye 'ime?"

Gabriel's direction of attention turned Daddy and Momma's heads toward us. They tried to understand what Gabriel was asking; so, did we to a certain point. Momma still touched Gabriel to balance him, to keep him from falling off the short stool he was standing on.

Gabriel, now standing even straighter, asked again, "Ere's 'eye 'ime?" A trickle of blood inched down his neck and over his Adam's apple---Eve ate it first, not fair.

Theodore searched through his pocket, moved through the crowd, and placed the dime into Gabriel's hand. Gabriel held the dime up to the light above the medicine cabinet and inspected it. Through his blood-crusted mouth, he smiled, somewhat toothless.

Seeing Gabriel's expression, Daddy barked. "All for money! A dime, a thin dime?"

Pivoting suddenly, Daddy exited the bathroom, disappearing down the steps toward his study, still muttering, "A thin dime, God help him." I heard his study door slam, and his first words to God were more than audible, they were loud.

The next Sunday, one of Daddy's rabbit trails during his sermon was about the root of all evil. He glared in Gabriel's direction during that part of the sermon and paused when he said, "Some people will do anything for one thin dime." I think Daddy was hoping someone else would benefit from Gabriel's mistake. "One thin dime now...your reputation and influence later!" Daddy shouted.

At that point in the sermon, Gabriel tried to appear repentant, but instead, his face looked repulsive, with scratches and scabs galore, and one eye nearly swollen shut.

Daddy preached in a Wednesday evening prayer service message, "Learning from your mistakes is how a person grows to become a mature Christian. It was that repentant and life-changing, soul-searching that changed King David's life and made him *a man after God's own heart.* David was sorry for his sin. Read Psalm fifty-one. It's all written in that chapter." Then, Daddy added, "It's beneficial to learn from your mistakes."

A preacher owns the ideal microcosm of a church at home with his family. The glass house that we all lived in was a unique greenhouse for growing plenteous sin and iniquity to assist my daddy in generating topic after exhaustive topic and convenient illustrations for Sunday sermons.

Daniel and me were hoping Gabriel would learn from his mistakes, but he never did, exactly. It wasn't long until he backslid, right into Clanton Butler's left hook.

One day at school, Gabriel overheard some fifth-grade boys talking about Clanton Butler's brag. Cliff Poston informed the boys, "Rooster said he would take anybody on in a boxing-glove match near the ditch after school today for a quarter, twenty-five cents."

Now, when it came to sense, Gabriel didn't have any or need any. He stayed bankrupt in his *common*-sense bank account. His favorite financial chapter was thirteen.

"I don't have to beat Rooster, Jake!" Gabriel argued to me at a third and fourth grade shared recess that day. "Use your head," he continued, "Rooster didn't say he would pay me a quarter if I *beat* him, only if I put the gloves on with him."

Gabriel sat there beneath that weeping willow tree, flipping twigs and small pebbles with his fingers at the sky. Above Gabriel's head, the tree wept long, bitter tears for him.

"Dang, anybody can do that, Jake!" he said. "I'm not crazy enough to foot-race Rooster!"

I tried to reason with him, telling him of how Clanton Butler had broken Anthony Pace's nose, and Anthony was in the ninth grade at the high school. I tried to think where I could come up with a quarter to replace the one Gabriel wanted to win so desperately. My pockets were rootless of all evil, no luck. I must have had too much debit of late, too many expenditures.

That day, after school, Gabriel met a group of boys behind the school building. The boys grouped around him like the entourage of a state dignitary. Gabriel disappeared behind the taller boys as they moved toward the ditch at the lower playground, down the hill.

The word martyr came to mind.

From a distance, the throng of boys kicked up a churn of dust like a posse on the trail of Jesse James or Billy the Kid. They trudged along, down the hill and toward the ditch. The ditch was quite deep and ran the length of the school's property side from the Enoree River to Highway 14. On the bottom part of the playground, the ditch's top was treeless and bare. Sometimes, the boys would try to jump this ditch, but the expanse was too wide, and no one could do it, almost. It seemed like a bottomless pit.

Rooster was the only boy in Pelham who had ever jumped the ditch. Because of his blinding speed, he cleared the chasm one day during school, when all the older kids were having recess. Everyone *ooed* and *aahed.* Rooster then proceeded to stroll on home for the remainder of the day, to the joy and delight of everyone, especially the teachers. All we talked about for weeks was the jump and subsequent escape.

Beside the ditch, alone, with a pair of garnet-colored boxing gloves over each shoulder, stood Rooster. Mr. Clanton Butler was gloating at the cluster of boyhood parading down the hill toward the ditch in his direction. His eyes lit up when he spotted Gabriel tucked into the mass. Tilting his left shoulder downward, Rooster let one pair of gloves slide off onto the ground. He moved away from that pair several feet and towed his own boxing gloves on.

Clanton Butler had belittled many a boy in foot races and fights. No one had ever beat him in either, and him losing just once is all us boys from Pelham wanted. We prayed for someone faster and tougher to beat him at something.

Daniel and me followed Gabriel's group. We kept our distance until the group stopped and Gabriel appeared alone, out of the group to the waiting boxing gloves on the ground near the edge of the bottomless ditch. Daniel and me rushed around to assist our older brother in his pursuit. Open-mouthed, Daniel stared at Rooster and was amazed at how Rooster could put his own gloves on, tying them with his teeth.

With my periodic glances, I could see that Rooster's left glove was slightly worn in one small spot; the right one was scar less.

I put Gabriel's gloves on him, one at a time, forcing them on, and then tying them tightly against his thin wrists. The gloves were too large and like-new with no visible marks on them at all. Someone said later, "Even though boys have worn those gloves against Rooster, the gloves have never made any contact with anything but the air."

I could tell that Gabriel's fists were shuffling around inside the gloves, enclosing sweaty palms.

While I was in the act of lacing Gabriel's second glove onto his wrist and beginning to tuck the loose strings inside the extra room around his wrist, Rooster hit Gabriel on the right temple with a gruesome left hook. Instantly, Gabriel vanished before my eyes. My hands were still in the string-tucking position. Naturally, my head followed Gabriel's path of departure, and my eyes jumped to the bottom of the ditch; Gabriel was there, knocked out on his side. One boxing glove was beside his face, the glove I had been lacing earlier, and the other one at his butt. He looked so peaceful. His head was closer to Enoree River than it was to Highway 14.

Clanton Butler removed his own gloves with his teeth and spit them onto the ground, while at the same time, reaching into his pocket. I was afraid to look at him. I was watching all of Rooster's moves by keeping an eye on his shadow; periodically, I cast quick glances at my older brother lying at the bottom of the ditch.

Suddenly, a quarter dropped to the ground between my feet, like an injured dove during bird hunting season. No sooner had it settled into the topsoil, than did Rooster speak. "Bring my gloves to school tomorrow...I'll pick 'em up at the swing set. Hang 'em on the end."

I figured he was talking to me since I was about to cry, and since I could feel his words like a stinging wind against my right ear.

“Okay.” I think I said.

Gabriel’s group quickly disintegrated into the sunset, having been disappointed again by Rooster’s ferociousness and firepower. Gabriel had become another notch on Rooster's belt, another empty promise in the quest to overcome evil. Besides me and Daniel, no one was left at the ditch. It took both of us nearly twenty minutes or so to wake Gabriel up. Attempting to get Gabriel out of the ditch, we all three fell back in several times. Each time, we would regroup and try again ‘til suddenly we emerged at the top, pushing Gabriel out and right onto a twenty-five cent piece that had gotten hot on its topside from the burning sun.

We managed to get Gabriel all the way home without Momma or Daddy seeing us, despite Gabriel’s intermittent outbursts, “What happened? Did I hit Rooster? Where are we? Where's my quarter?”

It was not until we put Gabriel to bed, that we noticed he was still wearing the boxing gloves. We left them on his hands in case--during a sound dream in the night--he might attempt to change the end result of the incident at the ditch, or in case he happened to touch the large bruise above his right cheek. The gloves would provide softness.

Not being able to go to sleep from the day's wild activities, from my perspective on my side of the bed, I could see out the window. In the slate gray sky, the only light that illuminated the planet--and *my* side of the bed--was the sun's faithful reflection onto a dizzy quarter-moon.

Small change.

18

I wanted so badly to tell Gabriel and Daniel about Josiah, but since Gabriel had been acting funny after the ditch incident, I didn't think he'd understand.

I wanted to tell them both that even though the river continued to flow beyond the tree line, that where the river touched the other bank, were a people who contained a wealth of value and character. That character, if left uncultivated and disregarded, however, could ultimately flood the bridge's foundation, collapsing the connection on which we must all coexist later.

I wanted to tell Momma and Daddy about Emmett and how the kids were treating him, and how he wasn't going to last long if the kids didn't leave him alone and quit asking him to walk the dam.

I wanted to tell Adam and Lillian about how, even though the highway was planted firmly in front of the parsonage and had lain there for a long time, making a suitable path for civilization in our state to travel up and down, to and from our ambitions and appointments, that the shallow and diminutive cracks and crevices across its surface would inevitably deepen and weaken the fragile state of affairs for all of us, if not prudently repaired.

I wanted to tell everyone to mind their own business, and if they didn't have something nice to say, then to shut their big fat mouths and move to Columbia!

19

Elijah Green died.

My dad received a phone call and the voice on the other side, a daughter-in-law, said, “Father died, Pastor. He passed on to glory this morning at seven.”

Of course, my daddy went directly to the home of this wonderful deacon of the church. Mr. Elijah Green’s whole family was there by the time my daddy got there, and so was Buford Jackson, the assistant chairman of the deacons.

“He was a great man, Pastor,” Mr. Jackson said.

“He sure was, yes he was, Buford,” my daddy responded.

"No one can fill those shoes."

Daddy didn't comment.

The funeral lasted two hours with more than five preachers preaching and seven groups or soloists and groups singing. The saddest moment in the whole proceeding came when Mr. Elijah Green's great-granddaughter, Ruth, stood to sing, without any accompaniment, "When They Ring Those Golden Bells." Her small voice painted a gate of pearl, a street of gold, and a river of life across the rainy hearts in the church. Not one dry eye could be found in the church house, and several of the church ladies stood with their hankies waving in the air, praising God, my momma included. When Ruth sang that part about "... in that far off sweet forever, by the shiny, golden river..." I couldn't help it. I cried. I hid it though. I'm pretty sure Gabriel didn't see me.

At the closing of the funeral, everyone stood, and the preachers awaited the quiet instructions from the funeral people. Nodding heads signaled the preachers to begin walking down the aisle near the front double doors that opened up toward the Enoree River. Behind the preachers, and the honorary pallbearers, the deacons, paraded. These men walked like weary soldiers behind their fallen comrade, with the exception of the next-to-be chairman, Mr. Buford Jackson, who proudly led in front with his large black Bible over his heart. Then the casket was turned to parallel the aisle, and six men grabbed it. They were Elijah's nephews. They hoisted the solid cedar chest upwards and moved in measured steps. The whole church was standing and crying. What made it worse were the ladies holding up Mrs. Green. They reached in to her and touched her as she passed, and some paced right beside her like mobile crutches. When old people cry, everybody cries. It's like a big oak crying in front of an acorn. Most of the huddled group of people trailing the casket were Elijah's family, which stretched up the aisle front to back. The funeral employees scattered out across the church, inconspicuously, like warning signs along Highway 25 in the mountains, gesturing silent instructions to the passers-by. The church emptied, somber but stately. My momma, sisters, brothers, and me were the last members left in the church besides Emmett, who had already begun to clean up around the pews by picking up a few scattered funeral home fans, tearfully tossed aside during the service.

Emmett looked across the church and showed his grungy teeth. I smiled back.

The funeral was all lined up in the parking lot outside the church. The police car, its red light silent, had its headlights on bright. Behind it was the preachers-car, our long, black Roadmaster Buick, packed with too many preachers. The family cars, two funeral cars to hold the immediate family, and eight more regular cars to carry those who couldn't fit in the Woods Funeral Home's cars, were sadly parked. The rest of the procession extended out of the parking lot, down the side of Highway 14, and into the pool hall across the street. At the side door of the church, busy funeral home workers, still arrayed in their three-piece suits with matching skinny ties and hankies, moved back and forth from a funeral home truck, toting flowers and flower stands, filling up the back of the truck like over-zealous gardeners in the springtime. Me, Momma, and us just stood on the porch, watching.

Beyond the top of the funeral cars, I could see the Enoree, still rolling, no sign of aging.

The cars started. They moved like a disjointed train, starting, stopping, rolling, pausing, until the entire spectacle was on Highway 14, headed toward Elijah's final resting place in Pleasant View Cemetery.

Momma escorted us to the bottom of the hill, to Moxley's store, where we were supposed to wait until Daddy would pick us up after the burial. We sat on a long deacon's bench in front of the store. It would be a few minutes before we felt comfortable enough to talk and play. We mostly sat and listened to Momma hum songs and cry. Somehow, it felt like the quiet before a thunderous summer storm. I cried too. Gabriel didn't see me though.

20

I made a couple of swings across the Enoree River in the first few weeks of third grade. I never told anyone at school or at home about it, because they would not have appreciated it. I felt uncomfortable about it, like I was lying, and I was. I knew inside that I should tell someone where I was going, but I couldn't.

I learned to sneak off from the backyard without being seen. I walked in a direct line from the back of the well house, through the open field, directly behind a stand of small saplings, past the twilight zone, and then made a mad sprint toward the tree line on my side of the River. With my limited foot-speed, I could still make the trek in less than two minutes.

Once there, I turned around to see if anyone had followed me or if anyone was stirring around in my back yard or near the school.

Out of habit, I reached into my pocket to feel the anvil, just for luck. I slid to the vine, loosened it from the roots around it, and stepping back to gain a grip, ran forward and cleared the river, landing past the rock.

Taking a breath, I proceeded down the riverbank toward Josiah's hiding place. Josiah had created the perfect place in the thickets along the bank that could not be seen with the naked eye. Me and him had decided to meet in the hiding place on the eighth of each month, because that's how old we both were, and it was easy to remember for both of us. So far, we had met three times, counting this one. I had secured a local drugstore twelve-month calendar for Josiah—my dad had four of them on his desk---so Josiah could mark the eighth's on each month to remind him of our meetings.

The large thickets were naturally dense and threatening. It was one of those types of landscapes, along the creek bank, that discouraged the average person from attempting to enter. Holding back a large bush with one hand, Josiah entered through a perfect hole cut in the back of the thicket. When we entered or exited the thicket, that bush would close across the hole like one of those magic glass doors at the A&P Grocery chain store in Pleasant Grove.

Daniel and me played on that magic door's rubber carpet about ten minutes one day before a man in a red and white apron came over to ask us to move on.

Inside the thicket, Josiah had two old peach-picking baskets, turned upside down, that him and me sat on. The only light in the thicket sifted through a narrow gap in the canopy overhead, next to a tree that had grown right smack in the middle of our thicket room, or, I guess the tree was there first--you know, the chicken or the egg argument. Me and Josiah decided to call our room, the *Eight Ball,* in honor of our ages, and because an eight ball is black and white, mostly black since we were on Josiah's side of the river.

We talked about a lot of things, all kinds of things, while we were hidden in the *Eight Ball.*

"Yall eat what for breakfast?" I asked him.

"Fat back."

"Raw?"

"Nope. Ma' mamma ca' fry so' goo' fat back, Jeck," Josiah answered.

Josiah had not called me sir or mister or anything like that in a month or so. I told him I would not talk to him anymore if he called me things like that. "Call me Jake, Josiah. I'm just Jake."

"Wha' yo' folks eats fa' brea'fas', Jeck?" he asked--he pronounced my name J-eck.

"Cereal sometimes, like Alphabet cereal, that's my favorite," I said.

"Wha' kine'?" he asked.

"Alphabet. You can spell your name in the spoon or any word with the letters of the alphabet, and then eat it." I paused to let this sink in. "I ate Brutus one day at breakfast." We both laughed at me eating a dog.

"Hey, we don's eats no dog, now, Jeck," he said, smiling. I had told him about Brutus at our very first meeting.

"No, you know what I mean," I said.

"Hows yo gats away to he-uh fro' yo house?" he asked me. He dug with a stick in the dirt floor. Looked like he was practicing the alphabet letters he had been learning.

"I've been slipping away without getting caught. I think as long as I get back pretty early, I'll be okay...with my momma's voice, when she calls me, I'll hear it. I'll just have to run fast as I can all the way there."

"Tha's nots vary fas'." His black hand grabbed his face; he snickered into it.

Nervously, we both sat still and looked around the *Eight Ball.*

I asked, "How do you get away from your parents?"

"I comes he-uh aw da time bys myse'f," Josiah said. "My folks just wants me home buh'fo suppa' time, dat be aw. Sometimes I has to wa'ch my sista."

"Now," I added, "I'm getting hungry."

Suddenly, a noise moved outside the thicket.

"Listen---"

"Wha's' it doin'?" he wondered aloud.

Both of us didn't move and listened collectively at the sound stirring, up the river, beyond the *Eight Ball.*

"Don's makes a soun'...shh..." he said softly.

The thicket actually made quite the sound barrier with its complete sphere of covering, but we could still hear, but not make out the noise near the river.

Josiah motioned to me with his hand to follow him. His bare feet picking precise spots between roots and rocks, I did my best to step in his footprints. We pushed against the bush, our front door, and eased out of the *Eight Ball* and toward the trees around the river.

Right away, I could recognize the voices of Ray, Stanley, Rocky, and some other kid. They were swinging across the river. *Surely not Daniel!* I thought. *He's too young.* I pulled up to the top of a small bush and looked for a cotton top. The three other boys were standing on the rock.

"Come on, Daniel, you can do it!" Ray said.

What? Momma'll kill him! He oughta know better'n sneakin' off without permission!

Laughing loudly down the river and making fun of Daniel to the others, Stanley said, "Swing, *baby*!"

"I can't!" I heard Daniel's voice cry. "I'm afraid!"

Why couldn't I have been so honest to tell the truth when I was afraid to swing?

"You little cotton-top nigger!" Stanley said, intimidating.

I could feel Josiah's pain as he sat with his head down, not even looking in the white boys' direction.

Finally, Daniel came flying through the air, tumbling past the three boys and onto the ground behind them. Rocky reached out to secure the vine.

“Back across!” Ray yelled.

All three boys zipped back across the river one after the other. Daniel was still on the rock. His face was in the pre-cry mode. His eyes were wet, and he was seconds from giving up.

I waited until I was sure the boys had gone and then slipped out into the open area near the vine. Daniel didn’t hear me.

“You stuck?” I asked.

My voice startled him. Almost choking on a throat of tears, he kept his balance on the rock. “Jake? What you doin’ here?” he asked. “How’d you get here?” He looked above me, like I had suddenly dropped in like Superman, rescuing Lois Lane. Daniel reminded me more of Jimmy, the young naïve reporter, though.

“Watching after you,” I answered.

“But how did you---” Daniel asked. His eyes still studied the trees, roots, and woods around us.

“Come on. Let’s go home,” I said. “I’ll help you get across.”

Taking a vine from the ground, I hooked the main vine in, and then, handing it to Daniel, said, “Just hold on and swing across.”

“I’m afraid, Jake. I don’t think I can.”

“What? You just did it...didn’t you?”

“Yes...well, but how did you know that I swung across?” Daniel asked. “Did you see me?”

“I saw you land,” I said back. “Here.” I continued to hold the vine out.

I supposed Josiah still had his head down, hiding.

“But, I’m afraid...I don’t think I can do it,” Daniel whined.

“Here. Hold the vine,” I said. I reached into my pocket and pulled out the anvil. “Here. Put this in your pocket. It’s what gave me courage the first time I ever went across the river. I take it with me every time I swing now.”

“Really?”

"That's right. Now, put it in your pocket and swing!" I said. I put the anvil in his pocket. "You can give it back on the other side. Hurry!"

Daniel looked at me, vine in hand, and then rotated his cotton-head around me suddenly toward the bushes; something behind me had caught his attention. Daniel's mouth dropped open and his buggy eyes were about to pop out of his head. "Who's that?" Daniel whispered. "Who's that?"

Looking back toward the bush too, I asked, "Huh?" Josiah was standing in broad daylight for all to see. "Oh, I'll tell you when we get home. Now, go."

"Jake, that's a nig---" Daniel started. I quickly put my hand over his mouth. "Go!" I said much more sternly, and Daniel felt it. He slipped right through my fingers and onto the other bank.

"Now, toss it back."

Daniel pushed the vine in my direction. I caught it. Taking one last look back at Josiah, I softly whispered, "See you on the eighth."

Josiah smiled and nodded. I swung out of sight.

Daniel and I talked all the way home about Josiah. I told him how secretive we must be about Josiah, because me and Josiah could get in trouble for talking. I also tried to explain how Josiah was a person who had feelings. Saying the N word would definitely hurt Josiah's feelings. I took my anvil back.

"Injun giver!" Daniel said. I wasn't allowing him to keep my anvil, no way.

Daniel swore he was all shut-mouth about the Josiah thing. I wanted to believe him, but my mind automatically took me back to the night he partnered with Mrs. Black in the nub club.

"You better be!" I threatened him.

Josiah and me talked every eighth, sometimes for longer times than others. He asked me a lot of questions about school and what we did in school. He really liked to hear about recess and the foot races.

"Dats my dream, Jeck," he said to me on one of our eighths together. "I wants to run in a race...a foots race, Jeck." He stood up in the *Eight Ball* then, dancing while he talked, using shy gestures to make his dream become a reality in the thicket's shadows. "I wants to hee-uh all da folks, whites and blacks, yellin' fo me, and my feets be a goin', Jeck, I tell you, dey'll be smokin'...makin' smoke likes a hay feeld on fi-uh. No body'll stops me'til I wins it all, Jeck...wins it all."

I tried to slow and hush his moment of glory inside the *Eight Ball*, but he couldn't be shushed. "Quiet, Jo." I started calling him Jo that day because he was too fast for Josiah. He would be talking too fast or running too fast to hear the whole name. "Jo, quiet!"

"...'til someones puts dat trophy in my hand."

He was wound up, and he *was* fast. One time, early for our eighth of the month meeting, I had seen him run with little effort from the bottom of his broom-brushed yard to the tree line on his side of the river, but with tremendous speed. I couldn't believe it, if I hadn't seen it with my own eyes, how far and how high he could jump. He was lightning on the loose, sure-footed, striking and bolting. His feet struck the earth, singeing the dirt with the balls of his feet and his toes. They thrust him forward through the field with the grace of a gazelle and the quickness of a mongoose. He was faster than a locomotive and just as tough.

21

One late-fall afternoon, near sunset, the trees of Pelham were lit up with yellows and reds, painting the Southern scenery, as an artist would render it on canvas. More leaves carpeted the ground, creating a crusty, earthen blanket.

"Get in the car, boys," Daddy said as he made a pass from the kitchen through the house and to the basement door.

"What did Daddy say, Gabriel?" Daniel asked.

"He said to get in the car...put your shoes on," Gabriel added.

We all three could tell the difference between a suggestion and a command from our daddy, and his most recent words were definitely a command. We heard the Roadmaster running in the driveway.

We hurried down the basement steps and out the door into the Buick. We sat in our four corners that we were accustomed to, whenever we four got to ride together in the family car vacant of any females. Daddy drove, of course, Gabriel sat passenger side, front seat, I sat behind Gabriel, and Daniel rode directly behind Daddy. We rode *four corners* before there was a Dean Smith in Chapel Hill.

Daddy eased the Buick down Highway 14, past Stuart's store, and across the Highway 14 bridge. We moved up into Blountville, and at first, I thought we were going to the Jackson's or Moxley's, but we went right past their houses and kept heading south on the highway.

Slowing at the next crossroad, the intersection of Highway 14 and Pelham Road, a dirt road that was an alternate route to Greenville, Daddy turned left. I knew something was different because we were passing the nigger-wash-hole, a low place in the river where the black people would sometimes bathe, wash their cars, or have a swimming party.

Immediately past the N wash hole, Daddy's Roadmaster Buick slowed, and curved down a side road, partly pressed with two sets of tire tracks, across a fresh green meadow. The tall grass had indentions where many cars and trucks had packed their paths into the top soil only moments before we had made our right turn.

When he came to the river, Daddy followed the compacted path and slowed again. There was another low place that allowed for vehicle crossings, albeit cautiously. The Buick swam the river and moved into an opening in the woods. Daddy's Buick trampled some small saplings and bushes that had been weakened earlier by the other cars and trucks.

Daddy killed his lights, and we cruised into the shadow of some trees, off to the right of the clearing, near several of the other vehicles that had parked there earlier. We had a direct view of the not-quite-so perfect circle in the woods.

In the middle of the circle stood a cross, like the one on the painting in my Sunday school class on the wall. Our interest peaked. No one breathed a word, and even Daniel was quiet. Daddy had taken us there for a lesson he didn't want us to miss. He parked the car, so we could see everything that was about to happen.

In a few moments, a group of people moved into the opening, dressed in all white robes and masks of some kind, carrying a red flag with an X of white stars. The robes looked like bedspreads or sheets. Eyeholes were cut in the pillow cases, so the people could see out. I was surprised to see how orderly and practiced this parade was. It marched out and circled the cross like Joshua and his people.

"K.K.K.," Daddy would explain a few months later.

Then, without warning, the cross went to burning, from the bottom to the top, on fire. All the people raised their hands and worshipped that cross. It was the most unusual worship service I ever attended, with no invitation, no Bartholomew Keller, no offering plates, no choir singing, and nobody getting saved.

As the sheet-covered people passed near our car on one of their loops around the cross, the only strangely familiar thing to me, marching under one of the white sheets in the front of the line, was a pair of alligator-skin cowboy boots, dyed red.

Exiting while the cross was still smoldering, Daddy drove us stunned and silent, through the woods, river, and grassy field, across the bridge, past the N-wash hole, and then turning the car's lights on, home. We went straight to bed without a discussion.

It was a gift from Daddy to our collective memories, a historical marker of sorts. We'd never forget it.

22

At least once a week, Emmett came to our house to cut the grass. He became our good friend. He let us sit in his car and blow the deep-sounding horn on his A-model. If we had asked him, he would have probably given us a ride in the rumble seat, but we didn't know how our parents would really feel about that. Emmett would on occasion, shake his leg and do his dance, without our even asking him. We felt awkward, not really wanting him to do it, afraid to tell him no.

He would cut the grass in one speed, fast and steady. He knew nothing else. He would cut until the sweat poured off his face, staining his shirt and bibbed overalls. Sometimes, his hatband even sweated, wetting and making a duplicate band around his hat.

Momma would bring Emmett a drink of water in one of her super big drinking glasses. She would pack that glass with ice and the water. The glass would be almost frozen, leaving it in Emmett's hand, perspiring. He would gulp the water, and in my mind, my mouth would go instantly dry, desiring to get somewhere near the opening of Emmett's glass. If I wanted water so bad, why did I drink so many R C Colas then?

Anytime that me, Gabriel, and Daniel got money, we headed to Stuart's store to buy our favorite stuff. I always bought four different things, depending on how much money I had at the time. I loved RC's, moon pies, bubble gum with baseball cards, peanuts, and Baby Ruth candy bars. Okay, five then.

I loved, on a hot day, to put the peanuts into the RC bottle and eat them as I drank. That was a trick Rocky showed me one day. The peanuts made the cola fizz.

When Daddy would go to the church to do some work, he would take one of us with him in case he needed us to do any chores for him while he was there, like getting him a pack of crackers at Moxley's store below the church. He would give us a small allowance for helping him at the church. It wasn't much money, but it would buy an RC Cola periodically.

I was at the church one day when Emmett was completing God's purpose for him, cleaning. He was in the main church dusting and shining the back of the pews with a rag. Sneaking in a swinging side door next to the church organ, I watched him. He sprayed a mist across the seats and then took a rag and turned the dull finish of the pew into a radiant shine. He took care with each pew, as if it was his own child, grunting his approval with his own flavor of positive criticism. He folded the rag to get into the tiny grooves, forcing secrets out of hiding. There was not a single spider web in that church building, and if there would have been, it would not be dusty.

As I lay there behind the organ, I could see Emmett's expression. He would strain, but always smile. He turned each hymn book around in the hymnbook rack on the backside of the pews, and then without a yardstick or ruler, would carefully measure with his eyes to space the hymnals the same distance from each other.

Down on his knees, Emmett would slide beneath the pews on the wood floor and check for bubble gum and stuff under the pews. Of course, I could tell you for a fact there was none under there, because he had checked the week before and the week before that one too. That made it very difficult for anyone to stick their gum there, since everyone sat mostly in the same spots each week in church, and you could be found out.

Emmett stayed at the church as much or more than he stayed at his own house during the week. He loved the church for a couple of reasons: one, he was born into the church, and it was the only place that accepted him just like he was, and two, there was a direct view of the Enoree Dam from the front porch of the church. Looking across the top of Moxley's store and past Mrs. Black's apartment, Emmett could see the dam off which his father fell, roaring and moaning all day and all night long, spewing foam and water through its three massive holes, into the deep water below the bridge. Emmett would spend some extra time on the front porch steps each week, mourning his Dad's memory.

After cleaning the main church, Emmett moved into each Sunday school class, dusting and sweeping. He picked up flower vases, globes, the plastic church, offering plates, Bibles, books, packs of sticky-stars, crayons, coloring books, and a statue of praying hands to make sure everything in the church building was immaculate and back where he had found it.

"He cleans that way every week," Daddy told me one time when I visited Daddy's church office. "He is so efficient, that

Emmett! If he could add numbers, he would make the perfect treasurer. He puts everything back in its place." I had no idea what efficient was, but I guessed it had something to do with good dusting.

When Emmett was finished, he placed his cleaning supplies back into the closet near the baptistery, where Daddy baptized people who got saved or joined the church. He picked his hat up as he left the building, locked the door from the outside, and left for his house in his A–model.

Before he departed on this particular afternoon, he said to me without looking up--as if he had known I was watching him the whole time, "Jake, want ta ride by my house and see'd it? I'll teck ya home lay'ta."

I didn't know what to answer. I couldn't believe he had asked me that question. Of course, I didn't want to go. I didn't know for sure what Daddy would want me to answer. "Uh… I guess. Let me ask Daddy."

I felt Daddy would say no. I ran quickly to his office to get there before Emmett did. I knocked on Daddy's study door.

"Come in."

I opened the door. "Daddy, Emmett out here wants me to ride by his house and then he'll take me home; that's probably not okay with you, right?" I asked with a definite uncertainty in my voice. "Just say no and I'll break the news to him."

Without me knowing about it, Emmett had slid in behind me at Daddy's study. I thought he was still outside in the hallway. Daddy looked past me and saw him.

"Why sure, Jake," Daddy said, surprising me. "You go with Emmett. Now you be careful not go and get his car dirty or track up his house, Jake. He takes pride in that car."

"What? You said yes?" I asked, confused. "Yes?"

"Yes," Daddy said, smiling even broader.

Emmett suddenly said, "I be carefa', Paster." Emmett's choppy speech and tangy breath entered the office, startling me.

"It's just fine, Emmett. If you drive half as well as you clean, you will be just fine," Daddy said.

"Oh, I we-uh, Sir. Not one mile ova' and stre't up Highway 14, oh, yes sir, Paster," Emmett said. Talking as he walked, he started to leave down the hallway toward the outside door. "You ken...trus' me." Once outside, his hat jumped on his head.

I made one last plea of desperation with my eyes at my daddy's face. He had already dropped his spiritual insight into the pages of God's Word. He released me to the plight of the Emmett-gyptians. As I stepped into Emmett's lumbering tracks, I prayed inwardly, *Yea, though I walk through the valley of the shadow of death, I will fear no evil.*

We both climbed up into a car that was from the past. The interior was simple with a long gear stick and a couple of gauges. Going up the Highway 14 hill from the church, I could feel the A-model motor begging for mercy. As we passed the parsonage, I entertained thoughts of bailing out, jumping ship, or even screaming for help.

The A-model worked overtime like a garden tractor and puttered and spit us all the way to Emmett's house. We didn't talk the whole way. Emmett sat tall in his seat and steered us north, sneering, his way of smiling. His eyes were set on the road, hardly blinking, his chin tensely rounded like our stone wall I might never see again.

Emmett's car turned into his driveway and backed into the barn's front shelter. He slid from his side of the car and shut the door. I was slow in getting out. I didn't know what to expect. I had heard too many stories about Emmett and his father. The house paint was scaly-looking, chipped. The yard was overgrown in the back.

It was common knowledge that Emmett's father had walked the Enoree Dam and jumped off. "Committed suicide," Rocky had told me. Others had said the same thing. "Mr. Jackson told my dad."

"It's because the doctors told Emmett's family that Emmett was retarded when he was born. Emmett's pa couldn't take it no more," Lanny had explained to me on the swing set at school. "That's what my momma said."

Emmett said, "Come on in, Jake. You will...see this."

I didn't argue.

His front porch was creepy, rotten boards and stuff. The screen door leaned and *eeked* when Emmett pulled on it. I thought it'd fall apart. It didn't. The house's exterior was years past a good painting. The door opened, and we eased inside. I took one last look behind me to see what the world was like just in case I was seeing it for the final time.

"Sit, Jake!" Emmett suddenly said.

I did. I sat down on a musty couch, covered with a worn quilt. Emmett disappeared into another room. "I'm in heah. I be back," he said; his echo bounced at my feet off the rough wood floor. There were a few spider webs, and the place needed a real good dusting.

Just loud enough for me to hear, I said, "Okay." I thought if I could talk to myself, I wouldn't be as lonely.

Above the stone-built mantel over the open fireplace, cold with gray ashes, a display of pictures hung lifelessly. One large picture was perfectly straight and clean, two other pictures nearby. I rose from the couch to get a closer view.

Not understanding why I was talking audibly, except to hear my own voice and to know I was still alive, I asked, "Who's in these pictures, Emmett? Huh?"

"My motha'...in the big place. Me in tha little. My father in tha middle," Emmett answered all the way from the other room; I guessed it to be the kitchen because I could hear what sounded like knives scraping against each other. To my question about the pictures, Emmett reacted as if he had memorized the answer

The little retarded boy in the picture looked to be about eight years old. He had a content face, but distantly blank, a blunt chin, protruding below warped lips. His unkempt hair and just-beginning-to-decay front teeth looked like a typical school kid, excited about being in school.

"Oh, I see." My answer was delayed. I wanted to sound really interested.

My eyes were drawn to his mother's portrait over the mantel. She was surprisingly striking. Her eyes were soft, hair shoulder length, and her face sharp all the way to her chin's keen tip. In the portrait, she appeared to be well above her room and board.

Stanley had told me one day on the playground, "My pa told me, Emmett's momma never wanted for things when she was alive, 'specially her cars."

"Cars?" I asked.

"She always drove a nice clean car... she kept it in her barn, spotless. Pa said she was somethin' else in her cars. She never had anything old or dirty." Then he paused, "And to think that Emmett drives that old beat-up A-model. He should'a got his hands on one of his momma's car after she kicked the bucket, huh."

With the emotional problems of the father, based on alleged suicide, I wondered why the mother's face was filled with life. Her eyes were focused and pleasant. She looked like she had received everything her life could afford to give her.

The father's picture--glass and frame--was broken and mildewed, difficult to see. The father's face was distorted behind the surface of the photo's wavy paper, which appeared to have been damaged from moisture in the past. I could only make out his arrow-straight lips and his beard, extending outward from a razor-sharp jaw.

Both parents have extremely pointed chins. Emmett's is rounded and dull. Weird. Would that be what made him retarded? A different kind of chin?

I guessed that Emmett's father was quite the busy man, keeping his wife up like he did with nice cars and caring for his only begotten son.

It made me think of John 3:16, my all-time favorite Bible verse: For God so loved the world, that He gave *his only begotten son,* that whosoever believeth in Him, should not perish, but have everlasting life.

My daddy preached one Sunday morning, "Jesus received both the sharpness of His Father's own vengeance and the bluntness of mankind's rejection." That Sunday morning message reminded me again of the cross with its blunt hammer and sharp nails.

Sharp? Knives! He's sharpening knives! I hate to be blunt, but I'm outta here!

I looked around the room to see if I could find something else to talk out loud about, to divert his attention. If I could find an alternate exit, I could make it to through the ditch, past the swing set, and home. I stepped toward a second room to the left. As I rounded the wall, I was surprised to discover a darker room filled with misarranged items you'd find in a blacksmith's shop on a Hop-along Cassidy Western Show episode on Saturday morning television.

Without warning, out of the blue and right behind me, Emmett's voice broke the silence. "That my father work." I almost bruised my back turning around to face him. As far as I could tell, he was knife-less. I hadn't even heard Emmett stir. He glided through the house like a cat.

"Oh, there you ar'!" I backed one step away from him, bumping into one of the items.

Emmett turned away from me, walking back into the other room. After reaching into a box, he lit a long match and ignited the wick of an oil lamp on a round table. The room started to glow brighter as the oil met the flame. Carrying the lamp into the dark room, Emmett held the lamp up, giving his face a more uncanny appearance. The dark room began to lighten. I turned away from Emmett toward the room. The various items, dust-covered, resembled the smithy's barn at the edge of a western town. I could almost see the bellows begin to push its breath out across the open flames of the blacksmith's shop.

"Father make horse shoes," Emmett said. "He melt things. Get 'em hot, and hits 'em hard with a hamma'...on his anvil. Seen a anvil, Jake?" Emmett gestured toward his father's former occupational tool. I was surprised that Emmett was talking so much. This topic was his specialty, his dance music.

Emmett's anvil sat against a wall. It was bitter and black. And cold.

Emmett moved to each piece and named it, touching it and looking back at me for validation.

"Bellows...anvil...hammer...Father make all the shoes fer all of Pelham and Bloun'ville. On this anvil...heah," Emmett said, pointing to the worn anvil. Emmett's face grabbed life, tightened, and appeared vital. It was obvious this was his favorite story to tell from his heart, what his dad did before he died.

The anvil looked like it had set under the crashing falls from the Enoree Dam for centuries. The oiled black surface was slick and cold, sharp at one end and dull at the far backside. It looked like somebody's heavy burden.

I kept thinking of the pictures over the mantel. It just seemed strange to me that *his parents both had extremely sharp chins like the anvil. He has a dull chin like the opposite end of the anvil.*

Emmett spoke reflectively, like an ancient poet or philosopher, above his retardation: "Anvil is quiet, alone. No one speak to it. They only beat on it, but it only get smootha' and harda', Jake."

I felt like Emmett was trying to teach me a deep lesson of some kind. I listened and the more I looked into his watery eyes, the more I began to understand the little retarded boy in the picture. Behind the vague expression on his face was a trusting heart, a contemplating mind. His whole life was composed of cleaning the church, his way of showing his love for God, and cutting grass, his way of showing his love for his fellow man. There was nothing else that was important to him, except maybe this blacksmith room, a representation of the father that he never knew. As people had beat on him, he had refused to become harder.

"Father," Emmett began more slowly, "father had a anvil in his hand with him all tha time. He have it on tha dam and in tha river below tha dam...in his hand." Emmett's eyes flooded and a couple of tears streaked down his cheeks to his dull, unshaven chin, and off the end onto the wooden floor, dotting the dust. He was trying to explain his father's death to me. I didn't care to hear it. "When he fall off." Emmett grunted to discard some internal tears.

Quietly, on the inside, I cried too. I liked to have not swallowed the tears, instead almost choking. They were over running my throat. I finally got my breath. “A small anvil?” I asked.

“He cut it from a rock. It look like...uh anvil.”

The anvil? That Josiah gave me? His pa found it below the dam when he was fishing.

Emmett continued. “Father cut his two names on bottom of tha anvil before...he die,” Emmett said. Emmett seemed relieved to be able to tell the story to someone who would listen. For some reason, I didn’t mind listening. I had suddenly forgotten about escaping. *I really don’t mind listening.* My hand moved to my pocket to feel the anvil. It was still there. If people would have listened to Emmett, his imaginative and honest feelings could be freed.

“How big? How big was the little anvil? That your father cut?” I asked, wondering if I had possession of it.

“Father make it tha same size as uh piece of fifty cent,” Emmett explained.

"You mean the anvil is the same size as a fifty-cent piece?" I asked.

"Yeah. Yeah, same size, Jake," Emmett said. "About this size," he added; he held up his fingers, making a circle with his left hand. I could see the black gunk beneath his finger nails.

Trying to say something to make conversation, I said, "That's something else, Emmett!" I stepped to the nearest wall and leaned back for support. I felt comfortable but confused. I touched my pocket to check the size. It fit right inside my circled fingers.

Wanting to check for the two names later, I asked, "What was your father's name, Emmett?" I hadn't noticed the bottom of my small anvil at all.

"Joe Longstreet."

JL, I whispered to my memory. *Remember the initials JL. Like…uh…Jello!*

"Here, Jake," Emmett said. He held out a small hammer, that in comparison, matched the same scale as the anvil. It too was a crude river-stone carving, but not smooth from being in the water for a long time. “You need this,” he continued. “If I not have father anvil, a hammer no good to me. You need it. Father cut this too. I no need it no more. You have it, Jake.”

I felt that he knew more than I had told him. Shocked yet surprised, I reached for the hammer without even saying thank you. I put it in my pocket, and it rested with a clink against the anvil. *Together, at last.*

Emmett and me talked about each piece of the blacksmith’s tools. He explained the purpose of each one in the whole scheme of turning iron into a useful product for society. As I watched him talk in his awkward voice and speech, he preached me a valuable message, in his own way, about how God molds each of us—though we are different—on his anvil of love to make something good out of our lives. How wonderfully God treats all his creation. A feeble-minded person can be used by God too. Amen!

That night, after Daddy and Momma asked me if I had a good time with Emmett, Gabriel and Daniel wanted me to tell them about my trip to Emmett's house, but I only told them parts of the story. I didn't elaborate. I told them more of the ride than I did of the rooms. Some things they just wouldn't have understood, not without seeing into Emmett's eyes, or listening about Emmett's father, or hearing his explanation of the anvil and hammer, or meeting a black boy, no way.

They seemed satisfied to hear a little of the story. I kept the other for my own dreams that night. It was a little peculiar to hear Momma's voice, reminding me at supper, "Eat your jello, Jake!" As if I needed a reminder.

Before I hit the sack, I turned the anvil upside down in my hand, and visible only to an eye that knew what shape to search for, was a faded JL. The J was worn almost away. I could hardly see it except for holding it right up next to the table lamp in our bedroom. It appeared someone had rubbed that J plum off. The L was practically fresh-carved, and to think I hadn't even noticed the two letters.

I placed the anvil and the hammer in my personal things box and covered them up with an old handkerchief of Daddy's that Momma had given me. Before turning in, I whispered, *Rest in Peace, Joe Longstreet.* The next morning, both pieces went back into my pocket. I figured I would need the extra courage someday.

23

My daddy preached, "Be sure your sin will find you out!" He never let us three boys forget that fact. He recalled that scripture each time we sinned and got caught. Just from hearing it so much, I felt Daddy knew when I had sinned, even though he would sometimes *not* bring it up to me.

Having made friends with Jo, I always wondered if anyone knew about it. I could hear "nigger lover" in my mind, and I knew how the kids at school would feel about me having a black friend. For sure, I would be killed if Clanton Butler knew about it. He hated blacks, period.

"What of it," Lanny told me at recess. "Everybody knows Rooster's pa is the head honcho in the KKK. Old man Butler has lynched a few niggers in his time, and he said he'd do it again, if the time was ripe for it. He lynched one black boy up in Dark Corners. They carried the boy up in the back of Mr. Clanton's truck."

Lanny told me that story before lunch one day. I was sick at my stomach and didn't eat until I sat down at the kitchen in the parsonage for supper. We had salmon patties and mashed potatoes with hot rolls and butter and green peas. Of course, Momma had baked a fresh three-layer coconut cake using pineapple for filling, and I ate a piece of that.

"Do we get jello, Momma?" Daniel asked.

I reached in my pocket. Both pieces were there.

At supper, Daddy asked me, "Jake, you been spending a lot of time down near the river. Who's been with you? I don't want you down there by yourself, son."

I sat still and ate my potatoes without answering, because Daddy hadn't ended his last statement with a question mark, so I figured that I---

"Jake, answer your father," Momma inserted. *Dang, why did she do that!*

Hoping to satisfy his questions and talking with my mouth partially full, distorting my response, I answered, "I've been down there with different people, Daddy. I'm doing safe stuff." *If you only knew how different the person was, Daddy!*

Daddy had just taken in quite a bite of salmon mixed with potatoes and chewed vigorously while looking at me. That was never a good sign. Daddy could study my face and read below the surface. I never knew how he could do that. He washed the mixture down with a large, prolonged gulp of sweet tea. He wiped his mouth. I nibbled on my roll, being nervous. That was such a give-away, and yet I always did it. I was a feeble liar, yet I practiced it often.

"Like who?" Daddy asked. He continued cleaning between his teeth and gums with his tongue. He leaned back in the chair and rested his arms on the chair's arms. Daddy was the only person at our table with arm rests on his chair. Our own arms were left up to us to find them a place of rest, which at this precise moment, across from my daddy and his intense stare, I was miserably readjusting, looking for a possible comfortable resting place for my arms.

"Like Stanley, Ray, Rocky..." I started listing everybody in my school, almost in the same seating chart of Miss Jenny's class. I knew I would be in trouble when I got to row three which was full of girls.

"That's all? No new friends I don't know about?" he asked. In my heart, I knew Daddy wanted to find out if I had been hanging around any of the hoodlums in Pelham, trouble-makers. There were a few of them, and the last thing Daddy wanted was to find out that I had befriended one of them, like Rooster or somebody.

I was in the spotlight now. Here was my chance to tell Daddy, Momma, and the family about Jo, to confess, to cleanse my soul of all its iniquity and sin. What a great opportunity to introduce my new friend who was so genuine and kind and thoughtful and had potential.

"And... Daniel." At the last minute, I remembered Daniel being down there that day and swinging across the river. So, I reached under the table and kicked him lightly as a reminder. If Daniel was going to squeal on me, now was his time. I wanted Daniel under the microscope, not me. I needed the bright lights outta my face. I waited to see what would happen next. My heart was playing "It's Howdy Doody Time!"

"Is that right, Daniel?" Daddy asked. He sounded like Raymond Burr, the TV Philadelphia lawyer. Daniel almost choked on his sip of tea.

"Daniel, aren't you going to answer your father?" Momma asked. *There she goes again. Who's the attorney and who's the judge here? Momma, back off!*

Daniel turned redder than the bottle of ketchup that always sat on our kitchen table, no matter the meal. "Yes Sir, Daddy," Daniel said; it was obvious a cry was imminent.

Don't cry you little retarded cotton top!

"Why are you crying, Daniel?" Daddy asked. "There's nothing to cry about, is there?" Daddy always looked at a cry as a weakness in our story. He was exploring that weakness.

Oh, God. Intervene now. Bring your heavenly and brightest glory to our table and blind us all, so that we may see you only and not the trivial matters that keep us so occupied, I prayed quietly, as if God was going to answer a sinner's prayer. *I'll take a falling comet from the celestial galaxy.*

"Because..." Daniel explained so eloquently.

Why didn't you say, because I love Jake so much that I accompany him wherever he leads me?

"Because why?" Daddy asked.

Drop the subject, Daddy! Please drop the subject! Daniel, don't say anything stupid!

"I don't know."

"Daniel," Momma said with her empathetic voice. "Daddy's not mad at you; he only wants to know why you're crying. Can't you answer him?"

"Yes, ma'am."

"Okay, then what is it?" Momma asked.

"I'm crying because I have to go to the bathroom *willy* bad," Daniel said.

I almost choked on the last bite of buttered roll. Brilli*ant! Absolutely brilliant! You're the greatest, Daniel, the absolute best! Me and you are the brightest brothers. We're both brilliant!*

"Well, now why didn't you say that, Daniel?" Momma asked. "You may be excused."

Daniel slid away from the table and to the bathroom. He shut the door, and even with the deathly silence that had followed Daddy's interrogation session at the supper table, I could not hear one trickle of urination hitting the toilet water. Daniel had become the best of liars, and I thought all along, I was the holder of that honor.

The little liar is sitting on the commode lid. He's brilliant! If Jesse James had only known Cotton Top, his trip to Boot Hill would have been delayed!

"Well," Daddy suddenly said, with fire in his eyes, causing me to drop my fork on the floor. "I had best not find out you boys are hanging out with any hooligans down there at the river. If I ever find out you boys have smoked or cussed, I will tan your hides. Do you understand me, Jake?"

"Yes, Sir." He had no idea about what his brother Joe had done to us that one week.

"When you boys start gallivanting and hobnobbing with this world, I will not let you rest until you get back into a right relationship with your heavenly father and your family," he preached. The kitchen table became his pulpit, arrayed with vegetables and one meat. "Be sure your sin will find you out!"

"Adam---" Momma started.

"Lillian?"

"Not at the table, please?" Momma asked.

Daddy looked at her, confused, paused to give me one last penetrating look, and then pushed away from the table, departing to his study.

I didn't even pick my fork up but ate with my knife instead. The knife reminded me of Emmett's house, and I felt like a spider was in my shirt, crawling up, poised to bite me.

"Momma, can I be excused?" I asked.

"Can or may?"

"May I be excused, please?"

"Yes."

I slid back, picked up my fork and put it on the table, thinking Momma had heard it fall, and then moved toward the hallway and my room.

"Jake," Momma suddenly stopped me.

"Yes," I responded, not even turning toward her.

"Anytime you need to talk to me, let me know."

I didn't say anything else. I went to my room and read a book, up until we had our family altar at bedtime.

As she did every night at our house, Momma announced, "In the living room, boys…girls!"

Into the living room, six of us—later on, eight of us filed. There were three older boys and three younger girls all sitting in chronological order, clockwise, around the coffee table in the center of our living room, near the upright piano.

As was our custom, Daddy and Momma sat in chairs at the head of the table. Daddy was the only one with a Bible. The rest of us came empty-handed.

"Let's read what God has to say to us," Daddy began. "If we confess our sins, He is faithful and just to forgive us our sins, and to cleanse us from all unrighteousness." Then, Daddy paused, and did a sweep with his eyes of the individuals who circled the outer edges of the table, pausing at me to give me a dad-ly stare.

Please, keep reading, oh father. Do not pauseth at me. I am not lying!

He had read from 1 John 1:9. I knew why he had paused. He wanted to pause before he read verse 10. "If we say that we have not sinned, we make him a *liar*, and his word is not in us."

Ouch! That hurts! Please, Jesus, forgive me. Please, Daddy, pray, and let's go to bed. There's no need in prolonging this pain. Shoot me and get it over with. Bring in the firing squad, line me up as did your brother Joe of yesteryear, and shooteth me!

For some reason, Daddy read long passages that night. He read the entire chapter of 1 John 2. It had 29 verses. He especially enjoyed dwelling on verse 15, which he read twice. "Love not the world, neither the things of the world. If any man love the world" --Daddy stopped to explain that the word *love* there meant hobnobbing and gallivanting—"...the love of the Father is not in him."

Finally, Daddy said, "Do we have any prayer requests before we pray?"

On any other usual night, Carol or Becky would have suggested a strange prayer request like praying for a bird that was hurt in a book that Momma had been reading to them or praying for some ant they'd seen crawling across the kitchen floor, but on this night, they were well asleep by the time Daddy had gotten to the final verse of 1 John 2.

"Let's pray."

24

My grandparents came down from the mountains to visit us. It was my birthday, and my grandpa had hand-built me a car, a small go-cart like vehicle with no motor. Grandpa was the foreman in the building department at the Balfour Plant in Hendersonville, North Carolina. He had access to sheet metal at the plant and had constructed the car for me. It had rubber wheels and a brake handle. It was a spit-polished, high-flying roller coaster.

I loved it. Grandpa parked the car in our basement. I spent time sitting on the car's seat, turning the perfect steering wheel on the column. I couldn't wait to get it on the hill next to the school. With that paved incline, I could see myself going top speed toward the school.

Grandpa was the king of storytelling. All you had to do was get him started, and he would talk forever, and then laugh. Perhaps I can assign him partial credit for my telling stories.

"J D," Daddy said to him, "tell us about the big rock down in Sumta," trying to say Sumter like Grandpa did when he told the story.

"Well, my foreman," Grandpa started, "old man Jefferson, uncovered this large rock at the foundation of the building in Sumta. Him and his dad-burn hired hands couldn't move it. This rock was a giant of a rock. It was partly in and partly out of the ground, 'bout the size of this room, I'd say." Grandpa would have told the story somewhat different had children and ladies not been standing by. I could tell when he paused, he was editing and being selective with his language.

Everybody sat up listening. Finally, Momma took Grandmother and the girls into another room, because she knew Grandpa's tongue was being restricted.

"Tell us what happened," I asked, already knowing like the rest of us, but wanting to have it painted in detail on the mind's canvas once more.

Grandpa finished his story like this:

Well, Mr. Jefferson walked over to where me and my boys were eating our lunch. I knew what he wanted. We just sat there though, waitin' for him to ask. The foreman said, "J D, why don't you and your boys come down here and see if 'all can move this dang rock." Well, me and my niggers, Old John and Benjamin--better known as Big Ben-- two of the biggest niggers in the South, we moseyed over to the rock, and I stood back and watched. Old John and Big Ben sauntered around the rock, like they were checking it out or something. The boss' men were all standing by now, seeing if it could actually be done. John and Benjamin positioned themselves at each end of it, and reaching way down and using their legs and backs, grunted like two old hogs before the slaughter. Up out o' that hole came that old rock like it was made o' feathers or something. John and Benjamin tossed it over onto the ground, bottom side up, and then got their breaths back again. Old John said, "Okay, Mr. J D, is that all?" I told 'em to go back to eatin'. They'd done a lot more in a few minutes than the rest o'em had done all the dag-gone day. Confound the luck, I went ahead and gave 'em a good ten minutes extra lunchtime.

"And would you know, Adam," Grandpa said to my daddy, "that anytime--then and now--that I want to walk through nigger town in Greenville, I can strut my stuff through there like it's nobody's business, 'cause John and Benjamin done told everybody there to leave Mr. J D alone."

Grandpa ended his famous story, and everybody sat back and listened to him laugh out loud at his fond memory. Grandpa came from the day when nobody questioned that kind of behavior or even took a second glance about it. He felt comfortable having two black giants who worked for him, and he told everybody about it at the drop of a hat, and sometimes, he would go ahead and drop the hat his'self.

A few minutes after Grandpa's stories, him and Grandmother packed up and went back to the mountains. I always wished Grandpa could have met Josiah. I believe, after having spent some time with him in the *Eight Ball*, they could have become good friends with a better understanding.

"Thanks for the car, Grandpa," was the last words I spoke to him that day.

"Watch that brake, Jake. I made it firm," he answered.

When spring sprung in Pelham, we took that car for a spin. Me, Gabriel, and Daniel took turns coming down the hill, after a stiff push from behind by the other two. The trip was fast, and the air would blow the hair back off our head like the window fan we used in the summer to keep us cool.

Finally, Gabriel came up with the idea of two riding the car at the same time. He said he would steer, if I would stand up on the back and hold on. Why I agreed with that, I'll never know. To take advice from a dime-off-a-block-wall person is not sensible. This is the same person who put boxing gloves on with Rooster. Someone should have placed a sign around my neck: Dumber than the dumbest.

We pushed the car to the top of the hill and turned it around.

"Now, get on," Gabriel yelled.

"Where?" I asked.

"Put your feet on the back and hold on to my shoulders," he said.

"Okay." I tentatively agreed.

I climbed on and leaned forward, placing most of my trust in Gabriel's shoulders, the same ones I had supported after he was knocked into the ditch. Daniel got us started down the hill.

More from gravity than from Daniel's weak push, we zoomed double time down the paved road. Where the road turned in front of the school was a slanted beach of sand that had washed down over time from the hill above the school. At the end of the beach, many grains of sand had been scattered out by the wind and weather and lay there in the spring sun, glinting like bits of broken glass, hot and sharp.

Flying full speed, Gabriel maneuvered us into the curve, and suddenly, without warning me or common sense, simultaneously swerved the car right and pulled back on the stiff brake Grandpa had warned me about.

It happened so fast, I can hardly recall the exact emotions or feeling or what it was like to go face-first into the sizzling, gritty sand that layered the blistering pavement. I do know for a fact, if you slide across that type of surface on your face for any length of time or distance, it is not pleasant or advisable.

Getting to my feet, I ran screaming to Momma. My face was on fire. I could feel the warm blood oozing around the sand that was embedded into my face. For what seemed like an eternity, Momma washed my face and tried to soothe my tears with words of comfort, but to no avail. I screamed incessantly.

Iodine is surely an instrument of anguish and torment invented by Satan. I feel sure that he will use it in Hell as a primary torture device throughout eternity.

Over the next few weeks, my skin would grow tight and sore, and then the scabs formed, and I would pick at them in school and church. Momma and Miss Jenny would fuss at me for pulling scabs off, but that fascinated me, the feel of dead skin. On one occasion, I had this flap of scab that hung from my nose, and when I turned my face toward a certain direction, would swing in the breeze like a kite off a cliff. I was the star of the playground for several days with my own kite, attached to my own gruesome nose.

Diane liked me then. She was in third grade too. When I went to the hospital to have my tonsils taken out, she was the one who told Miss Jenny to have the whole class to draw me pictures and write me notes. Then, Miss Jenny made the whole collection into one large scrapbook and sent it to me.

I read those notes forever and ever. I especially enjoyed reading Diane's because she put the word *love* at the end of her note. I knew what she meant.

I could tell she liked me, when at recess I would look up at the bank, and she would be watching me. I tried to run extra hard when she watched, but didn't go any faster, even strengthened by her undying love. One day, I got Bradley Smith to race me so Diane could see me run. Bradley was the fattest boy in the third grade. He sat in a larger chair than the rest of us did. He needed the additional room.

This race was only a few feet. We started it right beside where Diane was playing outside Miss Jenny's classroom. I talked louder when announcing the race's rules, so that Diane could hear my instructions to Bradley.

"Okay, Bradley," I practically yelled, "we're racing to that post there." The post was only about fifteen feet away. Taking advantage, I leaned forward while Bradley was still assimilating the instructions of the race--that was my plan--Diane was watching closely. I felt she liked my take-control attitude. She punched two of her friends, getting their attention, and I could tell they were taking notice of my prowess. “Now, Bradley, I’m countin’ to three, and then we’re gonna run as fast as we can to that pole over there...to see which of us is the fastest...*once and for all.*”

I started the countdown in reverse. “One, two, three, go!” I yelled quickly, before Bradley could realign himself.

My first two steps were gazelle-like, graceful and exact, pushing my one leg ahead of the other in perfect form like Maury Wills running the base paths for the Dodgers. There were only about seven or eight steps in the entire race, if that many. However, my third step was a horrible disaster. While looking back at Bradley and his flab, I tried to display my crowd-pleasing skills by glancing and grinning at my love and her two friends. That was a mistake. I should have watched where I was going.

My right foot tangled with Mary Lou Thatcher’s long leg, extended onto the race track. She was sitting halfway along the path to the pole, reading her fiftieth book of the year. I hadn't even noticed her long, lanky leg sticking onto the course.

Suddenly, and without warning, my world collapsed beneath me, and down I went. "Ouwwch!" I landed face first on my nose. My kite came off and fell to the ground.

Bradley, seconds later, passed by me, crossing the finish line first, all of him. The crowd was quiet, unimpressed. I lay on the ground and grimaced, realizing that my only saving grace would be to act more hurt than I actually was. I did. "Ouch. Oh, that hurts." I cried, moaning. I tried to stand up but crumpled again in pain upon the dusty and unforgiving racetrack. "Oh! My legs!"

I peeped at my injury to see if this academy award performance was affecting my audience.

All three of the girls did rise to their feet. *My plan is coming together beautifully.* I yelled even more loudly, "Oh, my legs! Owww! Shoot!"

The girls walked right toward me...and then...*past* me, toward Bradley.

"Good race, Bradley," they chimed. They disappeared into Miss Jenny's classroom.

Bradley was already swaying side to side, heaving in a raspy breath. He needed medical attention, too. He looked at me for support.

Pulling myself up and dusting me off, I stuck my tongue out at Bradley and headed back down the hill to where the boys were playing tag. I was afraid Bradley might have fallen on me if he had gotten too close to me, writhing on the ground.

I can't stand that old Mary Lou Thatcher!

25

Jo and me met every eighth in *The Eight Ball.* We only missed on January eighth and March eighth, when I had the flu and he had a toothache. The way we communicated with each other on those days was by dropping messages into our hideaway, and then eagerly coming to check for those messages a couple of times per month.

He knew I had been sick, because I brought an empty bottle of Bayer aspirins and dropped it into the *Eight Ball,* and I knew he had had a toothache because he dropped his old decayed tooth into the hideaway. It was laying right on the dirt floor, like a pearl in the darkness of a deep ocean.

Each time we met, we became better friends, understanding more about each other's worlds. I never said the N word, and he agreed to never say the C or H words: cracker or honky. There were some other words he said he would tell me about later, which blacks said privately about whites. I said that'd be good. There would be a time for that, we were sure.

All Jo talked about was running and jumping. Needless to say, he talked me into racing him through the corn stalks behind his house one day. I agreed. It was springtime, and I had these newfound hopes about being faster than I was the year before, since winter. I knew I had grown some during third grade, because my clothes didn't fit exactly right, and my speed had probably increased too. Boy was I mistaken about the speed part. I suppose as the body lengthens, it tends to be more awkward or clumsy, at least until the mind and motor skills are practiced and coordinated better.

Jo toed a line at the end of the corn row and then came back to me to go over the rules of the race.

"See dat line n' da dirts, Jeck?" he asked me. Of course, from where we were standing, about a hundred feet or so from the toed mark, I couldn't see a thing on the ground's surface.

"Yep."

"When da rock hits da groun', we lickety-splits fo da line, gots it?"

"What rock?" I looked around for a possible comet falling from space.

Picking up a small rock near his feet, he said, "Dis rock. I throws it up, it hits, we skedaddle t'wards da line, gots it?" Now, I was glad my grandmother had used skedaddle when she scooted me out of the kitchen so she could work.

"Okay," I answered. "I'm ready." I stood with both hands swinging at my sides and my eyes staring straight ahead at the line I still couldn't see. My knees were flexed and ready. Jo held the rock and was flexing to release it into the air.

"He-uh go!" he yelled; into the crystal-blue sky flew the rock, up, up, up and down, down to the ground. *thump.* I tried not to think of what had happened the last time I waited for the parsonage screen door to squeak before I darted all alone to the swing set.

I felt my hamstrings and thigh muscles tighten. I extended my chest outwards in front of me, trying to match its example, and churned my arms like a locomotive's connecting rod. For seven or so whole corn stalks, I led the race, but since there were many more than seven or so stalks in a hundred feet, I mostly ate Jo's dust. He beat me so badly, that by the time I arrived at the end of the row, he was already resting on the ground on one elbow, legs crossed, and his other arm draped behind him like he was scratching his butt.

"Whats takes yo'self so long, Jeck?" he asked. "Dids yo stops fer uh drank o' wata... or a naps?"

I wasn't amused by Josiah's taunting and sarcasm at my expense.

"Shut up!" I heaved, out of breath and near mad-ville. *Dumb nigger.*

He pulled his other arm around into the spring light, and there in his hand was the same exact rock he had thrown up in the air earlier. Not only had he beat me, but he had slowed along the way to scoop up the rock.

"You're kiddin' me!" I snarled, looking behind me, hoping I'd see a lone rock lying in our racing path. *No way.*

"He-uh it be, Jeck…right cheer 'n my han'."

"That's not fair, Jo. You know I'm not fast…as fast as you," I whined, pivoting around to face him.

Jo studied me, and knew without a doubt I was easy fixins, so he cooked me in the hot spring sun like a wiener dog over a Boy Scout campfire. "I gots a friend yo can beats… sho do," he beamed. "Sometimes, yo cans race 'im."

"Who? You mean there's a slow nig…black boy I can beat?"

Jo sat up a little, hearing the *nig* sound, offended, but then laid back on the ground, after a deep sigh. "If'n yo cant beats *this* nigga, yo sho aint gonna beats 'notha one," he offered. His feelings were hurt, I could tell.

"Sorry, Jo," I began. "I'm just upset 'cause you beat me so bad. I thought I was gettin' faster after winter, but I guess I ain't."

"I thinks yo is, Jeck, I ree'ly does," he said, sympathetic.

Questioningly, I looked at him.

"Why, yo dones run much fasta thans yo dids las ye-uh," he said, now starting to sit up. "Las ye-uh, you'd stills be plowin' my pappa's groun' up dare like Mr. Jackson's mule."

I began to smile a little, and my breathing was back. "Well, then, who's that feller you want me to whoop up on in a race? I think I'm ready for him."

"His names Lightning. He be my bes' friend."

"Where's he at?" I asked. I looked around toward Jo's house.

Jumping up to his feet, Jo asked, "He be in da barn...wants go see 'im?"

“I can’t go to your barn, Jo. If your folks see me, they’ll hang me…won’t they?” I wasn’t sure and was only relying on what I’d been told on the monkey bars at school.

Lanny had told me one day at recess, *Them niggers’ll hang you out ‘til you are drain ‘o all ya blood, then they will cut you in small pieces and eat ya.*

As if Jo could read my mind, he suddenly said, “But we’s wont’s eats yo ‘til yo is tard and cants fite bac’…then, we eats yo.” Jo stopped mid-pace, looking me in the eyes. Taking a soft pinch of my white skin, he added, “Yo be quites the catch, I do say.” Then, he let go of my skin and started walking again toward the barn.

“Hey, wait, Jo. You’re just joshin’ me, ain’t you?” I asked.

He never looked back. He knew I’d follow him like the lost puppy I was.

We both walked into the barn, me last. The barn had an overhang that was barely hanging. Beneath it was rotting fire wood piled about waist high, sheltered with a single piece of tin roof, about four feet square. Jo explained the piece of tin: "I use that tin when it rains to get me to the house dry." Inside the barn, an aging cow chomped on straws of hay and looked me over.

"How come you got a black cow, Josiah?" I asked. "You don't like white?"

Josiah kneeled down, near an empty stall, and stirred the mustiness around with a small wooden crate that was partially hay-covered. "Miss Nelly, she be black, but she give white milk, Jeck...and they aint be no white cows, no way."

He fiddled in the crate and pulled out a large turtle. He stood and faced me. "Missuh Jeck, meets Missuh Lightning."

"What! This is Mr. Lightning? This is who you think I can beat?" Jo just stood there, holding Mr. Lightning. Jo grinned so broad you could have tied the smile's corners into a nappy bow at the back of his head.

"I thinks...he likes you."

Suddenly, a lady's voice yelled from Jo's house, "J'siah! J'siah!"

"Who's that, Jo?"

"Momma. She pra'bly need me to go to da sto fah huh...I be rat bac'." He did a double take to see what to do with Mr. Lightning. "He-uh... hol' 'im." Josiah handed the turtle over to me and exited the barn, leaving the door partway opened.

I looked at Mr. Lightning, and he tucked his head completely inside his shell and didn't come out again, like he'd never seen a white person before. I dropped him into the crate. *Lightning. I'd say more like Pokey would be a better name.*

I walked to the crack in the barn doorway and watched and listened. Jo was talking and listening to his momma. She looked like a nice lady, kinda tall-like and steady. Jo turned around toward the barn and pointed.

He's pointing at me! Why is he pointing at me?

Jo began a sprint toward the barn and in a split moment was at its door. "Momma...she say com' to da house. She wants yo to com on."

"I *can'ts* come to your house, Jo. I..." I tried to explain, talking like him outta frustration.

Without warning, Jo pulled the barn door wide open and there in the bright sunlight I stood, and his momma looking right at me. She signaled, waving her arm, for me to come up to the house. I began moving, but slowly. Jo shut the barn door behind us, and then catching up, walked beside me, like a warden escorting his prisoner. I spoke as we walked, “Why did you name him...*Lightning*...the turtle? He’s a turtle for mercy’s sake.”

“’Cause on da groun’, he be slow...I mean tear-uh-blee slow...but ‘n da wata’, ‘n dat wata’, I cants evun ketch ‘im. Yo puts him wher he belong...wher he be feeling lik’ he belong dare...and he be like *lightning.*”

I didn’t say another word.

26

Josiah's momma seemed to be a shy, but friendly person. She seemed afraid of me. Eventually, she did talk to me, but not too long nor loudly. I wanted to smile at her but was afraid too. She acted as if I were the adult at times. Scanning the surroundings, I couldn't help but notice the sagging wood steps leading up to the back porch, decayed and propped up on a couple of river stones. Behind Josiah's mother's skirt, I could see the kitchen floor, worn and patched with bits and pieces of cardboard and old linoleum.

His momma had a deep scar across her neck. Later, Josiah told me his momma had gotten the scar one evening from two white men who threw stuff out of their truck as they passed Jo's momma on Pickett Road. I was surprised by the name Pickett Road, because there was not one picket fence in any yard on the whole road.

Josiah's momma and me said hello, and then after a few awkward seconds with our eyes staring at the ground, I left to go home.

When I got to the parsonage back yard, Gabriel and Daniel were raking an area near the field, where Gabriel had been sling-blading earlier. I circled around and sneaked up on them, so they wouldn't be able to tell from which direction I had come.

"What yall doin?" I asked.

"Fixin' Gabriel's dog place," Daniel answered.

"We gettin' a dog?" I asked.

"*I'm* getting' uh dog, you need to say," Gabriel corrected me. "Daddy's gone to get it for me."

"He is? What kind's it gonna be?"

"Beagle," Gabriel said.

"You seen it already?" I asked.

"Nope."

Daniel added, "He's brown and white, Momma said."

"She's seen it?" I asked.

"Nope," Gabriel weighed in. "She ran into Mr. Rufus Suttles up at the grocery store, and he told her he had four pups left that he was giving away, free. Momma told Daddy, and he's gone to get one. He said we'd have to feed it and take care of it."

"That's not like Mr. Suttles...I mean, to give one of his dogs away, free," I said, wondering out loud. "He only raises purebreds...beagles...for show. He makes people pay big bucks for one of his dogs."

"Momma said the dogs were *free*," Gabriel repeated.

"Oh," I answered, not wanting to beleaguer the point. "I bet the dog *is* free, but Mr. Suttles only raises pure bred beagles."

Gabriel kept raking, pulling back dead weeds and some young grass, leveling out a place about the size of a medium doghouse.

Changing the subject, I asked, “And you know it’s brown and white?”

“Momma said,” Daniel explained, “that beagles are brown and white.”

Gabriel said, “The momma dog is a brown and white beagle, but Mr. Rufus didn’t say what the daddy was.”

“The daddy? Do dogs have daddies?” Daniel asked. He leaned over with a curiosity we didn’t have time to address.

“No,” Gabriel teased, “they are born out of eggs, Cotton-top. Didn’t you know that? Every boy in Pelham knows dogs are born from eggs!”

I could tell that Gabriel would rather joke Daniel than to think that his new dog might not be an AKC purebred beagle.

Daniel straightened up to think about it. “Eggs?”

“Yep,” I chided in. “Uh...eggs as big as a baseball.” Gabriel gave me a knowing grin.

Daniel didn't ask any more questions about dog eggs that day, but I did see him playing with the pup later in the week, trying to get the dog to sit down on the baseball.

Daddy pulled up.

"The dog!" Daniel yelled excitedly. He ran. I didn't dare race him.

Me and Gabriel trotted up to the back of the Buick. Daddy was already out of the car and walking to the trunk. He reached over with his keys and unlocked it. The darkness of the trunk gradually changed into light, and there sat, in an Esso Oil cardboard box with newspaper flooring, a jet-black pup with a single white spot across one ear. The tip of his back-left paw looked like it had been accidentally dipped in chalk dust, just the tip. He had brown puppy eyes.

At first, he didn't move. His tail was well tucked and still. Daniel tried to reach him but couldn't.

"Dad?" Daniel asked.

“Let’s get the box out and get him used to you three,” Daddy said. Daddy picked up the box and moved it near the well house. The pup rolled side to side as Daddy carried the box. As soon as Daddy sat the box down, Gabriel reached in and put the pup on the ground. Relaxing a little, after seeing we were all non-threatening, the pup rose up on its front paws, but then shied away as we made a few sudden movements.

Daddy said, “Mr. Suttles said he hoped you boys enjoyed the dog. He also said that the dog’s momma was a pure-bred beagle---”

“What about the dog’s daddy, Daddy?” Daniel interrupted.

“Mr. Suttles said he didn’t know exactly, because the momma dog dug out of its outside kennel and was gone for a short spell.”

“Does the momma dog lay eggs, Daddy?” Daniel asked.

Gabriel and my eyes met, hoping Daddy would cover for us. He looked our way.

"Daniel, where do you come up with those crazy ideas of yours?" Daddy asked.

I quickly answered for Daniel, "Daniel thinks dogs are born when the momma dog lays eggs, Daddy." I smiled one of those go-to-bat-for-me-Daddy smiles.

"I see," Daddy surmised... "Well, you just have to be careful around this pup here, Daniel. She won't lay eggs for a long time to come." Daddy smiled, shut the trunk, and left for the basement. I heard him laughing all the way up the steps.

Peeping underneath the pup, Gabriel said, "It's a bitch."

"A what, Gabriel?" Daniel asked.

"It's a hen, Cotton-top," Gabriel said, patting Daniel on his head and smiling.

After an afternoon of smelling the yard and using it too, the pup began to run and jump and play in the green grass.

"What's his name?" Daniel asked Gabriel. "What ya goin' to call him?"

"I thought of Rusty...Buster...Rover..." Gabriel rolled off a list of names.

"He's black," I added.

"So?" Gabriel asked.

"And he's a girl dog."

"And?"

Well, call him something that has to do with something black, or dark...or like night."

"How 'bout Midnight? Or Blacky?" Gabriel suggested. "Grease gun?"

"Nigga," Daniel said, trying to fit in.

Giving Daniel a parent-like look, I said, "Pearl."

We all paused. Our eyes darted around at the surroundings, speechless.

Gabriel broke the silence. "Yeah, that's smart, Jake. Let's call this *black* dog Pearl... dang, Jake, a pearl is white, even I know that. Momma wears her pearl necklace to church, and it's white, uh...dufus! Pearls are white, Jake."

“Yeah, but there are *black* pearls,” I answered. “‘cept they cost more money…‘cause they’re harder to find. There’s lots of white pearls…but black pearls are way more valuable,” I said. I had read about pearls in a book report for Miss Jenny in the third grade. I saw a picture of a raw black pearl in the library book, and it was ugly.

“Pearl,” Gabriel said, to see how it sounded.

“Pearl,” Daniel said after Gabriel said it, like a cotton-topped echo.

“Pearl. Sounds pretty good, don’t it?” I asked.

Gabriel jumped up, turned, and ran toward the school driveway at the end of our yard and suddenly twisted toward us. “Pearl, girl. Come here, Pearl,” he commanded.

Pearl, the black and kinda white pup, lay down beside Daniel and licked his bare feet. Then, she tilted her head, flopping her charcoal ear over, and growled at Gabriel who squatted at the edge of the grass like another dog, still ordering, “Come, Pearl, come here.”

Finally, Daniel got up and ran, and snapping at his heels, Pearl chased him all the way to Gabriel.

I sat back on the ground and watched Gabriel begin to work Pearl to make her, not just a good family dog, but also a prize-winning dog. He knew how to pull things out of this canine to make her a champion, and he did. Later on, Pearl would take the first-place ribbon in the Greenville County Rabbit Dog Championship. She wasn't even a purebred Beagle. As a matter of fact, Mr. Suttles' son told us after church one Sunday that the daddy of Gabriel's pup was a large coonhound from the Suttles' neighbor's farm. I guess that speaks volumes for being pure.

When Gabriel's dog won at the GCRDC, not even looking like a beagle but more like a large coon hound, she stood out like a pearl, a rare and precious mutt, different, yet in her environment.

27

Daddy had exhausted three of his nights at the church in deacon meetings. Mr. Buford Jackson had suddenly thought it his duty to call meetings to discuss every blamed piece of church business that he could uncover.

Daddy hadn't taken a like'in' to Mr. Jackson's meetings. Hiding behind the basement steps, I overheard Daddy telling Momma in the basement between meeting nights, "He's trying to change everything about the church, Lillian, and it's not right. Do I ever miss Brother Elijah Green right now!"

It seems that Mr. Buford Jackson had been watching a couple of people real closely in our church and didn't feel they were qualified to serve in their respective duties.

"Pastor..." Mr. Jackson said in one of his summoned meetings, "Emmett is untrustworthy. I've seen him before, cleaning the church, and lifting a coin to his pocket, without once asking someone in authority what's to be done with it."

In each meeting, Mr. Jackson would have a new list of issues about Emmett. If one night hadn't been a success in damaging Emmett's reputation, then the next night would bring even more damning evidence that Mr. Jackson had dug up.

"And..." Mr. Jackson continued on another night, "my daughter saw Emmett throw away, in the large trash can in the Sunday School room, a hymn book, just because it only had a few pages missing. Now, that's waste...a waste of good money. Why, one of our pitiful orphanage kids in Africa could have used that hymnal to sing praises to God...and

Emmett tossed it aside like a worn-out old shoe. Gentlemen, I tried to warn you years ago about his mental disability."

Each night brought a different set of allegations about Emmett. Daddy tossed in his sleep that week, trying to figure why someone would set out to ruin another person, especially one who is *not all there*, and has done an exceptional job cleaning the church. "... a *damn* good job!" Daddy told Momma, after getting angry about it one day in his study downstairs in the parsonage.

Mr. Jackson agreed to conclude the meetings until more evidence surfaced and a more watchful eye could be given toward Emmett's duties and attitudes. "We will," Mr. Jackson spoke at the last meeting, "...we will let this issue rest for now, but all our eyes will watch Emmett. If we see any reason for reconvening to discuss his future here at Pelham Baptist Church, then we'll call the meeting and act quickly." Mr. Jackson then dismissed the meeting in prayer, remembering in his prayer the orphans in Africa.

The following Sunday morning, my daddy preached on Phillip and the Ethiopian Eunuch in the book of Acts in the New Testament. However, Mr. Jackson and his family were not present. They had chosen to go to the lake for the day instead.

28

Under a wide tree, Gabriel and me felt it our duty to sit Daniel down on a lazy summer day to give him *the talk*, as best we could with our own limited knowledge. Our readily available tool in teaching Daniel was what he had recently witnessed Brutus do to another dog, while we were all three walking to the store for a RC Cola. It seems Brutus had discovered a neighborhood girl dog was in heat. Right before our eyes *and* Daniel's, Brutus was becoming a daddy. On the walk back from the store, Daniel had asked more questions than Miss Jenny would have asked on a reading test, and for that reason, we decided to give him *the talk*.

"Wouldn't a dog have babies in the winter, then?" Daniel asked.

"What do you mean by that?" Gabriel asked him.

"Well, you said Brutus would be a daddy *in heat.* What about in cold?"

I could tell that Daniel's immature concrete logic would probably hinder our efforts to explain such an abstract idea as dog's having babies. Perhaps the egg idea was working against us.

Put out by Daniel's shallow understanding, Gabriel barked, "Never mind!"

"Let's put it this way, Daniel," I said. "Dogs do something together...like what we saw with Brutus and that dog---"

"What was he doing to that dog, Jake?" Daniel asked. "Was he hurting him?"

"No," I quickly said, "no...that was a girl dog, not a boy dog."

"They were," Gabriel said, without confidence, "...uh...having...love for each other?"

Everything me and Gabriel said to Daniel sounded awkward and unscientific. We stumbled and left Daniel's expression distorted with confusion and stress.

Daniel finally asked, "Does Brutus love that dog...like a girlfriend...like you and Diane, Jake?"

I paused, shocked, my mouth dropped open. Gabriel scooted around like his butt was asleep.

"What do you mean *Diane*?" I questioned.

"You like Diane, don't you?"

Wondering where this little white-headed munchkin got his information, I asked, "What?" No one knew about Diane. I had sworn myself to secrecy and only shared her name with the heavens, my mind, and a private space inside my notebook. Daniel knew way too much for his age.

Pushing Daniel's shoulder around to face him, Gabriel inserted, "Now, Daniel, let's get back to the humping dogs." Gabriel paused, waiting for Daniel's eyes to focus on him. "Look at me, Daniel." Then, I saw Gabriel wink solidly at

Daniel, a wink that never registered in Cotton-top's mental landscape.

Pulling Daniel's shoulder back around toward me again, I emphasized loudly, "*How*...how did you know about Diane? Who told you?"

Daniel's young brain was not only being overly bamboozled by The Unscientific and pre-*The Talk* approach to an Explanation of Canine Procreation in the heat, but was also being physically traumatized by one sudden shoulder-jerk after another.

Gabriel cleared his throat and lightly kicked Daniel's leg, saying, "Why don't you go get us a snack from Momma and bring it back to us, Daniel? I'm starving." Gabriel's voice changed as he said Daniel's name, like he was more interested in the "niel" part than he was in the "Dan" part.

"No...wait a minute here!" I nearly yelled. I was suddenly feeling like someone had broken into my private bank and forcibly taken my personal thoughts out. "How, Daniel, did you know about Diane? Answer me!" I knew he couldn't read well enough to decipher my love notes and poems. They were too deep and delved into the higher thinking skills.

As if there were a whole flock of cotton-tops seated beneath the wide green tree, Daniel asked, “Me?”

“Yes, you!”

“I---” he started but was suddenly interrupted by Gabriel again.

“Daniel, go and get us something to eat!”

He couldn’t have read what I had written in my notebook, because I had written it in cursive.

Now, on my knees, I waited a few seconds to sense the mood around the brotherly conference. There was a definite tension under the shade tree in the heat.

I pushed Daniel back to the ground. He fell backwards, and at first, whined, “What? What did I do? I won’t tell Daddy about the dogs loving each other, I promise---”

“No, that’s not it,” I said. I pulled my fist back in a threatening posture. Suspending my anger, I gradually lowered my fist, and calming my emotions, continued, “I want *you* to tell *me* how you knew about Diane." I kneeled above Daniel like a referee at a wrestling match on the television set and looked him sternly in the eyes. "How, Daniel? I'm waitin'."

Daniel gazed around me at Gabriel, who had suddenly thought it necessary with his eyes to inspect at a distance the field below the parsonage property. Daniel then looked back at me and then toward Gabriel, then back at me and then toward Gabriel for a longer period of time. Daniel was attempting to communicate to me with his eyes.

I turned to look at Gabriel whose eyes were pretending to comb the field. Gabriel glared back at me. "What? Why you lookin' at me for?"

"Did you tell Daniel?"

"I didn't have to...he saw it with his own eyes...you were there too!" he explained. Gabriel pointed in the direction of where we all saw Brutus having...love.

"You know what I mean!" I said. "I'm talkin' about Daniel knowing about Diane. Did-you-tell-him?" I emphasized each word.

By this time, Gabriel was beginning to stand, wiping his pants-bottom off. Grass and dirt fell to the ground. Turning toward the house, he said, "I'm going to get something to eat," He didn't look back.

I threw Daniel's leg off of mine and stood. "Did you snoop in my notebook and read my stuff?" I asked, loud enough, I thought. No answer. He just kept walking, not looking back.

I couldn't help but think of a specific episode of Wyatt Earp, when Wyatt had to run and jump on the bad guy's back in order to bring him down to the ground to fight him. Normally, I would have let these events slide, or tell Momma, or hit Daniel because he was closer to me than Gabriel, and younger. But, this was a matter of the heart, my heart.

I started in a sprint, which was not that fast, of course, but landed in a whirl of angry energy, onto Gabriel's shoulders, riding him to the ground.

"What you doin'?" Gabriel yelled on the way down. "You crazy?"

I pinned Gabriel to the ground face first. I knew he had already met the ground before, near the foundation of the curved stonewall under a bicycle; I was only re-introducing him. "You read my notebook, didn't you?" I screamed like a lawyer in *Perry Mason*. "You sneaked and got my notebook when I wasn't around and then told Daniel about it."

"Wha' chew talkin' 'bout?" Gabriel tried to say, his lips blowing dirt away from his mouth. "Get up, Jake! I can't breathe!"

There was no way I was going to get up until I heard him confess to the crime. I pressed more heavily on his back with my weight. I believed I would recognize when Gabriel would be near death, and then, and only then, would I get up to mercifully accept his final confession before he would cross over to the Promised Land, conscience cleared.

Suddenly, Daniel rushed past us in a wild gallop. "I'm telling!"

Attempting to take advantage of Daniel's warning, Gabriel murmured, "You better get up! Daddy'll be down here in a minute."

"I don't care. He can come with a legion of angels if he wants to...and set-up camp ... I don't care!" I *had* to be angry to say that and mean it.

"If you let me up, I'll tell you the truth," Gabriel agreed. To think I would be that gullible! I'd seen the same trick on *The Lone Ranger* and now, I would be falling for it.

"Kee-ma-sob-ee, oldest son trick middle son. Middle son real dumb!"

I stood. Gabriel stood and wiped his mouth off, spitting dirt. Then, he jumped on me, straight against me and we both fell, and rolled, and rolled. We finally stopped rolling and stumbled to our feet.

Both of us took a two-fisted fighting position, facing each other. Gabriel socked me with a right fist against my left arm. It shocked me at first, and I felt like crying, but I kept imagining myself winning my love from the other knight...Bradley the Fattest, at school.

'Tis no way that he shall rideth off into the sunset with my true love Diane. En garde!

I punched Gabriel on his arm. He winced.

He returned the favor and knocked me back. I jumped him again and got him in the sleeper hold. He bit me on the chest. I screamed and let go.

We faced off again.

"You stupid dummy!" I said, breathing heavily.

"You ass!" he said. I had never heard Gabriel say such a bad word as that before. He was really mad. I had caught him red-handed. He was a thief.

"You stupid, dumb...dummy!" I retaliated with a double-dummy statement, hoping that clever threat would slow Gabriel in this violent confrontation.

Louder and more sternly, Gabriel said, "You nigger!"

That did it. I charged him...and missed. I landed on the ground, hard. I turned over, thinking he would be landing on me, but looked up to see him standing *over* me, grinning. "You nigger!"

Behind Gabriel, a sudden movement caught my eye. It was Daddy and Daniel. I would find out later Daddy and Daniel had been hiding near the well house, watching the melee. Maybe, that explains Daddy's interest in the Friday Night Fights on Grandpa's television set when we would visit there.

Gabriel did not see Daddy *or* Daniel, though. They were behind him.

"Nigger, nigger, nigger," Gabriel jeered, more bravely with each syllable. I tried to signal to him that Daddy was right behind him, but Gabriel had already passed the point of no return. "Nigger, nig---"

"What'd you say, son?" Daddy's voice separated the *ger* from the *nig* with his authoritarian tone of voice. "What did you say, Gabriel?"

"Nothing," Gabriel offered. His blood instantly transfused with ice.

"What did you say?" Daddy asked. "I stood right behind you and heard you with my own ears."

If Daddy was behind Gabriel like he said, why didn't he hear what Gabriel said? I didn't ask.

"He said nigger," Daniel said smartly. Daddy turned to Daniel and popped his butt with an open hand. "Was I talking to you?" Daddy howled. "Did I call your name?"

For a moment, Gabriel felt off the hook, as long as Daniel was getting slapped, but Daddy jerked suddenly back around and faced Gabriel. "I want all three of you to march up to your bedroom...right now!" Daddy commanded. Whenever he would say things to us like that, using the *you-three* reference, it was as if he was preaching to a church full of people.

Immediately, Gabriel reached over to give me a hand in getting up, and we all headed to the bedroom, somberly. It's funny how a scolding from Daddy or Momma could make us three more cognizant of our brotherhood.

We moved toward the basement steps. Daniel, who would normally be crying loudly from the recent pop on his rear, was deathly quiet. Even he had learned at his young age not to waste tears on a trivial pop when you know a more profound chastisement would be forthcoming.

Once on the bed, we all three sat in the stillness of our room, looking for Daddy's shadow that would precede his actual self. Of course, the big warning would be his shoes clomping down the hallway. Daddy usually delayed his arrival for the whipping sessions, fueling our anxieties while we nervously sat there. He was training us for a doctor's waiting room in the future, I suppose.

During those times, sitting together on the bedside, many plans were passed between us that never, not in a thousand light years, would have ever materialized.

"Why don't we act like one of us is sick? That would get even with him."

"Why don't one of us throw up or act like we're dead?"

“Maybe Daddy will fall down the steps and break both of his legs!”

No matter the suggestion, it was always suddenly forgotten with, “Here he comes… *shhhh*.”

Daddy closed our bedroom door behind him. He stood with his hands busily pulling his belt off from around his pant’s waist. Watching his belt moving through the loops on his pants was like watching a long train disappear around a mountainous pass and then reappear through and across the last railroad tie. Even the *snap-snap-snap* sound of the belt passing each loop was easily imagined as the *click-click-click* sound of a train on the tracks.

These disciplinary experiences would cause me to have nightmares about cabooses later in life.

Daddy’s punishment speech was typically short, unlike his sermons at church. He made very few scriptural references, all of them memorized and personalized and mostly pertaining to chastisement, rarely mentioning reconciliation. He even threw in the bastard verses. That didn't make me feel too good. His temperament fluctuated from mild to super-hot-sauce-onion-coated-fire-and-brimstone by the time he quit chastising us about our iniquities. Had he spanked us right away, before the spiritual pep rally, the punishment would have been much quicker and more lenient. But he didn't. I wanted so badly to yell out, "Stop preaching about it and get it over with, Adam!" but that would have been extremely counter-productive.

Daddy always began his whipping with Gabriel. I suppose he felt if he could conquer Gabriel's bold will, with Gabriel's indignant attitude toward discipline, that by the time he got to us, we would be more convinced of his fatherly authority. I learned much earlier, however, not to question the person who had the belt in his hand, a lesson learned from our experiences with Evangelist Bartholomew Keller in his short stints at the parsonage.

Daddy would pull us one at a time, from the bedside, onto the dance floor beside him. He would grab one of our arms and then proceed to aim for our legs and butt with his belt. With each lick applied, our cries became louder and more dramatic. Of course, the dramatics paid off, and I became adept at theatrics with my wailing and gnashing of teeth. On occasion, I have had my daddy, out of breath, declare, “I see you’ve learned your lesson.”

He was so right, so right.

On that day, though, since the topic was so controversial, and somewhat Bible-related and current events, according to my daddy’s explanation, our discipline came in three parts. Three was a favorite number to my daddy. He loved that number in his sermons. *Three days and three nights in the belly of the whale, God the Father, Son, and Holy Ghost, three days in the heart of the earth*, to name three of them--Oh, and *you three*, not Bible-related.

The first part of the discipline included the whipping. The second part was the mouth-washing ordeal in the bathroom, and the final part was a prayer and Bible session, including confession, in my daddy’s home office downstairs.

Daddy and Momma both administered the mouth-washing. Being that we were not Freewill Baptist, our church didn't believe in the foot-washing ordinance of the church. We only did the Lord's Supper and Baptism. Several years before he was even saved, Daniel would eat the wafers and drink the grape juice at the Lord's Supper, and was the only one who ever complained about it. "I'm still hungry!"

I always thought that mouth-washing should be added to the church ordinances since we encountered it so much at home. It did include an emphasis on fellowship and holiness. If Baptists had added mouth-washing, that would have made three ordinances, three, Daddy's number; however, Momma was not ordained by the church for mouth-washing, but that oversight seemed to make little difference to *Reverend* Adam.

Daddy held us. Momma coated our tongues, completely back to the gagging part of the tongue, with Ivory soap. Momma bought Ivory soap because it floated, and the bars were large. I believe we wasted more soap playing with the Ivory in the tub water trying to see it resurface from constant dunks below the water, than she saved buying it. I never used Ivory soap after I left home for college. The smell reminded me of the crowded bathroom ordinance in Pelham.

After all our mouths were totally cleansed of vulgarity for eternity, except for the next day when Gabriel would call me a *nigger* in the field for showing Pearl where he hid the fake rabbit, Momma came to our bedroom, where we were supposed to be meditating on the bedside about our sins. All of us bowed our heads and closed our eyes as soon as we saw Momma's shadow coming down the hallway. She told us that Daddy was ready for us in the home office. None of us wanted to take that walk to Daddy's study. It was like meeting God in a back alley with our arms full of Achan's stash.

We knocked. We entered. We sat. We listened.

Daddy took us on an Old Testament survey, through Exodus, Psalms, Daniel and the Lions' Den, and ended up in Revelation with "Even so, come quickly, Lord Jesus!" That had been my same prayer immediately before Daddy had set forth his belt's locomotive run through the loops in our bedroom. Daddy spoke about prejudice and how the Egyptians and Philistines had belittled the Jewish people and how God took up for the underdog. Daddy asked, "Do you want God to be on your side? Then, walk with Him and do His will. You and God make the majority! You need to treat everyone as you wished to be treated. It's not the skin color that makes the difference...it's the attitude of the heart."

As soon as Daddy finished his sermon to us, he asked, "Are there any questions?" There never was. What kid in his right mind would ask God's irate man of the cloth a question so soon after feeling his wrath of Ivory and indignation?

"Daddy," Daniel asked, "why does Brutus hump that dog in the heat?"

Daddy didn't answer Daniel's question, but only bit his lip and pointed toward the home office door signaling our exit, and quickly we did. Once we had exited, Daddy either fell into a holy laughter or fit of crying, because I heard him expelling breath everywhere in his home office like a car tire with a large cut in the rubber.

We survived the three-part discipline, intact once again. All three of us walked away with no lasting damage: a few stripes under the pants legs, a purified palate, and a severely deflated ego.

As we three moved up the steps to our bedroom, Gabriel whispered, “Dogs come from eggs, Cotton Top.”

29

I was worried Gabriel was not accepting Daddy's messages and would have to suffer more pain in the future. Gabriel seemed so set in his ways...so determined to speak his mind. I didn't know what it was going to take to change him.

Gabriel, out of the blue, said to me one day in May behind the well house, "Daniel's already told me, Jake."

Before Gabriel had arrived at the well house, I had sat there earlier to rendezvous with Private Leroy, my black soldier. I was contemplating giving Pvt. Leroy a promotion to sergeant. The weather yielded signs of heat, brushing the last loose ends of winter far away from our shoulders and minds.

Curious, I asked Gabriel, “Daniel told you *what*?”

“About the nigger you met at the creek,” Gabriel said.

Oh, no. Do we have to go through this all over again?

“Don’t say that word, Gabriel. You know---” I said. I slyly slipping Pvt. Leroy into my pants pocket.

“I know.” Gabriel moved closer beside me, talking more quietly. “How many times have you seen him?”

“Once a month,” I said. A plane’s shadow rolled across our back yard. Its roar vibrated the ground.

“Once a month?” Gabriel asked. “How do you do that? I haven’t seen him around here or anything...only them other black boys that walk down the road sometimes, with their heads down to the ground.”

“We meet at the river---”

“At the river...once a month?!”

“Yes,” I said. “On the eighth of each month...or as close to the eighth as we can... every month.” Gabriel’s bewildered expression drew him even closer toward me.

“Once a month? You go to the river and see that nig...that boy...once a month?”

Attempting to clarify the story, I answered, “Yes...we meet in the...the *Eight Ball.*” Gabriel turned to look me in the eyes. I continued, “... It’s a hideout...in the thicket on the other side of the river’s inlet---”

“The *other* side?” Gabriel asked. “You’ve never swung to the other side...by yourself, I mean...except that day that all of us tricked you and...left you there.”

“Right. That’s the day. That’s the same day, the day I met him...the boy.”

“Because you couldn’t get back across the river?”

“Yes. I was stuck. The vine dangled over the river, and so, I went out the other side of the woods...to get some help to get back across the river, and there in a row of corn, I met him---”

"The boy?"

"Josiah. The boy's name is Josiah, Gabriel." Gabriel leaned forward with his elbows on his knees, thinking, straight out toward the river's direction. I said, "He's a nice person...Josiah," I kept explaining, "...but I call him Jo.... he runs way too fast to say Josiah to him ...he runs like a deer, and before you know it, he's already past you."

Sitting back against the well house, Gabriel apologized. "Then, it's *my* fault...you met him...'cause we tricked you...Sorry 'bout that, Jake." .

"No. I mean, no, it's *nobody's* fault, 'cause he's a nice person. Josiah is a real good... boy."

"What if you catch something, Jake?" Gabriel suddenly asked. "I mean...what if you get one of their...strange diseases?" He pivoted toward the parsonage, looking up at the windows, like he was counting them.

"Catch something? Who put that dumb idea in your head?"

“The boys and other people...they talk about it around different places.”

“*Who* talks about it? The boys you hang with?” I asked. “Do you really think they know what they’re talking about anyhow?”

“Their daddies and mommas told ‘em.”

“And don’t you know that their daddies are part of the KKK? Huh?” I asked. “You know that they were all there that night, walking around that burning cross under those sheets...most of ‘em.”

“Some probably.”

“Yeah,” I added, “and the other daddies are too afraid to stand up and tell the others what the truth is, Gabriel.”

“Truth?”

“Yes. The *truth.*” Both of us settled down against the well house and took a breath, facing the lazy sun. I talked softly. “The truth is...that black people are nice people... who have been treated wrong for a long time...very wrong.”

Gabriel looked at the distant sky like it was a span of time to the past. He studied the scattered puffy, white clouds and rested his tired eyes upon them. The sky paled.

"Truth?" he asked again.

"The KKK burned a cross in Jo's front yard," I said, "and some men in a truck came by on Pickett Road one afternoon and threw something out of the truck window at Jo's momma. After she bled for two days in their house with nobody to help her, she finally got to a hospital."

"That boy told you all that?"

"Jo."

"Jo told you that?"

"Yes. He told me, and he had tears in his eyes when he told me...and a couple rolled down his face," I said. "Something's not right about it, Gabriel. Don't you think?"

Gabriel never answered me, so we just sat there. We talked about the black people we both knew together, like Nora, Mitch, and Mattie, and I told him about the three-quartered buried onyx in the center of the black man's picket-fenced eyes, the man who worked for the moving company. Our conversation went from black people to school to church to the river's inlet to the main river basin, and we sat solid against the well house's side until the late-spring, orange sky transformed into a black canvas speckled with lightning, made by bugs.

30

Emmett pushed his smoking mower under a wide oak tree in our front yard. His reel mower was in the shop, and he had borrowed a pull-rope, motor-driven mower to cut our yard. He sat down against the tree, removing his hat, wiping his forehead and face with his red handkerchief from his back pocket. He exposed his scaly teeth in the shade, and his face wrinkled below his eyes with twisted, dirty crow's feet. His pulled his red bandana across his blunt chin and down his neck to sweep all the lingering sweat drops away.

The grass had been quickly and evenly cut.

"Emmett," I said, startling him.

"Jake," he whispered from his expanding and sinking chest. "Hot!"

"I know. Want some water? Momma'll get you some...I can call her."

"Guess so," he answered, still wiping his head and face.

"I'll go tell her," I said, standing.

Before I had a chance to turn and go to the house, Momma had already appeared on the front porch. "Jake...come here...and get this water for Emmett." She held the large glass in one hand, cupped beneath with the other.

"Okay!" I ran as fast as I could, which wasn't fast enough, and took the water from her hands.

"Do not run with that glass...if you fall, Jake...it could..." she said.

I walked fast and avoided her last few words.

Emmett made cold love to the glass of water, taking slow gulping swells into his parched throat. He let the glass touch his face all over and smiled when the water escaped his rounded chin and raced down into his overalls. He didn't waste a drop, licking the sides of the glass and swallowing ice, crushed with his coarse teeth. We didn't talk while he was cooling off.

"He-ah," he said, holding out the empty glass.

I took it, ran with it, left it in the kitchen, and raced back to Emmett.

"You through with the grass?" I asked.

"Uh huh...purt-neer...just gotta...trim...little bit," Emmett said, looking around me toward the bottoms of the trees and hedges.

"Emmett?"

"Huh."

Pointing at the bush-covered ditch past the end of the school building near Highway 14, I asked, "Is that your land...right there on the other side of the ditch...past the swing set?"

"Yeah," he answered. "Lands crooked."

“You mean the land runs crooked ‘cause the land is narrow there?”

“Uh huh,” he said. He pulled his short, rounded jaw into his face in taut concentration.

“Your land is right behind Mr. Rose’s house? That’s your land?”

“All way...to the wata...all the way,” Emmett tried to say.

“Your land touches the ditch...there...ain’t that somethin’!” I said. Emmett was putting his red rag back. He looked like he might be getting up...to start mowing again.

“Why?” he asked. He stood and leaned his attention toward me.

“What?”

“Why you know that? Why?” he asked.

“Just wondering...” I stammered. Emmett’s eyes locked on my face. “I thought that that land was Mr. Rose’s land...that land there.”

“Nope...ain’t...mine.”

While we sat still, a car sped by the front of the parsonage along Highway 14, down the road toward Columbia. Emmett watched the backside of the car disappear. He tilted his head back and thought about the car. He said, “Fast...too fast.”

Emmett stood, stooping down, and looked all around the bottom of his mower, wiping the excess grass from around the edge, and then stood back up. “Gotta trim.”

“You already cleaned the church today?” I asked, hoping to talk some more.

“No. Gotta go today...after the grass.”

“Okay,” I said. “I’ll let you trim. I’m going inside to check on Daniel.”

“Tot-en-top.”

“Yeah, cotton-top.”

“Got the hamma, Jake?”

“Yes.”

While running toward the front brick steps, I could hear a couple of quick pulls of the wrapped rope, against the stubborn Briggs and Stratton engine. Momentarily, the mower cranked, and the blades leveled the grass around the bottoms, trimming immaculately. Emmett trimmed until, eventually, he climbed into his car and rolled toward the river bridge.

31

Mr. Jackson had two boys and one daughter. His oldest son Purnell was in the sixth grade. Purnell's best friend just happened to be Clanton Butler, who came to Purnell's house a lot to ride horses. Mr. Jackson's other boy, Oliver, was Daniel's age. So, his two boys were either older than Gabriel or younger than me. However, his daughter, Francesca, was Gabriel's age. She was lovely, to say the least, and had a heart of pure gold and eyes like blueberry jello.

On the very rare occasions that we would get to go to the Jackson's house in the daytime, we rode the boys' horses and played in and around their barn and large pasture.

Most of the time, we went to their house at night, like right after church for sandwiches and Christian fellowship. That's when Daddy and Mr. Jackson would sit around telling stories and laughing while Momma and Mrs. Jackson would move about in the kitchen, cleaning or sharing recipes.

The Jacksons had eleven horses because one had died.

"Well, dad shot him..." Oliver had said to us. "He kicked at Dad once in the barn...and Dad didn't take it!"

"Shot him?" Gabriel interrupted.

"Yep," Purnell weighed in. "Dad shot him right behind the ears and buried him next to the river," Purnell continued, "where the river curves back to the South...down there," he explained, pointing. We all looked.

"Shot him?" I asked again.

"Yep."

"Couldn't he train him not to kick?" Gabriel asked.

“Nope,” Purnell answered, not flinching. “He, the horse, was black...and his eyes were cloudy and skittish...’too far gone,’ Dad said.”

“Too far gone,” Oliver added.

“But he was definitely fast...I’ll say that much for him,” Purnell said.

Purnell was almost as tall as Clanton Butler. Some of the boys at school thought Purnell was our best chance at beating Clanton at something, but since they were bosom buddies and traveled in a set like their fathers, it was hard to imagine that ever happening.

Gabriel and Purnell got along pretty well too. There were only a couple of things that bugged Gabriel about Purnell. Like the way Purnell talked about preachers as if they were second-class people. Gabriel got really mad about that, and once, I saw Gabriel’s tough white fist ball up beside his right pants pocket, but nothing happened, and I was glad. I thought Gabriel might get hurt if he was to tangle with Purnell. Also, Gabriel didn’t like it when Purnell beat the horses with a strap. Oftentimes, Purnell would pull his horse aside, one that had many marks and scars on it already, and Purnell would beat it unmercifully.

"Trying to break it..." Purnell would say. "You know...show 'em who's the boss in the pasture," Purnell would say through his devious smirk.

"Why don't you try riding him or something...instead of...?" Gabriel had said out of frustration.

Anytime Purnell beat a horse, Daniel would go to the house and stay until it was time to go home. Watching the tethered horse jump around to get away from the vicious strap was a horrifying sight.

Gabriel told me later, after Purnell had hit the horse, "I should have punched him."

On this particular day, however, Daddy and Mr. Jackson went together to an auto sale in the lower part of the state and left us with the Jackson boys to play all day. When we arrived at the Jackson's, Purnell and Oliver had already saddled up and were dressed in brand new cowboy outfits with matching cap pistols. As we got out of the Roadmaster, we could see their horses in the pasture past the back of the barn. The Jackson brothers were waiting on us. They had sent the message by phone for us to wear our outfits and bring our guns. We did. We wore the ones we had gotten for Christmas.

Gabriel was dressed in a Paladin outfit with a vest, gray derby, a concealed derringer pistol in his belt buckle, with business cards that read "Have Gun, Will Travel." I had my Wyatt Earp guns and holster set on. My pistols were long-barreled revolvers with pearl-like handles. I also brought three boxes of dry red-rolled caps, extra ammo. One problem with gunfights on the Jackson ranch was when you shot a Jackson, they would never fell. In their minds, they were invincible. Daniel wore his *Dead or Alive* sawed-off shotgun outfit. He could do some real damage if he shot you up close, but Daniel was impossible to kill.

I killed him once behind the house, and he wouldn't die unless I would let him take a bath first on Saturday night.

Finally, he died for me, and I took a bath in dirty water. It was little reward for killing your brother. I sang, "Happy trails to you, 'til we meet again," while I was soaking in the nasty water.

Purnell pulled back on his horse, brown and white spotted. The dust whirled around its hooves. Purnell said the horse was an Appaloosa, whatever that was. It was brown and white spotted is all I could tell. Oliver was on his Palomino horse, a blonde-headed horse. Both the boys and their sister took horse-riding lessons. Francesca, the boys' sister, had won several tournaments and had the trophies to prove it. In the saddle, she looked like Annie Oakley and Kate McCoy. I know Kate never rode a horse; I just had a crush on her from watching *The Real McCoys* at my grandma's house.

When Daddy's car stopped, Gabriel, Daniel, and me ran from the car toward our horses that were already saddled and tied near the barn door. Hearing that we were coming, the Jackson boys had gotten them ready earlier. Daniel always rode a brown medium-sized horse, a pony actually, Gabriel a brown horse with a diamond white shape between its eyes, and I rode this gray-looking mare that hated me as much as I hated her. She was stubborn. Usually when I wanted to go forward, she wanted to go backwards, or not at all. If not for her less-than-pure breed and her horse-like features, I would have called her a jackass, and often did under my breath.

Once, when I was in a soft gallop in the Jackson's pasture, Ghost, the horse I always rode and hated, stopped...on a dime...a large brown dime, not shiny at all, but quite mushy. I cleared her head and landed on my butt in the horse stuff, *ska-splutt*!

Ghost looked down at me and shook her head. She knew exactly what she had done and took extreme pleasure in it.

On this day, though, we all decided that me, Daniel, and Oliver would be the bad guys and we would be hiding from Gabriel and Purnell, the posse. We mounted and then took off on our horses in a strong gallop. Running in unison, our horses' hooves clopped like three synchronized garden tillers, digging up the red clay in the pasture. We followed Oliver's faster horse as he took us into some trees near the Enoree's blunted edge. We stopped along the river.

"We can hide here," Oliver said.

"Where?" Daniel asked.

"Right here...behind these trees."

I pulled my reins against Ghost's left side, and of course, she moved to the right instead. The fact that she turned in either direction at my request was an accomplishment for her. Oliver and Daniel dismounted and tied their horses to a bush, then sat down, loading their guns, checking for caps.

I dismounted too. While I tried to get Ghost to the same bush, she resisted my pull. I was not in the mood for a battle with her. I gave in and tied her reins to another bush behind me. Joining my hombres, I sat down wheeling out my box of caps.

"Where'd you get that many caps, Jake?" Oliver asked.

"Been saving them since last year."

“Wow, that’s a lot of caps,” he said. “I usually use all my caps up on the day I get ‘em.”

The horses ate the grass around their hooves, and occasionally, one of the horses would shake his or her head and sputter their lips, slinging slobber all around the ground. Their tails were busy swishing the flies, slicing the summer air.

“Let’s hide behind that rock over there,” Oliver said.

We all jumped up, not questioning the youngest brother of Purnell. After all, he was one of the Jackson’s who owned the horses, barn, and pasture where we were getting to play cowboys...free of charge.

“Okay,” me and Daniel said together.

We ran and hid behind the rock and waited for the posse.

Trying to be the first one to notice any noise and be the hero, Daniel whispered, “I think I hear ‘em,”

“Keep your gun ready,” I suggested. I loaded my caps in both revolvers.

We all quieted, listening. The Enoree to our backside was whipping and rolling, distracting one of our senses. "Can't hear anything," Daniel said.

My ears were drawn to a thumping noise on the ground. "What's that?" I asked.

We all stood some, to see over the rock. About that time, unexpectedly, a rope, large, stiff, and round, came draping down over and around us, and then retracted tightly, capturing all three of us with one frail swoop. Lassoed.

On the rock above us was Purnell, holding to the other end of the rope, and in front of us, untying our horses was Gabriel...Paladin, sorry. He shooed our horses off, and in doing so, stripped them of their bridles and saddles, which he conveniently dropped on the ground near our feet. "Adios, senores," Gabriel said. Paladin was not Spanish. Gabriel was mixed up and was probably thinking of The Cisco Kid. *Oh Poncho...oh See-sco!*

Purnell tied the rope loosely to a limb on a nearby bush above our heads and then him and Gabriel rode off in the untimely one o'clock sunset, yelling, "We're the outlaws now! Come and find *us*!"

First, we had to get untied and find our horses. I was hoping Ghost would run so far away that I couldn't find her. *That would be an answer to prayer*!

Finally, I heard something, and looking up, saw Ghost, coming back to where me, Oliver, and Daniel were trying to break free from our roping, and quite unsuccessfully, I should add. Ghost moved in closer and scratched the ground with her hooves, dropping her head like a bull fixin' to charge. She jumped around and then came directly to us, opening her mouth to bite the rope.

"Is she goin' to bite me?" I asked Oliver.

"I don't know," Oliver answered. "I've never seen her act like this before."

With a shade of fear in my throat, knowing she'd never obeyed any of my earlier commands, I whispered, "Easy, Ghost." It would probably have proven more beneficial for me to say, *Do not untie us; kill us instead, you jackass.* “Easy, girl.”

Ghost chewed until she had chewed the rope in two. I threw the rope off and stood up, not knowing what crazy thing this horse might do next. Ghost just stood there, but then, turned and picked her bridle up with her teeth, tossing it toward me.

“I believe,” Oliver said, “I believe she wants you to put the bridle on her...wild. I can’t believe this. My dad wanted to shoot Ghost one day...he said she was useless.”

I eased over with the bridle in my hand and slid the halter over her head. She willingly submitted. I was still nervous though. I thought back about the pile of horse stuff she had thrown me into a few weeks earlier. “Woe, girl...easy.” I bridled her.

Then, without thinking, I jumped up on her back, saddle-less. Grabbing her mane, I sat quietly and unsure on her back. She knew I was there and blew a quick snort of air through her nostrils. Her right hoof sketched upon the hard dirt.

"Jake," Oliver said, "...get *our* horses. Take the two bridles with you."

"Okay," I answered. I pulled on the bridle, and miraculously, Ghost floated across the hot air and into a blinding gallop. Her legs were extended as her body flexed and pulsated. She flew me across the pasture as if I was in the Kentucky Derby, and I wished I had been the way she was running that day.

We cornered the other two horses and rounded them up. I dismounted, re-bridling both of them. Remounting, I guided them back to their riders.

"Good job, Jake," Daniel said. He was smiling with all his face. "Wanna carry my sawed-off shotgun?"

"Naw, that's alright." I involuntarily started talking like a cowboy. "I'll just hang out up here on my old mare."

As soon as my two companions had re-saddled their beasts, we moseyed off toward the trail of the two bandits. I went bareback. Ghost seemed to prefer that method. For sure, I wasn't going to press my luck.

Purnell knew all the good hideouts on the Jackson ranch. He led Gabriel to a deep gorge near the Enoree Dam. Between two large boulders, behind some bushes, they hid. We searched for them high and low, just not low enough.

Ghost kept tugging me toward the dam, so I yielded. The other two deputies of mine continued on the main trail. "Catch you two later!" I yelled. Ghost continued to take me on a shortcut of some kind. We moved down a couple of places that almost dismounted me, because of the steep angle, and up a few places that made me hang more tightly to her mane to keep from falling off her backside. Eventually, she stopped right above the two outlaws. Looking down, I could see them as clear as day. They were joking and laughing, knowing that none of us could ever find them, and they would have been right, if it hadn't of been for my old gray mare, Ghost, who for some reason, took me right to the spot where I could see them plainly. I got off of Ghost and hitched her. She made no noise, but gladly breathed quietly while she picked from the green and brown grasses. Her job was over for now.

From my perspective, above Purnell and Gabriel, I could see the thunderous waters of the Enoree. I'd never looked down on such crushing power. As innocent as the placid waters appeared above the dam, the dastardly wicked ravine below the Highway 14 Bridge discounted that preconceived notion. The silence of the highway expanded the river, but the river daily embattled it, knowing one day, somehow, as time passed, nature would win over man's industriousness. As I stared and watched the two bandits, my attention was drawn back toward the massive force of water and its will power.

Suddenly, I saw Purnell jump up. He had seen Daniel and Oliver, who unwittingly rode within a few feet of the bandits' location. Purnell, hearing my two riders, stood. He seemed surprised to see Oliver and Daniel, untied. He spoke in hand signals to Gabriel who looked clueless himself.

Finally, Gabriel and Purnell opened up fire on my two amigos, shooting them both in cold blood. Oliver fell off his horse and tied it to a tree before dying in the hot sun. Daniel dismounted, tied his pony and then relocated to die under the shade of nearby tree, relaxing beneath his large cowboy hat.

So exhilarated by the successful ambush, Purnell and Gabriel had forgotten about me. I moved into a strategic position right above the two outlaws and leaped out from my rock right onto their backs. They both, bewildered, fell to the ground. I jumped up, and with my gun in hand, yelled, "You're under arrest, partners!" *What a western accent!* "Hands up!"

Dusting themselves off, they both got up, and my two dead comrades came racing down from boot hill to witness the heroic arrest.

"Way to go, Wyatt!" Oliver yelled.

"Good job, Jake!" Daniel jumped in.

"How'd you find us?" Gabriel asked.

Quite aggravated, Purnell breathed summer fire. "Yeah...nobody has ever found this hideout...nobody!"

I said, almost grinning, "You might say that a ghost helped me find it." I looked up and Ghost was still on the high ground, eating.

"Ghost found us for you?" Purnell asked. "The horse?"

"Yep, I didn't even pull on her reins..." I explained, "and she kept walking until I could see you two."

"The horse?" Gabriel asked.

"Yep."

I could tell that Purnell had exceeded the city limits of mad-ville. He was fuming. More steaming air was coming from his nostrils than all the horses combined. He said, "I'll kill that horse!'

"What?" I asked. "What did you say?"

Spying up the hill toward my gray compadre, Punell said, "When we get through down here, I'm gonna kill that horse...she knows better than to give my secrets away." Purnell growled.

“You’re not touching her!” I argued. “She’s a good horse…and smart.”

“You watch me, *PK*,” Purnell said. He always called me and my brothers P.K.’s when he got mad. It was his way of getting back at us. P.K. meant *preacher’s kid.*

With righteous indignation, I spurted, “I said you’re not touching Ghost!”

Purnell quickly dropped his hands, like the game was over. He no longer looked like he was being arrested but more like he was fixin’ to be in a saloon brawl with Hoss Cartwright, but I was more the size of Little Joe or the Cartwright’s Chinese cook. Purnell began to walk toward me. I was hoping Gabriel would step in to help me out; after all, Purnell did call me a *P.K.* and those were almost fighting words for Gabriel.

Subsequently, Purnell’s shadow covered me. I looked up at him. He growled again, more in a strangely lowered voice. “I said I will beat Ghost when I get her to the barn, and if I don’t break her, I’ll kill her.” Purnell stayed there, staring down at me, stubbornly. I didn't feel I could afford to blink my eyes. I kept them wide open. They were drying.

"I said..." I started to say, and then gulped real loud as I forced myself to swallow.

"You said what?" Purnell barked. "I'm waiting to hear what you have to say...you little...bastard nigger." *The apple don't fall far from the tree.*

All of a sudden, Purnell's teeth were quickly slammed shut by a lightning-quick shot to the mouth from Gabriel's closed fist, not just one, but a combination of rights and lefts and overhands that sent Purnell backwards against the large bolder and onto his butt. His mouth was bleeding and the taste of it must have frightened him because he started crying, at first a whimper and then a full-blown bellow like an overgrown baby with a dirty diaper.

Purnell tearfully said, "You hit me, Gabriel, and I'm going to tell your dad...you'll be sorry for this." He shakily stood, and gaining his balance, mounted his stead. Turning his horse around, he concluded, "...*and* Clanton!" Then furiously he galloped his horse toward his house outside the pasture.

I looked at Gabriel who stood tall and examined his fists for damage, of which I couldn't see any. To me, his fists were as good as a box full of caps, popping off on Purnell's chin and nose.

"Who needs guns, when you got weapons like those," I said to Gabriel.

Oliver whined, "He's telling on y'all."

Daniel moved to me and Gabriel. We all stared at Oliver, who silently mounted and also galloped back in his brother's trail of tears, toward his house.

"You kicked his butt, Gabriel," Daniel said. "You bloodied his face."

"I had to," Gabriel started. "He called Jake a bad word."

"Bastard?" Daniel asked.

"No, the other word..."

"Oh, nig---" Daniel tried to say, but Gabriel reached across me and shut Daniel's mouth.

"No more, Daniel. Do you hear me? No more," Gabriel warned. "We don't say that word."

Daniel nodded with Gabriel's hand covering his mouth.

"Okay," Gabriel answered. Looking around to survey the situation, releasing Daniel's mouth, Gabriel added, "Let's go home, boys. Our job is done here." A sunset and a beautiful cowgirl would have put the final touches on this showdown.

Suddenly, Ghost, who had been left alone at the summit, let out a shrilling cry, trying to gain our attention. We all looked up at her, the sun sizzlin' behind her, and Gabriel muffled a soft laugh.

"What is it?" I asked.

"Old Purnell looked like he had just *saw* a ghost, didn't he?" Gabriel said.

We all began to laugh and actually had to sit back down before we could get it under control. Once we did, we took our horses back to the barn, unsaddled and unbridled them, placed them in their stalls, and headed home up Highway 14, on foot.

We didn't laugh once along the way, until Gabriel, after a long pause, laughed, and said, "He looked like he had saw a ghost."

Intermittently touching each other and tossing a few loose rocks along the roadside, we laughed all the rest of the way home on Highway 14.

Now, I *knew* Gabriel was ready to meet Jo.

32

Like a raging river, out of control and violently and desperately pushing things out of its way, events began to overflow toward the end of the school year in that first week of June. The word had gotten out that Gabriel had punched Purnell in the mouth, and Clanton Butler was mad. His buddies had passed the word to me and Gabriel that Clanton wanted a part of us, even if he had to take both of us on at the same time, he wanted revenge.

This was the old west revisited. One gunslinger climbs to the top of the field until a new and up-and-coming young buck comes along and knocks him off. Then, the word gets out and the rest of the field starts showing up to take the new guys on, and *we* were the new guys. All gunslingers are awarded new names--nicknames of sorts—once they become famous. For instance, me and Gabriel had sent Pouty-mouth Purnell and his little brother Oily Oliver home to their momma. I guess our nicknames would be *little bastard* Jake and *nigger-lover* Gabriel, respectively. As far as Daniel's nickname was concerned, you couldn't beat the one he already had: *Cotton-top.*

Not only had Gabriel's punching episode stirred up the KKK's champion's son's dander, but it had also flooded Mr. Jackson's emotions until he was almost drowning the deacons with phone call after phone call about Emmett and his hastily documented mishandling of his janitorial duties. Mr. Jackson had called for an urgent meeting on the next-to-last-day of school, June the seventh, saying he had crucial and damaging evidence that Emmett had conducted himself in an inappropriate manner related to his duties at the church.

Who would have thought that me standing up for a crazy gray horse and Gabriel's subsequent punching episode could collapse Pelham's social dam and inundate the low land with controversy?

Since the news of the deacons' meeting about Emmett, Daddy had mostly been shut up in his home office, praying all day and reading his Bible, except for the times that he would be with Momma in the kitchen, getting her advice and talking the problem out.

"Lillian, you know Emmett worships his job. I have *never* seen him do anything out of line at the church. He is there a lot of the times that I'm there, and no matter what time I check in on him, he is always working extra hard to keep that place spotless," Daddy said. "I've never seen anybody so dedicated to his job like Emmett is to the keeping the church clean."

"Adam, I know you don't want me to say this, but I'm gonna," Momma said. "Buford is after Emmett for some reason... I don't know what it is, but it's something more than a few dusty pews or a penny here and there that Emmett might have pocketed for himself. There's more to it than that. It goes deeper. I wonder if Emmett has ever said anything to Buford or anything."

The answer could have been framed on Emmett's mantel.

After a moment of silence in the kitchen, like the sound of a room when the body lays in the funeral home, Daddy said, "Lillian, let's pray." They both held hands, because I sneaked in and watched some of it, and they both cried, not for themselves, but for Emmett and the church...and for Buford Jackson and his family.

"Help Buford, Lord," Momma prayed. "Keep him safe in your hands. Change Buford's heart. He has such a good family. Do your will, Lord..."

"In Jesus name, Amen," my daddy ended the prayer.

With a week left in school, I decided it was time for Gabriel and Daniel to meet Jo.

Right after school, they followed me down to the river, which by the way, was a good place to hide from Clanton and the others anyhow. Clanton had already been passing the news around at school that something big was going to be happening as soon as school was out, no specific date or time.

Gabriel and Daniel followed close behind me, and as we got to the vine, I lifted it and didn't hesitate a second, but swung across the rock and landed, sending the vine back to my brothers who were waiting for it, mouths gaping, never having seen me clear the river before. The vine bumped Daniel's face. I landed and stood on the rock watching Daniel and Gabriel decide who was next. I reached in my pocket and touched the anvil. It was still there. I had learned to depend on it, and like Jo had told me, the anvil had given me courage, in more situations that simply swinging across the river inlet below the school. *It'sa cur-idge stone, Jeck.* And to think I had carried this anvil all through my third grade year...and now along with the anvil in my pocket, Emmett's hammer clanged against it as I walked, making music with every step I took.

Daniel went first, then Gabriel.

"This way," I said, as we moved through the trees on the other side of the river. I led them out into the cornfield like a safari leader in a Tarzan television movie. The cornfield was a relatively new one, with fresh silk and ears reaching up in the hot sun.

"Where is Jo, Jake?" Daniel asked.

"Hold on," I said. "We'll see him soon. He's a lot like you, Daniel. He can't stand still for very long...keep your eyes peeled."

We moved quietly and curiously slow through the field, me going first and the other two watching side to side like an army recon force, preceding the main assault.

Suddenly, we heard singing. Up on the porch of Jo's house, sat six or seven black women, all scattered out in various postures, breaking beans, it looked like, or doing something with their aprons full. One of 'em was singing, unusual-like. She sang like a moan, and then the others would kinda repeat what she moaned, in a sing-song way. They all sounded like mourners at a funeral in an old black and white movie. They were singing about crossing chilly Jordan. I could make out a few words. None of us stirred any further. We froze and watched and listened, as the sweet sounds made their royal entrance into our eternal memory.

"That's Mattie," I whispered. "That's Mattie singing."

"Huh?" Gabriel asked. "Mattie?"

"Yes. That's her singing," I answered.

"How do you know?" he asked.

"The feet...her feet."

"What?" Gabriel asked.

"I'd know them feet anywhere," I explained.

Sitting against the back-porch wall, on the floor, was Mattie, and she was a' singing' like you never heard. Her voice was carrying into the trees and down the river, like floating music, angel-like.

"Well, I never thought she could sing like that!" Daniel said. "She mostly yelled at us."

"She kept that song a secret," I said. "Somehow, we only got the hums."

"Uh huh," Gabriel chirped in.

Unexpectedly, right in the middle of this cornfield worship service, a voice inserted, "Jeck?" We all turned around at the same time, and there was Jo, who had sneaked right in behind us. Gabriel and Daniel stared at him, like he was the wizard in Oz, curtain pulled.

As they looked to me to do the talking, I said, "Told you he was fast." I searched for the right words. "I wanted you to meet my brothers...I mean, they wanted to meet you," I explained.

Even though that was kind of a hint that an introduction was taking place, nobody said nothing or did nothing. They just stood there.

"This is Gabriel, my oldest brother, and this is Daniel."

Jo nodded and smiled, shy-like. Finally, his hand rose, almost waist high.

"Jo," Gabriel softly said.

"Hiya," Jo replied.

We all stood in the cornfield, and with the late, gentle spring winds pushing sun-blonde and sandy brown hair in varied directions, we awkwardly stared at each other and at Jo.

"Let's take 'em to the *Eight Ball*, Jo," I said, to break the tension.

"Okay."

Jo sprinted ahead of us all, like a young stallion on the loose. He jumped a small briar bush and vanished into the woods. We trailed behind, me way behind. Eventually, we were all in the woods, and the river's voice welcomed us with a steady, cool hum, like Mattie's solo.

Jo moved toward the hideout, and reaching for the doorway, pulled it back so that we could all enter. We did.

Inside, we all sat on the baskets and ground and talked about our different lives and ideas.

Gabriel and Daniel laughed heartily at Jo's dramatics, and how he had to stand up in the center of the hideout, so he could demonstrate every tale of his family and use his hands and dance moves to make it all come to life. Jo's accent drew us all in to his antics and crude articulation. After a while, Daniel was up boogieing with him, round and round, in a dance hall style. We laughed and talked until the sun hid behind the *Eight Ball's* back wall.

Gabriel relayed the story of his short-lived boxing match with Clanton Butler. Jo laughed, and I had to intercede on his behalf by telling of Gabriel's triumph over Purnell, repeating the word that caused Gabriel to bust Purnell in the first place. Jo smiled at Gabriel.

Jo told us again how his dream was to be in a race and run in front of white and black people to win a trophy of his very own. "I wants' dat trophy right he'uh in my hand...at da very end, when it be all o-ver...whiles' all the white folks and blacks...stares right at me."

"Maybe...you'll get your chance someday," I said.

After a few more stories and exchanges, Gabriel suddenly said, "We ought to get going. It's getting' late. We'll get in trouble."

We started toward the exit, when Gabriel stopped us. He turned toward Jo, who was following close behind us. "Jo...thanks for letting us meet you. It was fun."

Jo grinned his contagious grin. "Me too."

In the next few minutes, we were gliding across the river and on our way home, walking side by side with a common bond from the other side. We all bounced and boogied across the parsonage's back yard, like helium balloons, over inflated, humming.

33

On the Wednesday in the last week of school, me and Gabriel met Daniel at his classroom door to head quickly home. We decided, for the safety and survival of our family name, we would exit to the northern end of the school building, not our normal route for going home after school. We did. Gabriel and me kept Daniel between us and moved like self-induced body guards around the school and toward the front paved car loop.

Once into the shade of that end of the building, however, a strange concoction of shadows filtered onto the sheltered grass in front of us. Suddenly, we stopped to face Clanton

Butler, Purnell Jackson, his face a pattern of blue, black, and swollen skin, Oily Oliver, and a group of about fifteen others, including Pudge McPhils. These were the boys who regularly clung to Clanton's heels like mature cow manure on new boots. Gabriel stopped Daniel with his hand. None of us spoke, but only looked at the large group ahead of us, wondering exactly what to do or say.

His mouth contorted, Clanton asked, "Y'all goin' somewhur?"

"Home," Gabriel said, his words hitting the group and stopping.

"You boys done punched my pal in the mouth…I ain't happy, ya know," Clanton snarled aloud. "What you punks gonna do next?"

"I don't know," I started to answer, not knowing what to say that might satisfy this giant and his sneering companions.

"What you want?" Gabriel asked. The other boys were peering around each other for the best vantage of the action.

Pudge McPhils was chewing tobacco and spit one spray of juice in our direction. Daniel watched it splatter at our feet.

"Well...now ya talkin'," Clanton said, his eyes looking to his group for approval. Purnell winced when he attempted to smile at Clanton. "I've got a plan for you boys...that is, if'n your interested."

We had no other choice, as I could see it. I could tell by Gabriel's hesitation that he might want to challenge Clanton right there at the northern shaded end of the school building, near Daniel's first grade class, that Daniel would be staying in for another year. I quickly responded, "We are!" Then, pausing and much softer, "Yes, we are interested...in the plan."

Gabriel cut his head toward me. I sensed it. So, I repeated it again. "We are."

Clanton let us off the hook with a quick and precise challenge: "On the last day of school, right after school, at the ditch, a foot race and leap of death, winner takes all."

I couldn't believe this challenge. He had put much thought into what he was going to say when he would see us, he had it memorized.

If you had given that much attention to your school work, Clanton, then you would be in junior high instead of elementary school.

I had to ask, "But...we *can't* race on the playground...can we?" I had remembered, suddenly, that Clanton had been expelled from the playground since he had skipped school the day he had jumped the ditch for a show. *I've got him now. Thanks, Mr. Mason!*

Clanton abruptly repeated his challenge, making the necessary changes on the spot, with no stuttering. I knew then, we were in trouble: "On the last day of school, right after school, at the other side of the ditch, behind Emmett's house, a foot race and—he swallowed--a leap of death, winner takes all."

I could tell he paused in his challenge when he came to the *leap of death* part, because Clanton had suddenly remembered, like the rest of us, that no one, including Mr. Clanton Butler himself, had *ever* jumped the ditch from Emmett's side of the ditch, because that side was lower than the school side of the ditch. I heard his swallow, a choking gulp past his extended Adam's apple.

He stammered a bit, short of breath, but said, "It's a deal...you little *niggers*."

Several of his followers *amen-ed* him with their grunts and under-the-breath snickers. Oliver grinned. Purnell turned his head very carefully toward Clanton. Pivoting and separating the group, Clanton walked quickly away and out of sight, his long silhouette trailing behind him.

We didn't move; we just stood there and watched the group disband around the corner of the building. I felt like puking, and no time recent had I even tasted a cigarette.

"Are they gone?" Daniel asked, about to cry.

"Yeah," I said. I placed my hand on his shoulder. "What now?" I asked looking across Cotton top's head to Gabriel. My heart had moved into my shirt pocket.

"Sounds like we'll be racing Clanton in two days…doesn't it?" Gabriel answered.

"We're in a heap of trouble, Gabriel…any suggestions?" I asked.

We all stiffened, stopping to listen for any movement past the corner of the building in front of us.

"Yeah," Gabriel said. Looking down at Daniel, whose eyes were pooled with tears, Gabriel added, "First, let's get home where we can talk about it." Gabriel eased ahead of me and Daniel, around the building's corner and onto the school's drop-off zone, toward our house, next door. Me and Daniel trudged behind. It seemed so long ago that from our Roadmaster's back seat, Daniel had said, "Nest to 'da skool!"

We went to our bedroom and shut the door.

"Momma's gonna know something's up, Jake…we can't talk in here…with the door closed," Gabriel said. He rose and walked toward the door.

I stopped to think.

I said to my brothers, "I know what to do…follow me."

I jumped up, opened the bedroom door, and slipped across the hallway to the attic door. I pulled, and it opened. Gabriel and Daniel leaned around me to get a good look up the shadowy stairway, leading up to the musty, dark space. Starting up the steps, I said, "Come on." Gabriel pushed Daniel into my backside, and then Gabriel pulled up the rear, closing the door. When the darkness enveloped all of us, we stopped mid-steps and took a collective breath.

"It's dark," Daniel whined. "Jake?"

"I'm right here, Daniel...wait 'til your eyes get used to it."

"Huh?" he asked.

"The dark...your eyes will get used to the dark," I explained.

I turned back up the steps and made the climb. At the top, I located my old hiding place and moved in that direction, sitting down. Gabriel guided Daniel to two boxes near my spot, and they both sat, carefully.

"How'd you know about this place, Jake?" Daniel asked me.

"I found it when Brother Keller chased us through the house with his belt that day. He stood right there for a few seconds," I said, gesturing with my hand toward the top of the stairs, "and he didn't even see me sitting here."

Breaking up the idle chatter and getting us back on the topic, Gabriel suddenly asked, "What about Clanton?"

"Gabriel? What do you think?" I asked back to him.

"Clanton and the whole gang's gonna be there---" Gabriel began.

Thinking out loud about the date of the *leap of death*, I added the details. "On the eighth...the last day of school is the eighth of June...today's the sixth---"

"... and all of them are going to be expecting us to be there..." Gabriel started, "and to get ourselves totally embarrassed to death by Clanton...there's no way we can win, and you know it."

"So," I said, "what should we do?"

"Tell Daddy," Daniel suggested.

"No!" Gabriel interrupted, "we're not telling Daddy. This is something we have to do on our own. Daddy's got enough on him right now. This way, we can help him out."

"We can't beat Clanton in a race; even Daniel, as fast as he is, can't beat him," I answered.

"What if---" Gabriel started, stooping to stand beneath the bare rafters above his head, "what if we start the race... and you accidentally trip Clanton, Jake...somehow."

"What? You want me to trip Clanton Butler? I can't---"

"You could fall or something, so he would have to step over you...and you could roll over with your legs in the air and kick straight up...and trip him," Gabriel explained.

"No! That won't work," I said, pointedly. "I don't want him stepping on me."

"Well, what else?" Gabriel asked, frustrated.

"Get somebody else to race him---" Daniel began to talk.

Gabriel said, with his mouth full of sarcasm, "Yeah...like Purnell? Good luck doing that!"

"Rocky or Stanley or ---" Daniel kicked back in, listing all of our friends in Pelham.

"Look," I inserted, "in two days on the eighth of June, we are going to be killed on Emmett's side of the ---" My talking suddenly stopped. "That's it! I've got it!" I almost yelled, breathless.

"Lanny or ---" Daniel tried to finish his list of unlikely prospects.

"Daniel, shut up!" Gabriel whispered. Turning to me, he asked, "What is it? What do you have, Jake?" Daniel eyed Gabriel's intensity, then joined in, moving closer to me. I had to stand.

"Josiah!" I breathed.

"What? Josiah...what?" Gabriel asked, puzzled.

Almost too taken back by my quick-witted idea, I said, "Let's get Jo to race Clanton Friday!"

"Huh?" Gabriel mumbled.

"What else could be more embarrassing," I started, "than for Clanton to have to race against a *nigger*, as Clanton or his daddy would say it?" I stood erect; Gabriel sat. Daniel sat. "First of all..." Relocating to a central point toward the wall vent, I pivoted back around to inspire the troops. "Clanton probably will *not* race against Jo 'cause he's black, and if he did, Jo would beat him to the ditch...and maybe across it...I think."

"Jo can't beat Clanton...can he?" Gabriel asked.

"He can...I tell you...he can," I said with confidence bubbling through my voice, and at the same time, with a hidden uncertainty in my chest.

"Jo probably wouldn't even do it either," Gabriel said. "He's too shy for one thing, and I bet he's afraid of the white boys."

"He's seen most of 'em... Jo has watched them near the river...from the *Eight Ball*, and I've told him about 'em too."

"But...how... I mean how are we---?" Gabriel asked, looking for a battle plan. I thought of how much I needed Ike.

"I'll go over the river tomorrow---" I said. Looking down at my brothers' faces, now glued to my every word and highlighted by some late-day glares through the attic vent, I added, "No...we'll *all* go over the river tomorrow...and we'll convince Jo to race against Clanton. If we sell him on the idea, and if he knows he will be racing against the top runner in Pelham, with an audience...he'll do it---"

"Where's his trophy?" Daniel asked. "How will he get a trophy?"

"I don't know that answer," I said. "Let's just hope he somehow gets a trophy...I don't know," I answered. "Maybe he'll be happy just to win the race."

"I like it," Gabriel said. "I like this plan...we will go tomorrow...after school." Gabriel stood, holding out his flat palm. Me and Daniel rose too, and ducking to miss the rafters, placed our hands onto Gabriel's palm. "Let's go for it!" Gabriel whispered. "One for all and all for one, and no one tells Daddy or anyone."

"Like the three musky-tears?" Daniel tried to say.

Gabriel and me fought off a nervous giggle and grinned at each other instead.

"You're right, Daniel. You're very right," Gabriel said.

I put my other hand on Daniel's nearest shoulder. "Thanks, little brother for the suggestion."

With our hands joined, our ears were drawn to Daddy's trumpet from his home office. Perhaps for encouragement, he was practicing the hymn, *All the Way My Savior Leads Me*. The last few words of that song read, "And I know what'ere befalls me, Jesus doeth all things well."

How timely and appropriate.

34

Momma asked my daddy in their bedroom. “But why a Thursday night, Adam? Why?” I could hear her voice. It sounded like an emergency siren in the distance. “Wednesday’s prayer service. He could have done this last night after church if he really needed to!”

“Lillian, I don’t understand it!” Daddy answered back. “Buford is determined to have Emmett fired. He’s been on the phone every day and night, calling the deacons, and I think he may have convinced them Emmett has to go."

"It'll kill Emmett, Adam, and you know it."

"That's what I'm afraid of too, but it would seem that Buford would realize that...and not push this issue so hard...wouldn't it, Lillian?" Daddy said, his voice wavering. Besides God, Momma was Daddy's closest avocate.

"Buford has got the devil in him...he's full of the devil."

"I can't figure him out. When he was the assistant, he did everything to appease the people of the church...he was always congenial---" Daddy said.

"... to get the job, Adam...to get the job. He was a deacon all these years to get the job of chairman...to fire Emmett," Momma thought aloud. "But *why*?"

"I don't understand it...it's something from the past... something worth waiting on for these many years...we may never know what it is that's bothering Brother Jackson---"

"No! Don't you say that! Never again! He's not your brother, Adam...no, he's not---"

"Lillian..." Daddy quickly said, "we're not judges---"

"No... we don't have to be judges...we only have to be witnesses...to a murder, I'm afraid," Momma explained. "God called us to represent the weak, not validate the wicked."

"Lillian! That's enough!"

The bedroom at the parsonage became deathly quiet. Both my daddy and momma were sitting silent, thinking of what to say or do next. Momma rose to look out the window across the backyard toward the river inlet. *It's in those quiet, hopeless moments almighty God steps in and works!* Daddy preached one Sunday morning. *And during those times, it's often hard to hear His voice.*

"Adam...what...what are you gonna do?" Momma cried. "It's not right! It's not right."

After a pause, Momma turned back and fell face first on the bed. I could tell, because her loud cries were suddenly stifled into the mattress and box springs like she was screaming into a pillow.

"God, why?" Daddy prayed. I had never heard him pray so hard before. Both passion and anger sparred for equal ground in his voice. As a preacher, he couldn't fight against Mr. Jackson, but Daddy was calling on God to fight for him. "You led the children of Israel across the Red Sea...you pulled the three Hebrew boys out of the jaws of the fiery furnace...you collapsed the city of Jericho with a slight breath from your mouth, and ... we need you to intervene here...in Pelham, God..."

Frustration and stress painted his tone of voice, like his throat was closing on him or his vocal chords were paralyzed. He continued praying and I could hear my momma's words earsplitting through the bed and wood floor. I sat down on my own bed and cried, and in my own way, prayed too.

35

All day during school on Thursday, me and Gabriel didn't speak when we passed each other. We sent eye signals instead and did a lot of head-turning to see if anyone was watching or coming near us. At a joint recess, because it was the day before school was to be out, me and Gabriel didn't get near each other but stayed on opposite ends of the upper playground, away from any other boys and near the school building, in case we had to run in for safety. "Staying apart is the best plan at school, Jake," Gabriel had told me before school. “One of us needs to safely get away.” We needed to survive one additional day of school after this final Thursday.

At the lower playground, the group of boys who had followed Clanton around the northern end of the school building on Wednesday, had more than doubled, and was gathered around him and Purnell next to the ditch. Clanton was kneeling at the edge of the ditch, like he was estimating the speed he would need to clear it, that is running in the *opposite* direction from Emmett’s lower side.

Suddenly, Miss Jenny gestured in Clanton’s direction. *Boy, she has nerve.* Clanton stood, and glaring in her direction, moved reluctantly back by himself to the upper playground. Miss Jenny had caught him where he wasn’t supposed to be, and she watched him the rest of the recess, and so did I.

At the end of the day, when the last school bell rang, I waited until the sidewalk emptied and then moved toward the house. Gabriel and Daniel were at the basement door looking for me.

"Where you been?" Daniel asked.

"I was waitin' for everybody to leave first."

"Let's go. You think Josiah will be there?" Gabriel asked.

"Where else would he be? He don't have school like we do," I answered.

Gabriel started across the backyard, and putting my schoolbooks behind the basement steps, I followed with Daniel. We made the trip with long strides and hurried steps. Daniel cleared the rock and sent the vine back to me. I took the run and cleared it too. Sending the vine back to Gabriel, he pulled another 9.5 with a perfect landing. Gabriel secured the vine, so it would be there when we would come back through the woods from the other side.

We all scampered through the tree line and into the cornfield. Once in the field, we paused, listening for Jo.

"I don't hear him," Daniel said.

"Shh, listen," I said. Near the barn, I could hear some stirring. "To the barn."

I led, and they followed. The crack in the barn door was wide enough for us to enter, but we didn't. We heard some voices that stopped us at the entrance.

"You feeds him a leaf, Josiah?" a little voice asked.

I peeked around the door to see if I could tell who was in the barn.

Jo's voice answered, "Yes, I can, girl." I saw a little black girl sitting on a bale of hay. Jo was standing in front of her, showing her how he fed Lightning, his turtle. "Puts it hee-uh, and then he eats it...like dis...watch Liz'buth," Jo kept repeating.

I hated to interrupt the conversation, but time was limited for me and my brothers, and this was an emergency. I opened the door a little wider, and we all moved inside.

"Wha's---" Jo started to ask.

"Jo," I said. Jo's heart settled back down. Liz'buth scooted off the bail and behind Jo, like a baby chick behind the mother hen. She kept her head down and didn't look back up, holding onto Jo's dirty pants.

Leaning over to put Lightning back in his place, Jo asked, "What's you all doin hee-uh?"

I said, "We need to talk to you, Jo. We got a big favor to ask...and we are going to make your dream come true at the same time." I sounded more like a car salesman than Mr. Jackson did.

"Wha' kin's 'a fa-vah?" Jo asked. He reached back to touch his sister on the arm.

Paying close attention to my choice of words, I asked, "Somebody wants to race you...in front of a crowd of people.",

"Race *me*?"

"This race will be the biggest race Pelham's ever had...in all time, Jo...in *all* time," I said.

"Who? Who wan's ta race *me*?" Jo asked.

"That's not important right now---" I said.

"Clanton Butler," Gabriel interrupted, sending cold chills down my neck.

"Clanton Butler...Mr. Butler's son?" Jo asked. Every black person on Pickett Road knew the name of Butler, and to hear it created an instant horror.

"Yes..." I conceded. "Clanton Butler is looking for a race...a *big* race can you do it?"

"I don's know, Jeck... I don's know... I been doin' som' aw-fah braggin' ta you, but I don's know."

"Yes, you do! You can do it, Jo. I've seen you run, and Clanton...you can beat him in an outright race...you can," I tried to assure him.

His sister glanced at us and then cut her face back to the ground when I looked at her.

"When?" Jo suddenly asked. "When da race be?"

"Tomorrow...after school...after our school is over," Gabriel said.

"Can you be there?" I asked. "Can you be on the other side of the ditch at the lower playground below the school? Is there a place to cross over the ditch off of Pickett Road?" I kept talking, thinking we might be able to convince him to run for us.

"They be's a place...up hee-uh...off da road to cross to the otha said of da ditch..." Jo said.

"Can you be there?" I asked again. "Right after school."

"Wait...I can nots," Jo said. "I can *nots* be dare."

"What do you mean, you can *nots*?" Gabriel asked.

"Yeah, what?" I asked.

Daniel was looking at Elizabeth like she was an animal at the zoo. She peeped at him through Jo's legs that were twitching nervously side to side.

"I has to wa'ch Liz'buth hee-uh in da barn, whiles my folks a workin' cross da road... in da field," he said. Jo's crude umbrella, the square piece of tin roofing I had seen on another day, was leaning against the nearest stall.

Trying to find a simple solution, Gabriel asked, "Well, can't she go with your folks to the field... just for tomorrow?"

"No... it be's my job to wa'ch Liz'buth...in da barn," Jo explained. "I likes to run...I wan's to run da race...but---"

"Is Elizabeth afraid to stay in the barn by herself...even for just a *little* while...I mean," I said, "it won't take that long to do the race...if you're there on time."

"Sometime, she be sleepin' in da barn...and I can sneeks off some distunce," Jo said. He changed hands to gently touch Elizabeth's head.

"What if," I started thinking out loud, "what if Daniel comes over to stay with Elizabeth?"

"No!" Daniel said abruptly. "I'm not staying in here with a nig...*her*."

Elizabeth looked around Jo's legs to find Daniel's voice. Her face was pained. Jo paid close attention to Daniel's cold comment and looking at Elizabeth's intimidated expression and feeling her frightened arms tightening around his legs, it made him think of all the times that people had hurt his family...of all the times he had been called boy or worse words. He thought of his momma's neck and the burning cross in his family's front yard. He suddenly *knew* what he had to do.

Abruptly, Jo inserted, "I...I try to gets her busy...for a shawt time...and be dare...I will be dare, Jeck, promise."

I could tell he meant it. I could tell by his determined face and his firm posture, his set eyes. His bare feet stopped shifting, establishing themselves securely on mother earth's surface in the barn.

"We are counting on you, Jo," Gabriel said.

"Counts on me, den," he said. "I will be dare, Gabriel. You a' sees me a'comin' through da briar field... ta-mar'ra."

Gabriel squared up and smiled. Jo smiled.

We finished our conversation and exited the barn, crossing the river, and racing toward the parsonage. Daniel won. Gabriel only beat me by the length of one back yard.

Momma spilled two glasses of tea at supper that evening. Daddy had gone to an emergency deacons' meeting that Mr. Jackson had called. Daddy didn't eat supper that night. Mr. Jackson brought the children's church bank into the meeting with him. The bank was broken and the money for the orphanage in Africa was missing. The white plastic church was empty.

"Gentlemen, do I need to show anything else?" Mr. Jackson asked the deacons in the conference room at the church. "Here's a broken church...empty...somebody has taken liberties with the money that should belong to the orphans in Africa. Without money, a church is worthless...that person is Emmett, brethren."

With that public accusation in front of the deacon board, the conference room door slowly opened, and in walked Francesca Jackson. She was beautifully dressed, and with her expression saddened and troubled, she entered and stood beside her daddy, head downward. Mr. Jackson asked one simple question, the answer to which condemned Emmett to his worst nightmare. "Francesca...did you see Emmett take the money from this bank?"

All the deacons leaned forward in their chairs to hear her answer. Without hesitation, as if rehearsed a thousand times, she acclaimed, “Yes, father.” Immediately, she turned, exiting the room. Waiting outside in the hallway, her mother swiftly removed her from the church property, across the bridge up to the south rounded side of town, the dull end of the anvil.

Daddy covered his mouth with his hands to keep from erupting. His heart throbbed, counter-acting an attack, his face stoic and pale.

The deacons, without any discussion, without delay, climbed onto Mr. Jackson’s motion of firing Emmett as custodian of the Pelham First Baptist Church. After the meeting, Daddy called Emmett into his office and told him the bad news. While Daddy spoke to him, Daddy cried, and cried even more after Emmett slowly walked out of the church office. Daddy also gave Emmett an envelope in which Daddy had placed fifty dollars of his own money. Later, during the next week, Daddy would find the money folded inside Emmett’s dusting rag, in the custodian’s closet.

Daddy knew Emmett would never take money that didn't belong to him.

It was hard for us to get to sleep that night. Daddy never came home while we were awake. We all stared at the ceiling and talked about the race, the deacon's meeting, Elizabeth's shyness, Clanton Butler, Buford Jackson, and, of course, the race again. Daniel slept between me and Gabriel and got so close to me from being afraid in the dark, he entered my circle and didn't realize it until the last day of school, early in the morning, in the bed. I think Daniel would rather have fallen into the ditch.

36

June eighth started off partly cloudy and hot. It wasn't a can't-make-up-my-mind hot; it was Pete's chili-cheese-with-Tabasco hot, and sultry. Heavily suspended across Pelham like a rain-soaked electric blanket, humidity saturated every pore. For the final time, school buses turned their wheels, rolling kids to the unloading zone and zooming out toward the junior high and high school up Highway 14. Steering the early arrivers into the cafeteria to watch Warner Brothers' cartoons and *The Three Stooges*, Mrs. Duncan and the other teachers monitored the front entrance of the school.

Cafeteria workers smiled broader than any other day, and the buildings yearned for a good summer cleaning and painting. It was the last day of school.

The day was long, terribly long. Large white and gray-trimmed clouds crissed-crossed the sky, keeping the sun guessing exactly as to where and when it was needed. Recess was confined to the upper playground, and the strangest thing of the day was Clanton Butler and Purnell Jackson did not even show up at school. Several times at the joint recess, I scanned the entire playground, locating neither of them. Gabriel confirmed that fact when I saw him at lunch. "They're not here today."

"Think they've forgotten about the race after school?"

Gabriel answered me with a question. "You think the devil ever forgets about sin?"

At the end of the day, crying and hugging each student, Miss Jenny stood at our classroom door. She told us goodbye for the year, her tears warm and caring. I wanted to settle into her arms for a longer time but slipped through her grip into the hot, muggy air. In the distance, the sky turned a dark gray. I could hear a threatening rumble. Pelham was fixin' to have its first summer storm.

Exiting Miss Jenny's room, I glanced toward the lower playground, and with my eyes, jumped the ditch, and there, on the other side, was a large group of boys, already assembled on Emmett's side of the ditch. In the center of the crowd, a tall, slender boy paced. Clanton Butler. Draped long beside him was puffy-faced Purnell Jackson, grimacing still.

The devil never forgets about sin.

I looked left to see Gabriel standing just outside the sidewalk cover. Our expressions revealed the whole story. We had a race to run and hopefully win. With sad news about his repeat year in the first grade, Daniel languished up the sidewalk. I secured his red-scarred report card in my back pocket. Near my classroom door, we all three gathered at the middle of the school's outside walkway.

"They're waiting," Gabriel said.

“We need to go, so we can be there when Jo shows up,” I said.

“You stay near me, Daniel,” Gabriel said, “and don’t get too close to the ditch.”

Sauntering around the edge of the northern end of the building, past the swing set, we three moved across the shrub-covered, shallow ditch, nearest Highway 14, and edged down the bush line into Emmett’s long, crooked property line.

Shuffling above Pelham, a mortar of black clouds packed together, thickening like dark gunpowder down a cavernous gun barrel. A spontaneous shot of thunder shook the ground, vibrating in the direction of the ditch. We slowed as we saw the crowd of boys open up to welcome us inside like a pit of asps.

Clanton Butler shifted away from his mass of followers, nearing the ditch’s rim. He removed his shoes. With his wide big toe, he cut a jump line within inches of the ditch. He bent over to roll up his britches legs to the top of his calves, and taking a final estimation of the ditch's expanse, straightened and paced to a racing distance away from the ditch.

Gabriel touched Daniel's shoulder. Me and Gabriel walked away from Daniel toward Clanton. Growling and spitting a few scattered rain drops, thunder boomed almost directly on top of us. Heavy to fall, held back by black paper-Mache clouds, the summer sky twisted like the waters of the Enoree below the dam. Uneasiness stirred my heart. Part of me wanted to run home to Momma. Another part of me needed to eye-witness the verdict with my own eyes.

Clanton's toed line was being steadily erased by some larger raindrops, released from the colliding clouds. A flash of lightning lit up the sky beyond the river. Everyone reacted. Oliver moved next to Purnell. They touched. Clanton's coal-black hair yielded in the stiff breeze.

Clanton's voice shrieked above the roar of the impending storm. "Well, let's get it on, boys!" He glared toward us. "Gonna take yo shoes off for the race?" With both hands on his hips, he faced us. “Hurry up, you little P.K.’s…we gotta outrun this storm!”

Methodically, my eyes scanned the tall weeds at the bottom of Emmett’s crooked stretch of land near Pickett Road. I looked past Clanton. At first, hard to discern clearly, in the briars and gray, wind-tossed bushes, I could see our solitary black hope, advancing through, barefooted, bold, shirtless and on time.

“Jo,” I whispered.

“What?” Gabriel asked.

Motioning with my head beyond Clanton, again I said, “Jo.” Gabriel and Daniel looked.

Behind Clanton’s sizeable silhouette moved a black boy, progressing toward the starting line. He kept walking, getting ever closer.

“Hey, look!” Purnell suddenly howled. “Clanton…a *nigger*!” Purnell stretched his arm outward toward Josiah’s direction. Purnell winced to talk.

Abruptly pivoting on his bare feet, Clanton reacted. "What?" He hawked his eyes, gaping. "Where?" Clanton held his hand up, shielding his eyes from the stiffening wind and rain. Clanton's oily hair whipped back and forth into his eyes, across his forehead. He yelled, "What's going on? What's he doin' here?" Clanton spit in the storm's face.

Especially loud enough for the whole crowd to hear, Gabriel yelled, "He's here for the race!" To validate everyone had clearly understood his words, Gabrield said, "He's racing *you,*...in our place...for us, Clanton!"

Clanton's head unexpectedly convulsed, jerking back toward Gabriel. His lips tightly twitched. "What? I'm 'posed to race *you two*...not some...*nigger*!"

I yelled back. "Josiah's racing you, Clanton. Ain't that okay with you?" Clanton's head swung around toward Jo. I added, "A race is a race, ain't it?"

The throng of onlookers moved in closer to see and hear above the thunder and wind, mounting. Rain stung in sudden surges; then off and on it subsided into a mild pelting, as if the hand of a large black man was opening God's spigot. My eyes watered, blinking blindly. I felt Daniel move in behind me, using me as a shield from the storm.

The wind had blown the crowd into a large, tight huddle, and for support against the first summer storm in Pelham, all leaned into each other.

"You gonna race a nigger, Clanton?" Pudge shrieked past the noise; he spit again.

"You ain't 'fraid o' no nigger, are you, Clanton?" Purnell asked.

Pudge added, "This is your chance, Clanton...this is what you been waitin' for, all along. Show this black boy you are the fastest."

Clanton scowled over his shoulder toward this barefooted, poorly-clad black boy, who edged closer to the start line. Clanton shouted, "No! I ain't 'fraid 'o no nigger, 'specially no little one! Brang 'em on!" With his hands stretching out to his sides, Clanton hollered, "Let's get this beatin' over with!" He wallowed in his own callous words.

Clamoring on top of each other to see the race, the crowd molded together. The battering wind blew against the wet wall of bodies.

Jo arrived on the start line. His expression was uncompromising yet shy. He stopped within a few inches of Clanton's bare feet and faced the ditch. Jo eyed me and my brothers for a quick second, and then turned back to the ditch. A storm brewed between him and Clanton, pounding the earth's surface, cutting holes in the dirt with solid sheets of hammering rain. Clanton pushed a clump of his wet hair back. The water flowed freely off Jo's face, down his bare chest into his overalls.

"Somebody yell go…" Clanton bellowed in the midst of the gale, "…so I can bury this nigger in my mud!" Once ready, Clanton refused to look at Jo; he focused his attention on his own kind, among his followers, and then back at the ditch.

I picked up a rock, freshly splattered by the rain, and immediately yelled, "I'll throw this rock into the air…and when it hits the ground in front of the runners, they will go!"

"Just yell go!" Clanton objected, still facing the ditch. "You're wasting time!"

"...and when it hits the ground," I repeated louder, spitting out some rain from my mouth and making my point, "*then* the runners will go!"

Clanton glared at me. His voice was inaudible, but his mouth formed the word *bastard.*

I searched one last time to make sure Daniel was near me. Clanton's throng appeared as weakness leaning against weakness. At the starting line, prejudice was on trial. The verdict lay at the threshold of a wide ditch, the *leap of death.*

Yelling, I tossed the rock into the air. It disappeared into the torrent, and then with a *plunk*, hit the ground a few feet ahead of the runners.

The rain became increasingly heavy, blurring the runners' path to the ditch. Clanton and Jo exploded from the starting position with an equal launch, evaporating into the heart of the storm. Jo made me think of Ghost, the way he jump-started. The horde inched itself toward the finish line like a long worm scurrying for shelter. Everything moved in slow motion; nothing stood still. I raced behind the two combatants, only distinguishing a tall and shorter shadow against an angry black background.

Suddenly, with three or four successive flashes, the lightning illuminated the ditch, making the scene look a lot like a clip from a Chaplin movie. I lined my sight up with the two shadows and sprinted quickly in that direction. Thunder fueled me forward, with Daniel pushing at my heels. Like mixed clumps of courage and fear, the mud from the racers' feet struck thudded and splashed in front of me. Me, Daniel, and Gabriel chased toward the ditch. Finally getting there, we stopped at its foremost edge, finding it occupied at the bottom with a new, shallow, and ever-swelling creek, a fresh feeder to the river inlet. Out of breath and motionless, Clanton's soaked body occupied the ditch bottom.

"There he goes, Jake!" Daniel yelled, pulling my hand. "Look."

Across the lower playground, running like a panther from its hunter, Jo dashed toward the tree line and the tree vine that would propel him back to the barn to safely escort Elizabeth from the barn to their house. "Jo!" I yelled, not knowing why.

Clanton's well-wishers disjointed toward Highway 14, up the edge of the ditch, defeated, racing home, and running to beat the brunt of the storm. Purnell forsook Clanton and left him in the ditch. Gabriel reached into his wet pants pocket and pulled out a few coins, and rearranging the contents inside his hand, lifted a damp quarter directly into the bottom of the ditch, onto Clanton's left temple with a thud.

"Nice shot!" Daniel said. The rain seemingly washed our sins away on Emmett's side of the ditch.

Gabriel whispered through the thunder, "Let's go!"

We three raced against the whipping rain and felt our faces on fire from the razor-like drops, diving feverishly from the black sky. I held Daniel's hand. Gabriel patrolled in front of us, cutting a path through the dense, rain-soaked air.

Getting closer to the parsonage, I could hear Momma's voice in the storm. It was more than panicky. It was desperate. "Boys! Get home, Boys!" She was screaming loudly. "Where are you?"

We scrambled up the back-porch steps and through the screen, where she was leaning out to yell. "Where have you boys been?" she barked. "Answer me...*now.*"

"We've been at the school..." Gabriel started to explain.

"Nevermind! Get your rain jackets and meet me and your daddy in the car...and *hurry*...hurry!" Momma left the kitchen, pulling her raincoat on and throwing her purse onto her arm as she moved. "*Hurry*!"

All three of us skated on our wet shoes into our bedroom, and like second-shift fireman, thrust into our closet spaces, yanking out our rain jackets. We threw them on, quickly gliding down the steps; a greased fire pole couldn't have been any faster. The Roadmaster was idling outside, its wipers on fast speed. Daddy's face was hidden by the fogged-up

vindow, and the back door of the car was already open for
ıs.

We dove in on top of each other, forcing the other into the
›ack seat, slamming the door. Per usual, I was last. Like
sparking gunfire on a John Wayne television war movie,
ightning struck all around the car. Daddy and Momma sat
n the front seat. Our sister was tucked between Daddy and
Momma, making no sounds. We could tell something was
serious. None of us dared ask. We could sense it.

Even though it was early afternoon on June the eighth,
he day was entombed with eternal night.

The Roadmaster sped around the river-stone wall, around
›ur driveway toward Highway 14. We rode with restrained
speed down the road toward the bridge. In the distance, red
ights pulsed. A few flashlights glared and blinked like stars
n a sinister sky. Close to the bridge, Daddy slowed the car
ınd eased it over against the loose muddy shoulder of the
oad. The storm and water from the dam were in a battle to

make the most noise. The storm would eventually lose because it kept supplying the dam water.

Daddy lowered his window. A flashlight bounced toward the driver's side. "Preacher…" the voice yelled, "his body's down there." With the flashlight, the voice pointed to where a few gathered men were huddled.

Opening his door, Daddy climbed out into the pouring rain. "Be right back." He pulled his hat down around his head, trialing the flashlight toward the water's edge. It was hard to see through the flooded windshield. It was like looking through the end of an empty R C bottle.

Like small warning lighthouses, the red lights kept tempo with my anxious heart. After a while, in the drowning rain, I could make out some of the men near the river by their shapes. Some were deacons. Some were lawmen, and one was the chairman, Mr. Buford Jackson. He was nearest the body.

The men stirred around and conversed loudly, conducting business in the blasting storm. Eventually two shadows moved away from the others toward our car. The closer they got, I could make out it was Daddy and Mr. Jackson. They stood right next to Daddy's door and talked, gesturing with soaked hands at each other and toward the river. Nothing seemed to make sense through Daddy's window, fogging with an infinite flow of water. It was as if the Enoree River was mourning.

I partially opened my own window to listen. Mr. Jackson said to my daddy, "He jumped, Preacher. He jumped."

"He did?" Daddy asked. "Are you sure?"

"Very sure."

Following a long flashlight, a shorter, feeble shadow had awkwardly been scaling the highway in the rain. It sauntered into the conversation, almost splitting the two men outside my window. Daddy asked, "Mrs. Black? What you doin' out in this weather...at this time of night?"

Mrs. Black said, "I *thought* this wuz yo car, preacher...even in the dark, I could tell yo black car." She spit her words out through the water, into the moisture-laden air.

"Emmett jumped, Mrs. Black," Daddy said. "I'm really sorry." He paused to let his words sink in. Pointing, Daddy added, "He's down there."

"I came up here to tell you what I sawed, preacher," she said. "I sawed two...maybe his father's ghost...from years befo'...up on top o' the dam. I saw two up thar, preacher!"

"Really? Are you sure?" Daddy asked.

Suddenly, putting his hand on her shoulder, attempting to turn her back toward home, Mr. Jackson said, "Now, Mrs. Black, you go back to your house 'afore you catch yo' death of a cold. It's not decent enough out here for a woman."

Still facing Daddy, Mrs. Black, twisting out of Mr. Jackson's grip and ignoring Mr. Jackson's claims, said, "I sawed two, preacher. Two on the dam, almost side by side. I was looking off my po'ch, and I sawed it...two of 'em, preacher. Eerie it was!"

Mr. Jackson seized both shoulders on the second attempt, coaxing Mrs. Black back onto the side of the Highway 14 toward her humble home. To make sure, he paced with her several steps. She swayed slightly and stumbled away, pointing her own flashlight toward the dam as she walked. She paused down the road aways, saying louder, “Two of ‘em, preacher!” She started walking again, her rays from her flashlight dancing off the road and onto the dam, and eventually out of sight.

“She got a strange imagination, that Mrs. Black!” Mr. Jackson quickly said. The thunder continued to scream. My soul convulsed.

Out my window, I struggled to see Emmett’s outline, lying in the muddy residue at the river’s edge. *There was no way that Emmett would ever get near the river…no way!* My insides dissolved like ice on a hot day. Tears dammed up my emotions, threatening to break loose. I cried, and didn’t even care if Gabriel saw me. My cry throbbed my body.

Searching my pocket, I grasped a hold on the blacksmith's hammer and squeezed it. I would keep it with me until Emmett's funeral, when I would drop it into his coffin, behind his head.

Suddenly, a red light rushed up on the back of our Roadmaster, pulling us over, while we were sitting still. As we twisted in our seats to see the police car, the red light pulsated *Jesus Saves* across our faces. Mr. Jackson disappeared towards the police car and left Daddy standing alone in the storm. After a short time, Mr. Jackson moved back to Daddy. I opened my window wider, to listen.

Mr. Jackson said, "Deputy Crewshaw says the lightning on Pickett Road hit a little nigger boy over there." He pointed back toward Pickett Road in the rain. "The boy was running in the storm."

"Oh, no," Daddy said.

Oh, God…Not Jo! Surely not Jo!

"Let's ride out there and see it, Adam!" Mr. Jackson suggested. "The deacons'll take care o' Emmett." He and

Daddy took a last look toward Emmett's body. "I'll get my truck. Follow me," Mr. Jackson yelled, sloshing toward his truck on the other side of the road, where earlier, it had been strategically parked, closer to the bridge. Daddy climbed in, soaked and drenched.

"Adam...what?" Momma asked. "What's going on?"

"Emmett's dead, Lillian...jumped, they say."

"No, Adam...oh, God no!" Momma cried. "Who says?" She pulled away from Daddy's side, facing her weeping window. My sister reached around her waist to hold her.

"We're following Buford," Daddy said. "We're going out Pickett Road. They said a black boy got hit by lightning a while ago."

Our car dislodged from the mud and spun on Highway 14 in a one-eighty and became hypnotized by the rear end of Mr. Jackson's truck.

Not looking away from her own window, Momma asked, "Don't you think we've followed him long enough, Adam?" She allowed that question to experience the potholes of

Pickett Road before saying, “Where is he *ever* gonna take us?” I could tell she wanted to say more than that but refrained.

Daddy didn’t answer. He kept his eyes on the back of Mr. Jackson’s new truck.

The Roadmaster bumped and splashed onto Pickett Road, and keeping pace with the truck, rolled and weaved across the flooding pavement, feeling each dip. Suddenly, the vehicles slowed and pulled over…onto a muddy shoulder in front of Josiah’s isolated home. On my knees in the back seat, out the rear windshield, I could see between me and the barn, the silhouette of a body beneath a rain-soaked white sheet.

Josiah! I cried on the inside. *Jo!*

Forcing my door open, I faced the storm head on, racing toward the white sheet on the ground, next to the square of tin. “Jo!” I cried as I ran. “Jo!”

Gabriel and Daniel were already moving from the car toward Jo. Momma was yelling at us, “Get in the car boys! You boys get in the car now!”

I neared the sheet first and stopped, kneeling down. The rain meshed with my tears. I sobbed Jo’s name. “Jo!” I bowed at the only part visible, Jo’s arm, extending from beneath the sheet. I bent over. From Jo’s open palm, I removed the same rock I had previously thrown into the air to start the race between him and Clanton. Lifting the small anvil from my own pocket, I placed it in Jo’s open palm, enclosing his fingers tightly around it. “Here’s your trophy, Jo!” I wept. “You won the race!”

I leaned over, kissing his hand. “I’ll keep the *Eight Ball* for us, Jo…for you and *Jeck*. Me and my brothers will keep it for you. We’ll call it Jo’s *Eight Ball* from now on.” I stopped speaking, crying even more. My heart emptied itself upon my face. “Keep running, Jo. Lots’a people there to cheer for you.”

With a fold of the sheet, I covered Jo's arm and could somehow still hear Mattie's voice singing about Chilly Jordan...where Josiah's greeting grandstands awaited him... at the paramount finish line.

Gabriel and Daniel had cautiously slid in behind me, splashing to a halt. They stood. Gabriel's hand made contact with my shoulder. Against my back rested Daniel's leg.

Daddy and Mr. Jackson followed us to the body. They situated on opposite ends of the white sheet. Momma was still screaming at us to get back into the car, *right this minute.* On Jo's porch in a frail straw chair, his momma held Elizabeth like a newborn, both of them weeping as one soul. The storm was subsiding, the rain steady.

Looking up at Daddy, I spoke. "Jo was trying to get his sister from the barn...out of the storm...her name's Elizabeth." I glanced toward Jo's back porch as a reference. Daddy did too. "He was supposed to watch her while his folks worked in ..." My words were fruitless and perished.

Mr. Jackson's eyes browsed the house, barn, and surroundings. Noticing the square of tin near Jo's body, Mr. Jackson croaked, "Nigga should'a knowed better!"

Instantly, Gabriel's head lifted. He moved closer to me. I stood, reaching to touch Gabriel for comfort. Suddenly, he spat straight across me into Mr. Jackson's face. The rain and spittle mixed, flowing off his blunt chin, onto his chest.

I spoke, "Emmett told me he was afraid to get near the river, Mr. Jackson. Said he was afraid to get near the water!"

Me and Gabriel turned together, easing away from Jo, toward the car. Daniel pivoted, glaring right at Mr. Jackson. Taking an additional step toward him, Daniel abruptly screamed, "Bas-tard!!"

Embarrassed, Daniel sprinted to catch up with me and Gabriel. Like a small funeral procession, we all three strode arm-around-shoulders toward the long black family car, still idling near the edge of Pickett Road. Momma's eyes beckoned us in, "Get in boys...and get warm." Holding my sister and humming, *I will not be a stranger when I get to that city*...Momma twisted again toward the back seat. Catching Gabriel's eye with her increase in volume, she wielded a warm smile, winking. She turned back to the front, mid-verse, *I'm acquainted with folks over there*...causing Gabriel to remember the silkworm.

Daddy stared at Mr. Jackson for a long while, until their collective eyes convened at the sheet-covered body. Then glancing back at each other after a short, silent sermon, they each comprehended the other's intentions.

Through intermittent mist and looming fog, behind the family car, the law's red light appeared, casting a peculiar blush upon the scene, like God's face refusing to honor man's feeble efforts at managing their affairs.

At last, Daddy whispered, "Well, Buford..." again taking a glimpse at the light, the body, and porch, "you finally got what you wanted." Mr. Jackson hoisted his grim face, thoughtlessly. "For God's sake, I hope you're satisfied now." Daddy paused. Then he departed Jo's house, leaving Mr. Jackson alone with his own black heart.

In Jo's back yard, between a barn and a house with a ickety, river-stone foundation, lay a champion at a coward's eet, embellished with muddy, red-dyed, rattlesnake-skin owboy boots.

Be sure to visit Jerry's website,

readJERRY.com

to investigate his other writings and novels.